black ghost knife fish

the emerging of jakub riser

SION JONES

black ghost knife fish

the emerging of jakub riser

by

SION JONES

Aethem Press - Austin

God rest your soul, Kilgore Trout.

Aethem Press - Austin, TX

ISBN: 978-1-956558-05-0

Table of Contents

apteronotus albifrons

In the end, everything apparently comes down to a *fish*.

His workmate Sedric dreamt up the bright idea, but then again, if it swims and stays wet, Sedric was familiar with it. Every little thing about him was aquatic. He took his vacations any place there was a body of water to sink himself into. They were plastered all over his cubicle, on his keyring, hanging from the mirror of his car. It was difficult to determine exactly how much of this guy was Steve Irwin and how much was Jacques Cousteau.

He was a vegetarian, he was a marine biologist, if mostly amateur, and it was he that noticed first the emotional spiral Jakub had sunk into. It was getting closer to that day, and each week bent him a little more. Somehow, Sedric could understand. He was such a mother hen at heart. A *huge* mother hen.

He was naturally too easy to talk to.

Sedric had ordered the fish. Wrote the name on a small spiral notebook in Latin with a meaty former linebacker paw, ripped the page from the book, and handed it over to Jakub with a sense of pride as if he were writing a prescription he knew would work. Jakub had enough prescriptions by this point to know, but none of them had worked. The story stuck

Seddy close to home. He handled the oddities as if they were the most normal thing he had ever heard and showed no reaction that anything seemed out of the ordinary.

"There are still a few things to arrange. I think I can help handle that. Go ask for Linda. She'll know what this is. You're about to learn more than you ever wanted to know about fish perhaps, but I promise it will be worth it," He had told Jakub.

"A fish?" Jakub had asked.

But Sedric smiled in a moment of self-satisfaction and purred, "You *need* this."

It was a strange request; they had kept the knife fish in stock more because Sedric Martin liked it. He was a frequent customer, always used their services when he had to go out of town, came into the shop like he was coming home. All the other employees at the shop loved him, too. He was like a giant teddy bear and had studied this stuff for real.

So when he called in the order, Linda was taken aback. When he told her everything he was purchasing in the package, her heart skipped a beat. What kind of person would an *apteronotus albifrons* be a "necessary perfection" for?

That was the exact phrase he had used, necessary perfection. He had enunciated it for effect.

"I'm sending a fellow named Jakub Riser to pick that little angel up. She's going to be a *necessary perfection* for him, so see that he doesn't get anything else. Don't try and sell him anything else. I mean it."

"Does he already have an aquarium?"

"No. I don't think he's ever owned a fish in his life."

The answer surprised her, and she knew she hadn't hidden it well. "You're aware we'll have to deliver, right?"

"Yeah, I know. And I want a year of aquarium service on top of that. Teach him everything you know. Go ahead and run my account for the total."

"Are you sure?"

"I've never been so sure of anything in my life," he had said.

When she heard the bell activate at the door, one glance convinced her that she was looking at Jakub. Thin, skinny jeans, bike-messenger guy with about two days of scruff on his face. Not a bad-looking fellow, all things considered. He had a sling over his shoulder with a black rabbit that he kept absentmindedly stroking on its head. It looked like a baby, and he had it nestled near his chest. She was about to say something, to tell him he couldn't bring his pet inside when she realized it wasn't a living rabbit. It was a stuffed children's toy bunny.

Bizarre.

Some people have their things, so this should become interesting real quick.

"Jakub, I imagine?" she addressed him.

"That would be me," he answered, nodding his head slightly. Weak smile, almost unsure. Something about him seemed off. Not a psychotic killer babbling to himself kind of "off", but rather sad. Not a manically depressed sad, more like he had lost a close family member and couldn't shake it. She almost hurt for him.

"I'm kinda new at this, but I do trust Seddy, so I'll go with it," his smile turning to a quizzical grin, "What *exactly* is this that he's lined up for me?"

She felt the corners of her mouth draw up in a grin herself. "*Apteronotus albifrons*," she announced. "In the common tongue, the Black Ghost Knife Fish. Wait until you see *this* beauty."

"I've heard that before..." his voice trailed off. He was thankfully still smiling.

The curiosity was growing with every step towards the rear of the shop, and she simply couldn't stop the question. "So what's the story with your little friend there," she asked, gesturing to the rabbit.

He looked quickly as a shock of realization seemed to jolt him to recognition. Another weak smile flashed on his face. "Oh. Luna. She was a gift," The pain exploded on his face and disappeared like a bolt of lightning, "A very *special* gift."

"I see. Well, you are now two for two on special gifts," Linda said, "And I'm not undercutting your friend there. M'ija over here is a very unique creature, and is really only for very unique individuals. The fact that Sedric picked her out for you says a lot. About *both* of you."

He blinked. Nothing negative. Right after the words came out of her mouth, she was afraid she'd offended him. Usually she wouldn't care, but there was something in the air with this guy. It was electric. It made you *want* to care. Maybe that led to Sedric's decision.

"You know much about Sedric? I know you guys work together..."

"Well, he knows damn near everything there is to know about a fish, whether you're asking or not, and the problem's that by the time he's done, you'll *want* to listen."

She couldn't help but laugh. That was Sedric all right. "You know that he went to University of Alabama, right?"

Jakub snorted, "You can't be within five feet of him and not know that. 2010 Championship. Blew by the Horns like they were standing still. Nobody really likes that story here in Austin." His jerked again as the laugh got louder. "I don't give a shit. I come from an Aggie family."

"Oh, boo hiss," she bantered. "Didja know he bailed out of college when he got drafted?"

He jerked, "Drafted? Where?"

"Um, he played professional. NFL. Don't remember where. I'm not a sports chick. He was a linebacker for about four years and tore a whole bunch of stuff. Career-ending."

"He's never mentioned any of that."

"Then you probably shouldn't remember any of it until he tells you." She paused, "Okay, I'm telling you that so you won't be sweating this gift. For him, it's something he wants to do, and that guy doesn't do anything without his heart in it. But he's got the money, and that's the real point. It ain't hurting him in the least. Trust me. He's smart."

"Then why is he still working a normal job with me?"

"Because he's smart. Ask him sometime. He loves explaining that part. Good education. I let him talk to me a few times, and I now have an actual portfolio for the first time." She glanced around and confided, "You can be sure I'm not really making jack shit here. But I love it. Wouldn't wanna be anywhere else."

They rounded a corner where the lighting was more reduced and she asked, "What's the lighting like at your place?"

"Honestly, I'm a geek. I keep everything pretty cave-like. I don't really like a lot of light inside. I can get enough of that outdoors." He ran a finger over the rabbit's head again. She could tell he wasn't thinking about it when he did it.

"Perfect. These guys are nocturnal. They don't like a lot of light, either. You'll get along just fine."

Jakub had never seen anything like the fish Seddy had picked out for him. The face was a little strange, but it had a single fin that ran along its underside, and that fin ran in a wavelike motion to propel it around. It was the strangest creature he had seen, but it was soothing at the same time.

Linda's voice shook him back into focus. "I said, she's a low electricity fish. She gives off an electrical impulse." She looked at him again to make sure he was paying attention this time and continued, "The females have a lower frequency than the males, but they use the power of their frequency to attract their mates. Lots of very interesting studies on these guys."

She was pretty in a strange way, but he wasn't there for that. No one had ever given him a fish before, and he knew better than to turn Sedric down. Now everything in his life was in a *go for it* mode, so he said yes without thinking too much on it. If he had any problems, he knew who to call.

"This breed is native to South America, which is why I call her M'ija. She doesn't have a name yet, not a real one anyway. From what I've been told, the natives in South America believed that the souls of those who had passed on actually went into these fish, which is why they're Ghosts. But then again, there are so many versions of that story you'll have to ask Sedric more on that one. I think they're beautiful. Don't know what they have inside them other than the normal fish guts. Don't really care to find out."

He watched her swirl from one end of the tank to the other like something out of a science fiction movie. Linda put her hand in, and the fish swam up immediately like a puppy dog.

"They're also very friendly once they know you and trust you. One of the few fish I can think of that you can actually *hold*. You can even hold her while she's eating, and she doesn't have scales, either. That's why she has that shark-like look to her. She's also a carnivore, I might add. Not like a piranha though. She likes shrimp and things of that sort. Not quite a Red Lobster kinda girl, but not a bad date."

"Angelica Luz," he said aloud.

"Excuse me?" Linda asked him. She appeared to have not understood him.

"Angelica Luz. Her name," Jakub announced, half pointing towards the tank. He saw Linda look up slightly in thought.

"Angel Light. That's like angel light, angelic light, something like that? I just pretend to speak Spanish on TV."

"That's the general idea."

"I like you. That's a good one. I think she'll be happy with that." She observed the fish for a moment and continued, "She can also detect her prey and communicate with her mates in pitch black. They have these little organs that run the length of their bodies and help them with something kinda like radar. They call it geolocation, but that's how I think of it. It's so cool."

He focused on what she was telling him and tried to take in the unbelievable creature that fit his worldview so perfectly.

"I want to make certain that I understand exactly what you're telling me. This is a fish that loves darkness, comes out at night, uses electrical impulses to do damned near everything, and is gentle enough to hold in your hand. On top of that, the female has the greater voltage and uses that for mating."

"And food. But yes."

"Wow. He *did* listen."

"Excuse me?" Linda asked.

"Nothing, never mind. Thinking out loud. Beautiful. She's perfect."

Jakub returned home after they had arranged delivery and prepared the money order he had picked up during lunch. He checked the address twice to verify it was correct. Who wouldn't be happy to see a grand pop up in the mailbox? He wanted to make sure it arrived at the right place, and that it was untraceable.

Maria Salazar. Jakub ensured the address was as it should be, took a breath, and popped it into the envelope.

One task down.

Acting on sound advice had helped life become a little easier. He had an appointment with his new therapist, and once a week they had a support group. The other meeting was more valuable to him.

Jeanette's friend lived in Austin, and she was teaching him to now speak in a new way, and in an uncommon language. One that he didn't imagine *existed* seven months ago.

all aboard

"What kinda crap is this?" Jakub asked the clerk behind the counter. He was at the register in a liquor store that had seen better days, the paneling looking as if it would fall apart at any second. This bastard jacked his bottle prices by two bucks! It wouldn't sound like much to the average Joe, but Jakub needed his supply line clean. He did business here, and a lot of it, too.

The clerk, Sally, stared blankly back at him with a bewildered look.

Sally was a dude.

"We don't really have to go over this shit again, do we Jakie? I mean, you're payin' five bucks more anywhere else you go. I'm not trying to screw ya, I swear. Look around you, does it *look* like I'm getting rich here? I have mouths to feed, and you got one you want to fill up with this stuff. Tryin' to help both of us here. Plus, the distribution's jacking me now, and I'm only passing half of that onto you. So *I'm* actually the one getting screwed here."

Jakub was stuck in the middle of a piss and vinegar moment, and trying to figure how to get out of it. The quickest way was the three bottles on the counter. But still, two fricking bucks apiece? That was more than a fiver right here!

He reached for his wallet because he knew he was walking out of that store with them even if Sally raised the price to a hundred bucks a bottle. Bourbon kept him from killing people and small animals. It was a public service. Sally was eyeballing him with a look of concern.

"I'm not gonna make a scene, Sally. But c'mon, help a brotha out every now and then."

"I *am* helping you out. I didn't raise the price a solid five bucks."

"You know what I mean..." Sally was looking around now. The scattered way he was shifting his attention meant he was about to break.

"Jesus," he breathed, reaching for a mouthwash bottle behind him and clunking it on the counter with the other three. "That's the best I can do. You know this is called enabling, right?"

"It's God's work you're doing here."

"I don't know I'd quite go *that* far."

"You say the word 'enabling' like it's a bad thing. If it helps, just say that you're helping fuel success."

Sally snorted. "We'll call it whatever you wanna call it." He rubbed his brow and cast Jakub a quick glance.

Jakub swiped the card and returned it to his wallet, slipping it into his inside jacket pocket. Easier to keep track of it if it's near your chest. Never know when someone will try the bump and grab and escape with all your hard-earned money. Or at least what you have left of it until payday.

He knew that he had a problem, but it was one problem that was an island in a sea of a million and one other problems. What are you going to do with it? Well, you can at least drink one of those problems away, and when the bottle was empty, you moved on to the next one.

His job was paying the bills and the booze, and apparently housing the bitch. Speaking of which, she was ringing his phone at the moment. And it wasn't to talk. It wasn't ever to talk, but to instruct.

"You haven't stopped for anything for dinner yet, have you?"

"Well..."

"Good. Be a dear and stop by Cafe Brazil. Pick me up a California Chicken. Whatever you're getting. Okay, thanks. See you when you get here."

The line went dead.

You've gotta be kidding me.

It wouldn't have mattered if he had gotten anything or not. She would have vetoed whatever he had picked up, and would have harangued him until he got back in the car and picked up what she wanted. He wondered why in the hell he put up with it to begin with.

She wasn't working any real jobs, she'd pick up little secretary gigs here and there, but being a privileged pain in the ass was enough of a full time job she couldn't keep consistent. On top of that, the girl was way too young for him, which was part of the problem. He was 31, and she wouldn't have been old enough to have graduated from junior college, if she had gone more than one semester to begin with.

Her name was Mitzi Granger. He'd never met her parents in person, just talked to them on the phone once or twice. Daddy was a seven figure LA executive, and always seemed to be off traveling somewhere for business. Given the moral aptitude of his daughter, and the stories she had of her mother's entertainment capabilities, he was out there sowing his wild seeds as well. Probably running off with girls his daughter's age.

We all make mistakes. Jakub's was ever letting Mitzi sink her claws into him. She was used to a certain type of lifestyle and now she pretty much demanded it out of Jakub's salary that wasn't near enough to support her tastes. No chance in hell that he was going to be competing with Daddy's wallet anytime soon.

Thankfully, the Café Brazil was only a few blocks from Sally, so it didn't take too long to get there. He walked up to place the order and surveyed their menu.

Twenty bucks.

Twenty bucks for a damned California Chicken. It wasn't the price of the meal that bothered him, they had incredible food there, but more that she entertained herself trying to pick the most expensive items on any menu, and instead of asking nicely, demanding them. The demanding got him the most worked up.

He had a larger problem. He was a wuss. Why deny it? He should have kicked her out on her ass about two months ago. She was one of the things you get at his friend Jermaine's parties, and that is not what you want to be taking home if you think about it long and hard.

He tacked on a few pasteis and called it a day. Pick your battles carefully. He wasn't feeling it tonight, and it had been a long day. He would get nothing out of her other than her eating her dinner and going back to whatever strange pecking text battle she was going to have with her friends as she took over his television.

Mostly reality TV shows. If the word Housewives was in the title, she was there with her little pack, all trying to figure out how they were going to get to that point. He was figuring out that he wasn't a boyfriend or a relationship of any kind, he was a career choice for the fledgling gold digger until she found the next lily pad to light on. While there were some points off and on that benefited him, for the most part, she was a house guest. She had overstayed her welcome and had no intention on ever becoming involved in anything outside her party girl world.

Weekends were pretty quiet, she would go off with her gal pals, and he would get volutold for mandatory fun by his other friends.

It was time to pick up the order, drive it back to the house and hook up with his mistresses in the brown paper bag. The Princess of La-La Land could go about surveying her kingdom and her royal subjects.

Jakub decided to take the backstreets home instead of trying to fight with the traffic on Venice. He could drive slower and munch one of the pastels before he pulled in and that would help his stomach for the evening. As he unwrapped one, he wondered exactly how in the hell he'd gotten himself into this. She had met his sister Willow, and while Willie had too much of that Texas decency to say anything stupid, he was confident she didn't approve.

That'd been about it on the social calendar. She wouldn't go anywhere with any of his other friends, and stayed in her own little circles. He wasn't sure if he was really her boyfriend, or her perceived sugar daddy that she would spread for when she needed to make sure she had a place to stay. He should've doubled down on that one.

It sounded like a crass discussion to have, but it had come down to that. She had spotted him at one of those damned head-spinning EDM soirées that Jermaine hosted. Hell, he was the one that introduced them. Kinda pushed her into him. Jakub wasn't going to fight it, she *was* that attractive, and she was that much of a turn on. At least until you'd been around her for a week when you were solidly on the hook.

His thoughts shattered by the phone ringing again, except it wasn't Mitzi. It was worse.

Mom.

She was the other person he didn't want to talk to tonight. Her problem was that she *thought* she was still 22. She had a delusion that she was a walking college coed dream when in fact she was on the fast track to becoming more accurately a geriatric nightmare.

Dump that one to voicemail.

Mom came with her own set of problems, most of them mental, and no one seemed to really know where it had started. She had gotten ill when he was in the 7th grade and ended up losing her career because she became bedridden. Dad had gotten her a nurse. But he didn't have the sense or the power to get an ugly older nurse, or maybe he hoped things had gone different. The nurse that was sent to practically live in was a hot little number named Vera.

She was really pretty, and in about nine months Mom was back in business. She had decided she was a lesbian, and with that silver tongue she had stitched up the lovely medical lass in more ways than one. Mom packed up and left Dad one fine morning after the kids had gone to school and figuring everything was quiet, she was going to sneak off.

The problem was, Dad actually loved her crazy ass. Which was why he spent so much money on Vera the Vixen in the first damned place. That night ended at about 1AM when the loud crack shattered what started as a painful but normal night for the kids. Willow found him and what parts of his cranial cavity were still identifiable all over the bathroom walls.

Mom carried on as if nothing had happened at all, and put on a decent enough show for the cops that they simply called it a suicide and kissed her ass until her quota was up. No real surprise that Willow got married young. She spent as much time out of the house as she possibly could, and once she was out, she tried to keep Jakub with her as much as they could stand.

Carl Samson was the young buck that married her. He was your typical Texas backwoods boy, the blue collar salt of the earth type, and of course Jakub approved of him.

Carl was just good people.

Mom convinced Vera to relocate to Houston. That started this whole mess and it was where the kids left her. She didn't have the physical or mental ability to leave anyone alone or take a hint. She called him a few times a week. When she was having one of her *I have to fuck with someone* episodes, she would ring Jakub's phone repeatedly until he answered. One night she rang 34 times in a row. She'd been known to call LAPD to perform a welfare check on him when he didn't answer. That was the girlfriend before Mitzi. He had considered marrying her. Took her back to Texas.

Mom tried to corner her in the bathroom, and it wasn't to talk about the relationship with her son. Her name was Janet. She was a smart girl 2 years his junior, and when they returned home to Los Angeles, they were in the middle of a steamy encounter when the cops began pounding on the door.

Janet packed that night, and he never heard from her again. She changed her number. He knew better than to hunt her down. He knew why she left, and couldn't blame her one bit.

Thankfully Vera's income didn't allow for them to come out to California, then again, Mom didn't offer, and he wasn't inviting. The phone thing was enough. Conversely, he saw Willow more frequently. They kept player points on gambling programs, and he would use her cards to play slots when he killed time in Las Vegas. That way they could afford to come out every year and meet, then he would go see them. Vegas was where Willow had met Mitzi, who tried to spend every last penny Jakub had, but not while shopping *with him*. The rest of the time she spent trying to wander off, snapping selfies for her social accounts like she was a rock star. Jakub was not in a single one of those pictures, either.

That's right, the guy that had actually funded the venture.

As he pulled into the parking garage he remembered he'd been put on the hook for something else, but wasn't listening to Jermaine long enough to recall exactly what it was. Jermaine Hutchens worked the mail room and spent his off time building himself as a show promoter. When he wasn't in the mail room, he tried to show off to the world like he made five times what he actually did and dressed the part.

He got his clothes the same place Jakub did, a thrift shop on the back side of Beverly Hills where all the rich people and production companies offloaded their practically new clothes. You had to get them before the sharks did. A Marc Jacobs for $25 ain't gonna last long on the rack. Janet had been in love with the place. Mitzi acted like she was being asked to step through a mud puddle while wearing white.

Jakub parked and sat still for a moment. He could feel the heat from the bag on his hand. He really didn't want to move, but knew he was going to have to. This all was so stupid because it was *his* apartment! He was being ruled and lorded over by some young clueless bitch in an apartment he *paid for*!

Willow said he needed to get some counseling or see a therapist. She thought he drank too much. She recognized how much Mom contributed to it and blamed Mom for the fact that his major life decisions, with the exception of moving from Texas to California after college were shit decisions.

She was correct for the most part. You couldn't deny it. But he wasn't ready to throw that towel in the ring yet.

something more

Jakub felt like he was coming apart at the seams. Work wasn't too bad of a gig, he did the things he needed to, and they weren't much of a challenge. He didn't want or need *too* much of a challenge. There was enough going on between his mother and the teenybopper leech he'd picked up. There were some big things still missing in life, and the bourbon wasn't filling them.

In the meantime, it'd have to do.

Mitzi clutched her food, gave the nod of approval that meant he was free from any further marching orders for the night. She set to the conquering of her Housewife fiefdom, wherever in the hell that was going to take place. Probably on her phone tittering about with her friends. You can unquestionably pick too young, even when they're adults.

He couldn't help but ask himself the question. *What in the hell are relationships really about, anyway?* It couldn't just be about the sex. Any idiot of either gender could easily pay for that. What was it he was looking for? Was it to have a living body next to him that he could turn to, even if they weren't going to pay the slightest attention to his existence? Maybe having someone there could be enough, but it certainly wasn't a workable long term solution.

Sometimes he looked at himself in the mirror and wondered who in the actual fuck he was, and did it really even matter in the end?

Why was he even here?

But the apparent fact was that he *was* here, and he might as well make everyone else suffer for that fact as much as he did. Still, there had to be something good out there, a life that was fulfilling, one that he could get joy out of, have a reason to live, and feel like he had some sense of purpose. This certainly wasn't it, though.

He'd heard enough of the self-help speeches and other feel-good mythologies to know there had to be something out there. Otherwise there wouldn't be anything to crow about.

How hard is it to find out who we really are, and what we're here for? It shouldn't be that big of a thing, he knew people that didn't give it a second thought or care in the least, but the problem was that he *did*. This wasn't the first time he'd went over this in his head, either. Jakub had made it a habit. An abusive habit, to be more exact.

It's like we come to Earth to be abused, he thought. Like humans need punishment because they all generally suck and someone needs to beat them all into shape for some bizarre reason. That's probably what God's for. Maybe everyone is in a big experiment like some universal ant farm. He runs around, figures out who he has a hard-on for, or a case of the ass with, and then he goes at them with a stick. Whack-whack-whack.

Who knows?

Then again, who cares? It all ends the same way, anyway. He reached out to take his glass again. You run around and suffer for however many decades, then you take a dirt nap and somebody sings songs from *The Lion King* over you. The worms eat you, shit you out, grass grows, it's the Circle of Life.

It is what it is.

Jakub hadn't remembered pouring the drink, but it was there in his hand, so might as well drink it all up. That *was* what he was paying the man for.

He could hear a celebrity woman whining about her first world problems again. He wished he could reach out and touch her. Preferably with a right hook or a blunt instrument. But that was the crap that Mitzi was into, and as long as Mitzi was quiet, relative peace reigned. He really didn't have the patience or energy to shake up her program.

Several problems were at play here. He had no idea what he wanted to do when he grew up, which should have been about a decade ago, and was getting no traction in anything he did. He had no purpose and the only goals he had was to not get Mitzi riled up, keep a paycheck, and most importantly keep his glass relatively full. Which kept him from hurting peoples feelings or testing their medical insurance plans. With Sally raising the prices, that mucked with his drunk budgeting. And that's exactly what it was... *drunk* budgeting.

Tony Robbins can't solve *all* your fucking problems for you.

When the room is slightly rotating, that's when you know you have entered the Plane of Don't Give A, and can relax a little. He had a mind full of F-bombs, and wanted to cut back here and there. It wasn't easy, and it became increasingly more difficult as the liquid in the bottle went away. But there was a little calm to enjoy.

The other bad part of the adventure was the age gap. Perhaps in another ten years it wouldn't have been a thing, but right now, it was a bit much. He was 31, supposed to be established, supposed to be in middle management or something. When he became 41, a girl in her 30s wouldn't be an issue. It would almost be expected. Then you're with someone that has earned their stripes, too. Just not as many as you.

In their case, he was like a professor macking on the students. Except she was about as sharp as a sack of wet leather and triple the personal drive for fame and popularity. Maybe if she had that much sexual drive, she'd be worth keeping around.

Why exactly *was* he keeping her around, anyway?

He heard a cat fight start on the reality show. There was tittering and tapping. Must be nice to not have to worry about what you're spending, what you're doing, or where you're going. Or, it might not be. He wouldn't know. He was having a hard enough time trying to keep his head straight to begin with.

He wanted to punch them all in the mouth, but it was easier to put the burning brown stuff into his. As long as he wasn't leaving the house it shouldn't be much of a problem to anyone. He opened his laptop to check sports scores and saw the new email. One of those heavy graphics money sucking machines his workmate Jermaine sent to let him know he had secured him admission to yet another party of his.

Who names a white kid "Jermaine"?

Jakub wasn't sure why he went to those things. Probably because he had a love for underdogs, and he liked rags-to-riches stories. He proceeded to open it. Jermaine had a tracker with his email campaigns, and Jakub didn't want to play the game, pretending he hadn't seen the message and then listening to a bunch of self-pity. Easier to show up to his parties and be a body. It gave him something to do. But it wasn't his group, and he wasn't sure where his group *was*.

Maybe he needed to get a hobby or find something a little more useful to do. It was work, eat, and then free time that wasn't free. For him, he was going back into lockup. There wasn't any issue with staying home, but if he left, he had to render a report, though she couldn't give a shit either way. She wasn't going to interact with him that much, but acted as if the world would end if she didn't have a GPS location on every place he decided to fart.

All of it was annoying. He was a free man, paying the bills and making his own way. Why was he having to answer to a young debutante? He couldn't score regularly while living in his own house. Something wasn't right with that whole equation, and something was going to have to be done about it. Figuring out what he would do and how to handle it were the two biggest problems.

Jakub had forgotten what number of glass he was on, but he was starting to feel it and the glass was empty. Those were the two determining factors on whether to get another drink or not. If it was empty, fill it. If he could still remember it, fill it. Fill it until he couldn't *feel* it. Then it was time to go to sleep and do it all over again tomorrow.

He shifted his way to the bedroom, curious why it was that he was always going to bed alone. If he didn't have any company, why bother? Perhaps it was Jakub being a little grumpy, because when he woke up in the morning, Mitzi was always there on her side of the bed next to him, usually facing away. She liked to sleep on her right side, and he liked to sleep on his left, or facing whichever way was off the bed. It was the way he did things, and he had no explanation for it.

It just was.

Sometimes he wondered how much of this was all in his head. For all he knew, life on Planet Mitzi could be rainbows and unicorns. He really had no way to gauge it other than she always did her thing, and he always did his. There really wasn't any twinsies type stuff going on, they weren't trying to dress the same or force themselves to always do the same things so they could be the socially acceptable "cute couple" and other than the occasional excursion out, she was pretty much a homebody and seemed to like it that way.

As he had predicted, when he woke the next morning, Mitzi was there, settled off into dreamland. He managed to force himself out of bed and get the coffee started as he prepared for work. There wasn't much to do, and today was supposed to be relatively quiet. He could expect Cliff to force most of his load off onto Jakub and play online games or something. Who knew what he was doing with all of that time?

Jakub ran through his head what he could remember of the service ticket lists. Some machines and laptops needed their operating systems wiped. There were network adjustments to make, user accounts in and out, it never ended, but the pace was a turtle race, so it didn't matter. At this point, he wasn't shooting for more. The corporate ladder had a few rungs missing, and jumping them didn't make sense.

By the time he had gulped down his first cup of coffee, Mitzi was stirring.

"What time are you gonna be home?" She asked him.

"The usual, about five or five-thirty," he responded. "Why?"

"I figured we could do something, go out to eat, or order in if you want. I wanted to get an idea of how to schedule my day."

Why the hell does it matter? You're not going to do anything but watch TV and text your friends...

"Okay. That sounds good," he answered, "We'll figure it all out when I get in, then."

He grabbed his bag and stepped into the hallway, almost bumping into the neighbor, Mrs. Costa. She was heading back to her apartment from who knows where that early in the morning. Her wispy thin robe was screaming for every male in a 50-foot vicinity to recognize the fact that she was wearing a thong.

It was a typical morning for her in that regard. She wanted to be desired in a much more animalistic way than Mitzi did. Mitzi craved people to see her for the recognition and fame, usual things for a girl her age in Los Angeles considering the pack she ran with.

Mrs. Costa was in her 50s and wanted to be lusted after and dry humped like she was practicing for a porn shoot. He couldn't remember ever having seen her with real clothes on more than a handful of times since he'd moved in. She was the prowling epitome of a cougar in the Beverly Hills wild.

"Goot Murning, Mr. *Riser*," she greeted him with an accent and an emphasis on his last name. He imagined that she always accentuated his last name as if it were a pun that she wanted him to recognize. The gaze she inflicted on him reminded him of prey at the zoo, and he had an image in his head of her feasting on his insides like that movie he'd seen on the nature channel. She was hungry, like a lioness. He made sure to keep his eyes at head level.

"Morning, Mrs. Costa," he responded, "Have a great day."

"Oh, I will," she purred.

He saw as he turned the corner in the hallway that she was stretching over slowly to retrieve the key without bending her knees for that extra showmanship. She fished it from under the mat and checked with a side glance to see if he was watching.

Of course, he was. It was difficult not to. She might have been in her 50s, but she had flaming red hair and still held together like she was 25 years younger. Besides, because there's a show going on for the public doesn't mean you don't observe it for curiosity's sake at the minimum. He was wondering why that cranky bastard Mr. Costa wasn't dead from a heart attack yet. The poor guy should have been over-worked in the sack by now if he was doing his job right. After all, she was *his* trophy wife.

Jakub didn't know what Mr. Costa did for a living, but he understood there was a substantial amount of money involved. Since they were living in that particular building, Signore Costa was most certainly a miser.

The drive into work was smooth for a change, after all, when you understand how to operate in Los Angeles traffic, you have half of the battle licked. It's all about timing. Once you figure out what your window is, you stick to it. Five minutes deviation screws everything up and adds an extra hour to your commute.

Cliff behaved exactly as predicted, leaving a large part of the work on Jakub, who didn't mind since it kept him occupied and in the eyes of the powers that were in the office. Having those eyes on him meant that usually they invited him to share in lunches the partners would order for clients.

Today was one of those days, and it was a Sam's Deli day. That's when a $10 sandwich tastes the best and at the peak of freshness...

When it's free.

Typical days with nothing but routine and a little perk here and there. The less excitement, the better for everyone, especially Jakub. Quiet, stability, and normalcy soothed him. Being able to predict what would happen in a typical day made it easy to work through it and plan everything else.

Like a date with the nighttime bottle. He didn't drink at work usually, although a time or two he slipped off at lunch and had a shot or two. Or three. But not if he was going to be face to face with the higher partners or any of the clients. That would be asking for trouble.

Given the perks today, that was the primary reason that Jakub drove back home stone-cold sober.

no turning back

As soon as he saw the khaki clad boy with the dreads and the Seattle grunge sock cap, he sensed something was off. He hadn't seen him before, but the boy cast an embarrassed side glance at him as he passed on the walkway. But he didn't enter the parking garage, he walked further down the sidewalk, away from the business district and towards the residential section.

Not a resident.

The other thing that had been strange was that for a change, Mitzi had not called in a dinner order. He had actually been relieved. Sometimes she didn't and they would go out. He would know if she was dressed to kill, and that would be another high bill that wasn't intended for the budget.

He could hear scurrying inside the apartment as he turned the key in the lock. The scent of fresh air freshener hit him full force as Jakub saw that Mitzi was in fact not even remotely close to being dressed to kill. She was in shorts and a t-shirt.

She wasn't wearing a bra. For some women that would be a normal thing for a domesticated couple, but not for her. She was always trying to be in television presentation mode as if she were going to be on TV herself.

"Hi," she said brightly with a smile. "Did you have a good day, honey?"

"It was okay. What did you do today?" Too cheerful. She was trying way too hard.

"Well, I lounged around for a little bit and tried to get into the work rotation. They say they might have something for me tomorrow." It was a Thursday. The temp agencies rarely put a worker out for the first day on a Friday. Now he was getting really itchy.

"Nice," he said, forcing a smile. "What else?"

"Oh, I went for a walk. I just got back a while ago. I wanna relax now. Maybe we should get something delivered tonight." She gave a coy look with her eyes. Mitzi wanted to play. The problem was that Jakub identified the scent she was trying to cover up with the air spray. She wanted to play in order to cover that up.

There is a feeling that is close to walking off a plank into the ocean. You know the water is there, it's cold, and you know what it's like to be wet. He could pretty much smell the salty sea air.

"Cool! I'll be back in a minute. Gotta go to the bathroom." He headed into the bathroom and turned on the exhaust fan.

I wonder of she's this amateur, he thought as he began pawing quietly through the trash can. He found a few pieces of paper, two toilet paper rolls, and saw nothing of note in there. Something in his gut told him to look again.

This time, he took the toilet paper rolls and actually looked inside them. The first one was empty. He knew what was in the second one before his brain identified it.

A blue condom wrapper.

It had been shoved inside along the wall so it wouldn't fall out and generally wouldn't be seen through the bag. Sneaky, but stupid. He was glad they hadn't thrown the used condom in the trash as well. That would have been messy and extremely irritating to find the hard way. They probably flushed it.

He examined himself in the mirror, contemplated what the next best move was. He surveyed his face, looking deeply into his own eyes, and realized something strange.

He wasn't angry.

This was an out, and it had been handed to him on a silver platter. He could do one of several things with it. Either store it up for later, or hide it back in the trash can and pretend he didn't see it.

It was the lack of emotion that he felt which presented the most strange shock to him. He had envisioned this before and figured he'd be one of those guys to go on a nuclear jealous tear and explode on anyone in a three-mile radius. But thinking of all the money he would now save, and the fact that he could actually get his television back made him wonder which way was the best in the long run. He had that damned nice guy streak that always seemed to get him screwed over.

Jakub took another long look into his own eyes, flushed the toilet, and stepped back into the hallway. Mitzi was parked with her buttocks against the top of the couch lightly bouncing, trying to arch her back in a tease. She was nervous. Even with the flirting, she wasn't hiding it well.

He smiled sweetly at her and said, "I have the *perfect* thing for us to do tonight."

She perked up.

Jakub produced the condom wrapper between his fingers and said, "It starts with you getting the fuck out of my house. Because I keep good track of what I put on *my* dick, and this ain't it. Considering it's been almost a month since I've been able to put anything on said dick, this ain't mine and you have a problem."

The color drained from her face.

"Here's what I'm gonna do," he paused, and it felt like daggers were leaving his eyes at mach four, "I'm going to be a gentleman and leave for one hour. When I get back, you and your shit will be gone. I don't care *how* it's gone, call up that Pearl Jam looking motherfucker and have him haul your shit on his bicycle for all I care. But if you *are* here, and anything I own is not intact, you will have the pleasure of being introduced to the Los Angeles County Sheriffs Department." He held up a finger, "No further discussions are necessary. I know what brands I use and don't use, and I'm really bad about picking out patterns and boys that are scared shitless of me. *You* decided to hit that young dick, so you can go see if that young dick can now behave like a man. Good luck with that one."

He grabbed his keys and walked to the door. Turning, he said, "One hour. Don't care where you go, but you ain't staying here. In case I was unclear in *any* way, you have my genuine invitation to get the fuck out of my house." Mitzi opened her mouth as if she were going to speak.

"O-U-W-T, out."

There was no waiting to see what happened next. He went straight to his car, turned the ignition and left. He headed down Venice towards the ocean without any particular destination in mind. He still couldn't feel anything. No anger, no real judgement. On one hand, he couldn't blame her because they were in vastly different worlds. Most women her age were beginning their careers or finishing college. It was a totally different set of friends and people. She had not incorporated into his world, and he had no desire to join hers, so the only real things that had connected them was that he had some consistent money, and they had sex.

The sex wasn't bad, of course, but it can't build anything. You could conceivably have a relationship without sex, not that he would *want* to, but you can't have a relationship, let alone a marriage without being able to relate. And at his age, he knew he needed to start finding that off ramp from the single life.

Jakub considered going to a club, but the fact was that he was driving, and he only had an hour or so to spare before he went back to the ranch. She didn't have that many possessions with her, so it really shouldn't take her that long to get everything together and leave. It was very likely that she spent more time calling for a ride than she did in actually leaving. Not that she would have a shortage of people to come pick her up. She seemed to have a black book many times the size of his.

He should develop his a little more.

A glance to his right helped him realize where he was. His favorite burger place. The perfect spot for him to spend an hour and reflect on what had happened. As he pulled into the parking lot, he was thankful it was a Thursday. Crowds were much lighter. For some reason everyone in LA seemed to think that the weekend was the time for fast food. That was usually when he stayed hid, or escaped the city. And he hadn't gone escaping in some time. Not since the last time he saw his sister Willow in Las Vegas.

He found the red-coated interior calming. The most plausible reason was that she wouldn't eat here, some crazy pop-culture pro-vegetarian protesting thing, although she was about as much of a vegetarian as a pack of coyotes. She thought it made her look cool, he thought it made him hungrier.

As he walked in and stepped up to the thankfully short line, he found himself standing behind a taller surfer-looking guy with blondish hair. Surfer guy actually wasn't the kid Jakub had first thought he was. In fact, he was about his age or a little older, with a shock of hair he kept flipping out of his face every couple of seconds. He looked over at Jakub and smiled, then with the hair finally getting to him, flipped it backwards over his head producing a soft ball cap from his back pocket and clapping it on this head.

"Gonna fix that bullshit," he muttered. Then he eyed Jakub again and asked, "What's goin' on? Good day so far?"

Jakub smiled, "Good *now*. I kicked my ex-girlfriend out of the house."

Surfer Guy jerked his head back. "Damn. Well, sometimes ya gotta change the oil in life, huh? I'm sure it'll all pick up for now. You get a clean slate to start over with. I know it hurts in there somewhere, but it's really more like pulling off a band-aid. Been there a few times."

Standing in silence for a few moments, he looked back over and said, "Name's Aiden. Aiden Jarrells. I know, I had flower child wannabe parents. You can't blame them, parents rarely know what the hell they're doing at the time. Now everyone's been asking me if I'm Irish my entire life. I'm thinking my momma had a crush on an actor, but she isn't copping to it." He put out his hand, and Jakub took it.

"Jakub Riser. You live near here?"

"Meh, I say here and there. I was doing the 9 to 5 grind for years and decided to take a break and float around."

The girl at the register called him forward. He ordered his meal and directed with a thumb backwards, "And whatever he's having, please." Jakub was confused at first, but Aiden turned and said, "It's your day, we might as well celebrate. On me."

How Angeleno was that?

The crew were on the ball tonight. Their order took no time to arrive at the counter, and Aiden invited Jakub to come sit with him at one of the red tables. It seemed like a good way to kill an hour. The ability to have an unattached conversation with a complete stranger had a therapeutic ring to it. He would be able to talk to someone who would actually listen to him.

"So tell me about yourself," Aiden began, " Where does this put you now that you're free? Have any plans, anything that you were really wanting to do that you couldn't do before? I know that for me when I was in those kinds of relationships there was always at least one thing that I wanted to do and couldn't because of her."

"Well, I know that I like socializing, and instead I end up going to parties with all of these rave kids that serve me no useful purpose. Wouldn't mind taking a road trip somewhere. Maybe across country, or go to Vegas for much too long."

"I'm picking up the South. Where are you from?"

"Texas."

"Ah, that would be the sound. I like Texas. I wandered around Austin and Dallas for a while. Went to San Antonio once. That's an entirely different world there. Really nice people."

"Yeah, it's certainly slower there," Jakub said, "It's quite a bit different than the world here."

"See, that's what I like. I'm from here, so I grew up in all of this mess. Then when I got older, I got way too far into the world as it is until I guess I broke. Last few years, I've been a bit of a bum, working enough to feed myself, keep a little in the bank, and fund my traveling to everywhere I wanted to go. If you get the chance or the notion, *take it*. It's worth it."

"Where did you come from this time?"

"Well, I spent about three weeks in Nepal and Tibet. Went to Kathmandu. It's kinda on the border. I figured that if it was good enough for Bob Seger to sing about, I might as well go. The square there is little but it proves that if you ever want to find where a town square is, ask a pigeon. Holy crap, there was like a million of them there. They even hang on the sides and ledges of all the surrounding little buildings. And the color, that's all some weird mahogany shade and you think you're gonna smell patchouli forever and a day, but um..." he gave a slight stink eye, "Yeah. Not quite that."

"Where are you gonna go next?"

"Haven't decided. I think I'll get some work with the studios a while, retool, then maybe Amsterdam again. If I get the right sale on tickets, it might go well. Could head to Australia, or Patagonia. You know, there's a group right in the smack middle of Argentina that speak Welsh. Odd. I like odd things, and then I like to go see them. But, if I go there, then I have to go to Rio, and holy god..." He leaned back with a relaxed smile on his face, "The women are *incredible*. I'd never get out of there alive. How about you? Have you done any traveling?"

"Not anything to really speak of, I've only been here in the States. Mostly what you see between here and Texas. I've been wasting too much time chasing women, and not enough time doing it effectively."

"You need *you* time, brah," Aiden said, "It's your life, and you're the only one that can live in your skin. Now you have a shot at doing exactly that, so maybe it's time to do some wild stuff. At the very least treat yourself better. The way you actually deserve to be treated. I get the gut feeling that the time for changes is headed your way like a runaway 18-wheeler. Just don't let it hit you, okay?" He laughed.

Jakub smiled, "Deal. I'll get right on that. Especially after I get back to make sure my apartment is clear of ex-girlfriends and their shady friends."

Aiden produced a business card. "You should probably hang on to this in case you need a rather unknown voice to talk to. I had these made up, you might want to consider it. You never know who you'll meet, and you might want to talk to them again, so you give them your card, and it doesn't matter where you work because it's yours. After all, you *are* a brand, whether you realize it or not, and you dictate what that brand's gonna be. Only you have that voice. I'd like to hear from you again, and if we're in the same place we can meet up for coffee or a drink or something."

"I'd like that," Jakub said, retrieving the card from Aiden.

They parted ways, and as Jakub drove home, he understood how exciting it was to leave the house and be on his own again.

The apartment was empty of Mitzi's belongings and the keys neatly laid upon the kitchen bar.

take a breath

The trash had been removed from the apartment, she had parted much differently than others in the past, and Jakub was grateful for that. Something nagged him in the back of his mind that none of this was right. It was the right action at the time for them to separate, but he mulled over the condom wrapper. Of all the shenanigans Mitzi would be prone to do, cheating wasn't one of them.

It made him wonder what it was about him that was so bad it could have driven her to it. For some reason the thought should have made him happier, but all it did was depress him because now he was reflective about his own shortcomings and failures instead of the beneficial chance he now happened upon.

He cracked a new bottle. Apparently she had walked with his open one, and he was somehow okay with that. If it was her best shot at revenge against him, then it didn't hurt, which he was good with. If it was because she wanted a strong drink after the shock of the day, then he owed her a drink at least.

Something about the sound of the ice popping and cracking after a stream of bourbon met it in the glass was soothing. It was like when you were a kid and someone like an aunt that had spent way too much time rearranging the skin on your cheeks moments ago in a death pinch poured Coke over ice.

The popping, the cracking, the fizz. The bliss of that first sip as the sun beat down on your neck. It was a straw short of heaven.

He plopped down on his couch, took in the faux tan suede that covered it and flipped the television to a non-interesting channel. It wasn't housewives, but he found himself equally bored with it.

In his own thoughts, Jakub tried to come to a sense of the day and knew soon he would have to prepare for tomorrow.

Friday.

And he could do almost anything he wanted to do with the weekend. Except for that damned thing Jermaine was throwing in a few weeks. He'd have to show up to that. Mitzi would probably skip his show thing to avoid Jakub, because unlike her, he was being roped into those first hand. She only came to them to meet her friends and dance to the oompa boompa music. It made them feel like little socialites, which was mostly her racket anyway.

The realization almost hurt. He had time on his hands, and the ability to do almost anything he wanted to do, but he didn't have any *real* friends. There was people he knew from work, and the on again, off again girls he had dated, but nobody he could really consider a friend that he wanted to call and unload his troubles on or invite over for a drink and a good stiff talk. He knew the drink was rather stiff, too, but that wasn't the point.

He'd met that cool guy at the burger shop tonight, but he didn't know Aiden well enough to call him up and invite him over. From the way he'd talked, Jakub figured he would probably do it.

Sometimes we invest in the wrong shit, Jakub thought to himself as he felt the liquid burn down the back of his throat. Drinking is a pastime, not a friend. And he hadn't really had a friendship with Mitzi. That was more of a fuckship with a live-in woman. They had no connection, really. Janet had been an obsession, she had smarts and power, and he felt important himself around her. Scoring her had actually put a feather in his cap that said he wasn't an idiot and wasn't complete trash. Mom responded, fixing his matrimonial situation for good with her well-timed obnoxious stunts that would be punishable by sexual harassment laws anywhere else.

Willie was about all he had in terms of people to talk to in an intimate sense. It was one of the perks of having a close sibling. And there was no way in hell he was going to call her this late to tell her what happened. *The Epic of Mitzi Granger* could wait until the next time he talked to her.

Jakub had those dreams from time to time that he imagined every male did. The perfect girl with the look that sent you over the edge, her voice led you around by the nose because it was so enticing. She was everything you ever wanted. You didn't care if she farted at dinner or told your mother to screw herself. However, in his case he would consider the possibility of paying off a date to tell his mother to kindly copulate with herself using a blunt, rusty implement. That wasn't a good litmus test.

He was feeling a little calmer and switched the channel again, where some Tony Robbins video was showing. He didn't know why, he just liked the guy. If Jakub took a little more of his advice and worked at what he was saying, he could get things to function better in his life. Maybe not. It's all a craps shoot, anyway.

Tony had a polite Marine drill sergeant demeanor about him, a suave *I'm gonna lead you to water, but you have to do the drinking* mentality. He was busy nailing some dude to the wall about his relationship at home. The poor sap squirmed out of the lines of questioning like he was being interrogated by an angry in-law.

Jakub had an instant shower thought:

I wonder if most in-laws know they are really outlaws?

That probably wasn't entirely fair, any girl he married would have an awesome sister-in-law. Her mother-in-law, not so much. Can't win 'em all. He'd just go shopping for good in-laws, that was all. Never know what you might dig up if you go to the right places, which obviously wasn't one of Jermaine's parties.

He knocked off the last of his alcohol as the burning seemed to taper from its antiseptic fury. Wandering aimlessly to his bedroom, he dove face-first into the over-priced yet insanely comfortable bed. The one he was noticing in a haze still had coffee-colored bachelor sheets that screamed Jakub was single and now alone. The latter fact was failing to register too much, possibly of his own intention, as he stepped off the plank of the good ship Jolly Jakub into the ocean of sleep.

He didn't swim too hard, either.

One would think that a night's sleep after such an eventful and satisfying ending to the day would be restful. After all, he wasn't sure that he had moved from the time he hit the mattress. When he woke the following morning, it felt like he was peeling himself away from the bed like the cellophane off the back of a fruit leather. Sure, today would help pay the bills, but that was about it. He wasn't curing cancer or refining the theory of relativity. He was going to be calming down executives that shouldn't otherwise be allowed near high value electronics, and pushing cables to and fro to accommodate the turnover.

Thank god for automatic coffee pots. One small, menial task that feels like decoding a blueprint on *Mission Impossible* in the first ten minutes of being awake when you didn't want to be. He wasn't putting too much effort into building his travel mug, either. A splash of cream, a light handful of sugar, topped with a good shot of hazelnut liqueur, it was close enough.

Off to another blurry day that really wouldn't have anything of note, no purpose, no meaning, and the best excitement he could hope for might be a good sandwich at lunch if he was lucky. A boy can be a sucker for a good sandwich in the right environment.

Paco, the other mail guy was at the door when he got to the office. "You seen Party Boy?" He was referring to Jermaine, of course.

"Nope. We ain't joined at the hip. I haven't seen him since I left work yesterday. Why? Did he get himself in trouble again?"

"I don't know yet, but I'm sure I'll find out soon." He grimaced with some pain and after letting Jakub through slid back into the door himself. The poor bastard was always hurting somewhere. Paco had two jobs, this was the second. From what he had said previously, he worked in a grocery store overnight. Liked to talk about all of the stars he'd seen lurking around in the middle of the night. It was like having a personal Joan Rivers show that never slept.

At his cubicle, he plopped into the "commander chair" he had confiscated from a former exec and slid into his own gray fabric cell. The phone had voicemails.

Of course.

Pawing at the arrows on the phone revealed a call from his sister, one from the front desk, and two from a disgruntled co-worker that he was not looking forward to seeing. He couldn't recall anyone right off that liked dealing with her, so he had to spend the extra time to blow sunshine and rainbows up her ass to keep her calm. Hell, if she'd maintain some sense of composure today, he might buy her a unicorn to go with them.

His eyes landed on a purple butterfly that had been pinned to the wall of the cubicle. He had no idea who the guilty party was, but he left it. Might be good luck somewhere.

After all, butterflies are cool.

He thought about the fact that Willie had called him. She didn't normally call him during the day, and usually spoke with him at night. He should probably check his email. She was the canary in the mine shaft when it came to having to deal with their mother. If she knew Mom's stupidity was about to go in a fire hose mode, she would normally give him a warning. Neither of them liked dealing with her.

And the only thing he disliked as much as talking to Mom was the ticking bomb of emails he knew he was about to uncover. He had organized them in a specific manner to safely ignore a large portion of them without getting too deep in the weeds.

Sarah's email was the one that stuck out. Yes, she was going to Jermaine's party too, and no, before he asked, he couldn't get a ride because her girlfriend Lindsey still couldn't stand his ass. He had no clue what he'd ever done to her. She had always been civil to him and vice versa, but it seemed that the only time Lindsey would let him within five feet of her was when he was loaded and they were all trying to get away from the "events" like extras in *Escape From New York.*

It was a shame that she didn't like him. He knew she and Sarah were a thing, he knew he wouldn't be able to get her attention, but at least he could be liked. That shouldn't be asking too much, especially for someone you've never even said a crosswise word to.

To be honest, she unnerved him, too. Very likely for the opposite reason. He had every reason to be jealous of Sarah. But Lindsey was quiet, kept mostly to herself and simply watched people. And he could not help but simply watch *her.* Maybe he was giving off a creep vibe and didn't realize it. That was probably it. There are some people that you can't help but look at. They grab your attention without trying any time they enter a room. She happened to be one of those people, that's all.

He forced the thoughts out of his mind. Being newly single didn't help in that area, anyway, and if you spend your life focusing on the women you can't have, a guy will go crazy.

Opening the email from his boss, he hoped it was a boring waste of digital space that had no impact on real life. He found himself almost excited to discover that was the case.

Delete. The key of the gods.

A bunch of tech ads belonging to mailing lists he'd forgotten to unsubscribe from, and the email he *did* make the mistake of opening was from some company hawking their latest gaming goggles. He had a friend in that business. Okay, not a friend, but more of a person of loyalty. They both had North Texas in common, and that's sometimes enough.

Anteryx. Sounded like an animal. Looked like birth control for the face. But the screenshots were neat, some new release in virtual reality. He was having enough issues with conventional reality as it was. Why add more bullshit to your life?

More status reports, server activity, push and pull lists, all things a growing boy needs to ignore while getting through the morning coffee, which in fact vanished. Jakub looked in the travel mug like a New Testament miracle was going to happen.

I never get any miracles and they won't happen to me. Either God's lazy, or he's off-shift.

He shook it, sucked the last few drops out, then wondered to himself exactly what in the hell he was doing.

There were cool companies that had staff in t-shirts and jeans, or cargo shorts, and they did all off the neat advanced techie things that made the trades. They played with really expensive gear, and people actually knew some of their names. He looked down on his chest at the tie Mitzi had given him last Christmas and realized there were two takeaways.

One, this was not that company of his dreams that he lusted after, and two, he was drinking entirely too much and way too hungover if he was wearing the tie that his ex had bought him the morning after he'd sacked her. He'd been too busy drinking to burn it. Maybe a ceremony was in order. Now he wouldn't have to make the call to see what was going to be bought for dinner. That was a plus. Less things to do made him happier.

It was easy to figure out why men ride the corporate ladder somewhere in the middle, maybe pump out a few kids and then rot in an easy chair until they're carted off and buried. It made sense at this point to wait a little longer until all the good ones got divorced, then maybe he could get a good wife on the rebound. It was like sports.

You needed a strategy. And a good plan for the random short-handed breakaway.

Lunch was a turkey club delivered by Cindy Moss in Accounts Receivable, which was a delight in and of itself. He was hoping her husband would buy a Harley and start chasing hookers in Columbia. That might be the break he needed. The fella could toss him an relationship alley-cop. He was a dick, anyway. He didn't deserve her.

As the day lulled closer to an end, he felt in his gut that he was going to have to deal with The Bitch when he got home. It was like a scene from a horror movie when you knew the bad guy was behind the door. And you wondered why the teenagers were mucking about like they had an IQ barely above plant life.

He was feeling like the teenager. And Jakub had no idea what was coming. And for that, God created cognac.

smoke and mirrors

"I'm not gay."

She was starting to piss him off again. No single person on Earth seemed to be able to get his blood pressure up like his mother. The bad habit of calling him for the sole purpose of giving him a hard time. He didn't know if she was bored, or full of angst, or just that crazy. Indubitably a combination of all three.

"Are you sure about that? You live alone, you know that girls don't work out well for you, and I hate that you are wasting away in that prison cell you've built for yourself. It's not healthy. I think that you have some deep seated issues that you really need to address with a therapist. They are wonderful. I *love* mine."

"Like you *love* your nurse?" Jakub fired back.

"Honey, that's not fair. You don't like Vera? What did she ever do to you?"

"I like Vera just fine. But I'm not going to go get an education in blowjobs just because you ran off on Dad and hooked up with your nurse. The two are simply *not* mutually inclusive. Quit trying to make it a thing." He could feel his skin getting hotter. She always picked the damnedest times to call with this nonsense.

"I'm sure there's a nice boy out there for you. Maybe a doctor or something."

"Have you fallen and hit your head recently?"

"No, I'm just saying..."

"I'm not gay. Look Mom, let me try and explain it to you like you're five. I'm not gay. I'm not *fabulous*. I have no desire to hook up with guys. *Any* guy. I'm not gonna do it. I'm not interested in justifying you, or your bullshit, or salving your wounded pride that you don't have a Macy's Day Parade with ticker tape celebrating that you came out because you had a hot nurse."

"Now you're just being mean."

"Realistic. I'm being realistic. It's an entirely human trait. You should try it sometime. And for the record, I live in California, about one mile from the Pacific Ocean. It's a magical place that you've never even visited! Once! So *not* a prison."

"You don't have to get so excited..." He knew she was clearly enjoying this whole martyr thing.

"I *should* go see a therapist. I don't have sexual identity issues. I have mommy and stupid narcissistic bitch issues, of which I solved one last week when *I* was the one that told *her* to, and I quote, 'Get the fuck out.'" He reached into the freezer for the ice and lined up his favorite crystal glass.

Silence.

"I can acknowledge that you have an issue with the fact that you are the only person in the family that is a lesbian, and I know that it has been pointed out that if there were more of you, there would be less of us. But that's not hate or wounding your tender pride. It's called fucking biology."

He clinked the ice into the glass so it would come off almost like a rimshot. Nothing like sound effects when you're trying to make a point. Especially when you want to slap the shit out of your parent and know that there's no real way you would even if they were in front of you. Throwing ice is much easier than dealing with a police report. Even if it would be justified.

Maybe.

"You don't have to be so harsh about it," she said softly. Great. Now the "wounded" card was coming out.

"No, harsh was what happened with Dad. Now in your defense, you had no way to know he would take things the way he did. No blame in that. He did what he did for whatever fucked up reasons he had. I, on the other hand, would have found hotter and sexier than Vera and paid her to find me irresistible at the next family function just to screw with your head. Make it so I couldn't walk to the dinner table without her cupping my balls like they were the fucking Faberge Egg. Those are *your* fine genetic codes that make me that way, in case you're keeping score on this. Go ahead and pat yourself on the back, Mom. Back on the topic, also realize that my generation is not *your* generation, and at this point nobody gives a good goddamn that you're a lesbian. Get it? *Nobody cares.* It's not a special status anymore. You might as well be an Astros fan."

"I am an Astros fan."

"You don't even *watch* baseball, Mom. You just live in Houston. The only reason you're claiming to be a fan is because they won a World Series, and somewhere on that planet of yours, you think it will help you score some ass. My advice to you is to stick with Vera. If you have any sense you'll stay *on* that."

"It still counts," she said, trying to put a pout into her voice. Her method was trying to pick and choose pressure points, and somehow you couldn't return her barbs with any effect. Even with sound logic. It was like water off of a duck's back.

This was a waste of time. Jakub had things to do. Even if it was absolutely nothing.

"Before I forget," Jakub began again, "I should also point out that she *did* in fact look and act like a cheerleader. She would have probably qualified as a Dallas Cowboys Cheerleader, she was *that* hot. Certainly not something I picked up from a grease trap somewhere." He cracked the top on his bottle and began to pour, the liquid cracking and popping the ice as it settled in the glass.

"Hey, I'm working a crossword, and I can't get this last clue. What's a word that's the opposite of sell?"

"Buy?"

"Exactly," he said and with a disconnect flung the phone onto the counter, where it landed with a clack. *And that's why I bought the expensive case*, he thought.

There are times when mothers make bourbon taste better.

He had managed to get over some of the pain of not having a father anymore. It takes time, but if you get caught up in the right things, the pain begins to fade and you quit trying to sort it all out. There are events in life that have no real reason to them, and the less they affect you, the better off you are.

He picked the phone back up and punched out another number. He heard the familiar "talk me off the ledge" voice pick up on the other end.

"Let me guess," she said.

"Willie, she's at it *again*."

"Trying to turn you gay?"

"Yes! It's like an obsession with her. I'm not understanding what the hell she's missing from my equation over here."

"Besides the fact that she's crazy?"

"I mean, I could understand pressuring your kid to join the football team, maybe pick a major, find a real job so they could get out of your house. But sucking dick?"

"Do you *honestly* have no other term for that?"

"Well... I'm pissed and it works. Besides, how many girls have I brought home? She's met almost every woman I've have any kind of a real relationship with."

"And hit on every one of them."

"Exactly! You see my point!"

"We know she's crazy. This ain't a news flash. It's been a thing for years."

"Decades," he injected, "She has at least two decades."

"Okay, so *more* than ten years..."

"The bitch has tenure. I should *not* want to get into an MMA octagon with my own mother and beat her within an inch of her life. It's not natural."

"*She's* not natural. She has a verified mental problem."

"I don't know anyone else like her. I live in freakin' Los Angeles! Half of my friends are either gay or lesbian, and I have never had any of them be anywhere *remotely* as obnoxious as her. That *includes* the guy who claimed he was my soul mate on the bus."

"You're comparing apples to oranges, Hon. She's crazy." She paused.

"I kicked Mitzi out."

"The princess?" She snorted, "Didn't see *that* one coming."

"Whaddaya mean by that?" His head was starting to swim again from the alcohol, which at this point was precisely where he wanted to be.

Willow was laughing.

"She couldn't hold a conversation with anything that had an IQ above plant life. The bitch could talk to brick walls for hours. She'd prefer to talk to mirrors."

"So you're saying she was conceited?"

She paused for him and then with a deadpan prompted, "C'mon."

Jakub took a deep breath. "Yeah, that was pretty much the problem. Never listened to shit, it was always her party and she couldn't seem to shut up. Made me nuts."

"You know why you picked her..."

"Huh?"

"She's a lot like Mom. *Vapid* is probably the term I would use for her, to be honest. Thinks she's much more than she is. Nothing in there upstairs. Admit it, the only reason you were with her was for the sex. We both know she was decent at that or you wouldn't have had her livin' with ya."

He stopped. She was right. That fact irritated the living piss out of him for some reason. He was hoping that he could get drunk enough to not care why.

"Guess I need to learn to make better decisions, then?"

"Kinda the point I'm aiming at, kid. You can do *so* much better. You deserve so much better. Where you comin' up with these girls, anyway?"

"Parties, usually."

"There's your problem. I don't know if I've heard of a relationship working that started at a bar."

"You guys did."

"No, that's not correct. Our first *date* was at a bar. We met online."

"That's even worse." He got up to pour again.

"Have you tried online?"

"That's how the two before Mitzi came about, remember? Online dating sucks for me. The ones I want to meet won't have anything to do with me, and the ones I don't somehow end up with my home address and Social Security number, and they have the will and strength to use them. It's pretty terrifying."

He took a slurp. Time to shift the subject.

"So how did you deal with Dad?" He heard a slight gasp, then silence. She was pausing, thinking. He wasn't taking a potshot at her, and he knew she understood that. She was probably seriously considering her next words.

"It takes time," she said softly, "It takes *life*. This whole thing with Mom is really starting to get to you, isn't it? Oh, hon, I'm so sorry you're having to deal with her like that. She's trying to get into your head. She got into Dad's head, and you know how that went down. When I say she's crazy, I *mean* that shit on its face. I do worry about Vera and her safety sometimes. Honestly, I think I wish Dad had ran off with Vera instead of Mom. The bitch ain't got all her screws in tight. Her marbles done fell out the bag.

She done dropped her basket. She's a few fries short of a Happy Meal."

"I get it," he interrupted.

"She ain't crazy ha-ha, she's fucking crazy certifiable, like 'Get in the round room and wear the shirt with the long sleeves' kinda crazy. Do *not* let her into your head. For any reason, at any time. When she's talking, pretend you're Helen Keller and try to go to your happy place."

"What about you?"

"The kids help deflect that. So does Carl. 'Cept sometimes I think Carl might be touchin' himself and daydreaming about havin' a close quarters huntin' accident with her. You know how he loves his gun collection. We minimize how much we deal with her ass. Hell, we see you more than we see her. You're over a thousand miles further away. Speakin' of kids and asses, I need to put 'em to bed."

"You need me to get off the phone?"

"Naw. Gimme a sec..." She covered the receiver and he still heard her yell in the background, "Kids! Git yer asses into bed! *Now!*"

"That works?"

"Like a charm. They know not to mess with momma anymore. We still live in a state where in the right community you can get off with murder just because 'He needed killin'. In my case, I kilt the TV."

"What?" Jakub asked, laughing.

"Bet yer ass. I told them to get to bed, they ignored me, I cut the TV power cable in half. Fixed that shit. 'Nothin to watch *now*, is there, bitch? Who's in charge now?' Carl wasn't too happy about it. He tried to rewire the cable twice, bless his heart, but he just couldn't get it. He was determined as hell he wasn't missin' a Stars game though. I got a new TV out of it. They're so much cheaper now."

"So who exactly is it that has the crazy mother?"

"There's a difference. I just make 'em behave. I'm not trying to turn 'em into the Village People."

"Fair enough. Any bright ideas on this situation, then?"

"Well, Carl bought these VR goggles. That virtual reality stuff that's all the rage now. They're pretty neat. You know you can travel anywhere in the world and it looks like you're actually there? You can also watch sports and crap like that with 'em, too. Looks like you're in the arena. I'm not allowed to let the kids anywhere near 'em, because we'd never see their fuckin' faces again. Hell, I don't know how many times I've seen Carl's eyes in the past three weeks, but it keeps him quiet until somebody screws up. Or he sees something that gets him all excited. I watched a few movies on it. Really nice. He's probably found some porn or something. I don't care about that, I get *mine*."

"I did not need to know that," Jakub answered flatly.

"I don't get much 'girl talk'. Suck it up,

Buttercup. Now, about the VR stuff?"

"I really haven't paid any attention to it, to be honest. Where do you get 'em?"

"Aren't *you* the tech guy? He got his at the store. As far as I know you can buy them online, too. You should be able to find them out there. Easier than here, anyway."

"Since you put it that way, I think I know someone that can get things like that. I'll give him a call tomorrow."

"It'll be good for ya. Besides, you need to do more traveling to exotic places, and with this, you can pretty much do it for free. I get to go to the beach at least once a week."

"Like Galveston?"

"Like Fiji. Hawaii. Bermuda."

"Look at you, all *fabulous* and stuff."

"Totally."

stealing time

Jakub knew who to shake down about all of this virtual reality junk. You wanted to talk to gamers and the people who supplied them for these types of things. He wasn't the best at that whole scene but Jefco was. He'd know exactly what to get, and as a gaming supplier, he likely had it in shop or could get his hands on it.

A few searches online looked good. The graphics on these things were incredible and the theory was that this was the wave of the future anyway. Might as well take a jump in and see what was going on. So much had happened in the past few years with technology.

It wasn't too long ago that you could break a plate glass window with a computer monitor or a television. Now they were the thickness of a plate glass window.

Times change.

Jefco didn't. He'd seen about everything there was to see when it came to gaming and the technologies around it. His real name was Jeffrey Cousins, but Jefco was easier and the nickname stuck. Probably 25 years or so ago, judging from his appearance. He was easily in his 40s, possibly his 50s, and the child in him had never left.

He moved to Los Angeles about 15 years ago from Oklahoma, and at the time he'd arrived, the tech industry was booming, people were buying hand-assembled gaming kits and sometimes the custom laptop. He did well for himself and established himself as a staple. The studios and CGI teams would come to his door for the hard to find items from him or milk his connections for the newest gadgets he could find.

But Jefco loved Jakub. Much of that had to do with home loyalty. Sometimes he assumed he and Jefco were the only Dallas Stars fans out west. He hated basketball, and didn't like the Texas Rangers, so they had become hockey fans. Jakub could solidly relate.

Jakub had explained what he was looking for, and Jefco's face lit up.

His grin grew almost wicked. "Wait until you see *this* beauty," he said while motioning to the workshop.

It was a black set of what almost looked like safety goggles gone wrong. They extended out from the eyes and had full head straps. Jakub had seen things similar, but had never actually had one on his head.

"This is *not* your general buy-in-the-store kinda thing," Jefco started, "They're a development model. Whoever had these before actually *coded* for virtual reality in some form or capacity. So you're gettin' a pristine advanced model. Or you were. I wiped it again when I got it, and I believe it had been reset once before that. I think they said it came from an estate sale or something. This should still be a better set than anything else you're gonna pick up in the stores, and that's why I'm passing it to you. Because I *like* you."

"Dude, they don't let you out much, do they?"

"It's now a gamer's world, buddy. I don't hafta go any damned where. I can tap a screen, order my groceries and have them delivered to me. I can have just about anything else I want delivered to me. Why would I ever want to leave the house? With those things right there," he said, pointing at the goggles, "I can go anywhere in the world I wanna go, and can't nobody say *shit* to me. I can stalk my ex-girlfriends and never get kicked off the lawn."

"If I start going nowhere, I'll get fired."

"Then you need to get yourself a new job, buddy."

"Think we got the Playoffs this year?"

"Man, we totally got this. We have a fricking beast in net. I think the Cup is coming home."

"That's the kinda talk I like to hear," Jakub said.

"Oh," Jefco blurted, "There was also this app on there that lets you see crap like all that wrasslin' stuff and sports, all kinds of junk. I even got to watch the Lakers on it. Don't really like the Lakers, but apparently they do. And the All Stars were on there, so there's a little hockey on it. Like being at the game. You're practically on the ice. You're gonna love that one. I've got another app loaded where you can go anywhere in the world that you can pretty much find on a map and you're right there in the middle of it."

"Really?"

"Dude! I *so* hooked you up! I also got sailing on there. You like sailing?"

"I've never been sailing. Why would I go sailing? You know where I'm from. The beaches are all hours away from me."

"Who gives a shit where you're from? It's all about where you are *now*. And now is where you could walk to a marina. It's relevant. You'll like sailing. Trust me. Knock down a baggie of weed and you can sail all day without worrying about falling off the boat and drowning. You might end up pissing yourself, but hey, that's happened before, right?"

"Um, nope, not usually..."

"First time for everything." He waved his hands in a shooing motion, "Take, take. You'll rike. I promise."

"You're starting to scare me, Jefco."

"Hell, I *always* scare you. That's why you love me and bring me money."

"No, I love you and bring you money because when it comes to good hardware, I want good shit, and you always have it."

"You're holding the best I got. It's a labor of love. Now give me my money and git outta here. I got hookers to rent and a dog to go slap."

"You ain't right in the head, son."

"I also ain't paid. I want $500."

"No."

"Give it back then. I can find some bastard that'll gimme $500 for this."

"No." Jakub thought that if he held his ground, he might still be able to bend Jefco a little more. He seemed to have a weird addiction to talking smack and haggling.

"$400. That's a steal." Jefco offered.

"How the hell do you figure? I can go to a box store and get one of these for $300."

Jefco snorted. "The hell you can... that device lists for $850, son. That's out of the box with nothin' special. You have a dev model, that pushes the bottom up to over a grand. At $450, I'm letting you rape my cat. My cat ain't even *that* ugly."

Jakub groaned, "You're one *sick* bastard, Jefco."

"$450. Take it or leave it. It'll be gone by noon tomorrow."

Jakub pulled out a wad of bills from his pocket and thumbed them over. Jefco pocketed the bills and said, "Nice doing business with ya, Jakie."

"Wait a minute," Jakub said, " Didn't you say $400 first?"

Jefco grinned with a devilish smile, "Did I? Oh, well. Hookers have to eat, too. When you need something else to get your jollies off, I'll be here."

"Screw you, " Jakub said, "See ya. Don't let my Stars lose. If they choke, I'm blamin' your sorry ass."

"Back atcha," Jefco said as he guided Jakub towards the door.

As he handed the parcel containing the goggles over, he said to Jakub, "You'll wanna follow the instructions. Make sure you read 'em first, or there's a potential of bad things happening, y'know what I'm sayin'?"

"I think I can get an instruction booklet down."

"I have to check," Jefco said with a rare moment of seriousness, "That's a high dollar piece, no joke. I'm not quite as familiar with it as I'd like to be, so you're almost swimming with sharks on the support end of that. I'll be able to answer some questions but I'm not gonna be able to do any real surgery on this thing."

Jakub nodded. He took the advice to heart. If Jefco was going to be that serious about it, he knew for a hard fact this was something he should be listening to. As he walked to his car he realized that perhaps the worst thing he could do was to rush home and plug it in. That was the impulse he felt, and after all of the havoc as of late, it was time to try getting those impulses under control for a change.

He knew he had problems. Impulses with women, all the impulses from drinking, spending half of his time trying to please other people and the rest of the time trying to medicate himself because of the result. Maybe today could be a little different, he could go visit a friend.

Except he didn't have any friends. He had acquaintances, but not friends. Right now was the wrong time to dwell on that. Hell, any time was a bad time to dwell on the point without a drink in hand.

He knew he didn't really have to leave the parking lot just yet. Fishing his wallet out of his coat pocket, Jakub retrieved the card that Aiden had given him at the burger shack the other night. He seemed to be a little more of a "man of the world" than Jakub, and might possibly be able to either meet up or at the very least be a friendly voice.

The card itself was a thing of beauty, a shot on the front of an open ocean with the sun breaking the horizon. It read THE WORLD IS MY HOME, and on the back provided the particulars in a deep aquamarine font. There was a website, a travel blog. Folks like him were doing that these days. He decided it would be a good idea to not think. Picking up his cellphone from the passengers' seat, he dialed the number from the card.

"Hello, person from Texas. How can I help you have a wonderful day today?" He heard Aiden's chipper voice on the line. A woman was giggling in the background. It took a second for him to register why he had answered the phone that way. Jakub remembered that from his cellphone, the caller ID adjusted the listing to read DALLAS, TX, instead of his name. A handy product when you didn't want everyone getting wind of who was calling them.

"Hi, Aiden. It's Jakub Riser. We met at..."

"The burger shack. I remember you. How ya been holding up?"

"Good, all things considered, of course. Been trying to figure out some new things to do, guess I'm just out of practice fending for myself and being left to my own devices."

"I know *exactly* where you're at," Aiden said, "You're at the point where ya don't really know what to do with the time you got on your hands now. Right? It's an icky sticky time, that. Been there before. If I didn't already have plans going tonight, I'd jump in myself. But I do have an assignment that will do ya some good and take your mind off things. The scenery will be nice too, I promise you."

"What would that be?" Jakub inquired.

"You like fish? Like good old England style fish? Fish and Chips fish, not that greasy chain junk."

"I guess so. What do you have in mind?"

"There's a place off of Santa Monica Boulevard, it's an English pub kinda place. Ye Olde King's Head. Best fish and chips on Earth, I promise you. Find a parking garage down there and get some grub, get a brew or two, and the Promenade's right there. I'd go after a Bass, or an Af-n-af."

"Af-n-af?"

"Guinness and Harp mixed, half and half. They might call it a Black and Tan, but screw it, ya wanna sound like ya know what you're talking about. Might as well do as the Romans do, though that's probably historically a bad metaphor."

"Oh."

"You also have the beach, but that's going to start thinning out soon. It's what, five something? The Promenade should be happening for a few more hours, though. Tip a busker somewhere. They need ta eat too. You'll thank me for the scenery, my man. It's one place the girls go to be seen, and we go to look at them. Just remember that the goal is to get your belly full, your heart light, and enjoy the view. This is a birdwatching session, not a hunting expedition. So for tonight, the rule is to look but don't touch, got it?"

"I think I can handle that."

"Good. I have your number right here, I'm gonna save it, and I'll call you tomorrow to check up on ya and see how everything went. Square?"

"Square. Thanks."

"Catch ya tomorrow, brotha. Have a good time tonight. No excuses. I'll be checking up on ya."

He wondered if Aiden would, or if it was all talk to get him off the phone. But the idea was a pretty good one. He hadn't spent a lot of time on the Promenade and had only been there a couple of times to go through the shops with Janet. She felt because she was an attorney she was owed certain things in life. Unlike Mitzi, he hadn't been saddled with having to pay for most of them.

Jakub found the restaurant online easily. They even had the blessing of a reservation widget right there on the website. He made a reservation for one at 7:30, although that felt a bit strange to him. Aiden was right. He needed to learn how to begin enjoying time alone, at least for now.

Twenty minutes later he found himself in a dark gray concrete parking garage on 2nd Street in Santa Monica. The package from Jefco fit nicely under the passenger's seat and he covered it with a few shopping bags so it would be mostly obstructed from view.

He casually strolled down Ocean and decided to take a few moments in the park. It was one of the things he'd forgotten about California. There was a reason you moved here, just like there was a reason so many moved to Texas. The palms and the sun heading towards the ocean as the hue of the sky changed right before your eyes. The smell of the salt in the heavenly sea air just outside the reach of the smog blanket is nothing to be experienced anywhere else. Sure, you paid for the privilege to live here, but moments like this were certainly worth it.

Like the twenty-something blonde in her jogging outfit checking her wrist for whatever device she had on it. She wore a safety orange baseball cap meant to look sporty and in fashion. She was watching her wrist. Jakub was watching her.

It's the little things that make the world go round.

Off to the right, a man was curled up on the manicured grass under a palm having a personal siesta. Seemed the perfect place for it. Deep down, he was delighted that no one seemed to care. Some things are just meant to be available to anyone. Jakub sidled up to the fence that helped keep drunk individuals from rolling into the Pacific Coast Highway and down the hill to the beach below. He could survey the beach from there and felt slightly self-conscious that he was scanning for bikinis, but who was really going to know? Perhaps they assumed naturally. After all, he was a single male in the park. Sure, he could be doing just about anything, but he wasn't a busker or a surfer type, which didn't leave much to wonder about.

Jakub could see the Santa Monica Pier off to the left, and decided it might be a good trip suggestion for another day. In the meantime, he took the option of strolling briefly up and down the walkway on the beach side of the grassy strip that ran from a veterans memorial to the visitors kiosk for the tourists. There were always tourists in Los Angeles. The almost perfect year round weather dictated it.

It crossed his mind that the sun was beginning to set, and that was something he usually missed because he was either too damned busy, or senselessly occupied. Maybe this was one of the things Aiden had in mind.

Watch a sunset. That's a bucket list item, Jakub thought as he stretched back on a pack bench facing

the horizon and watched the daylight prepare to
close another day of life.

appetite

The scene transfixed with the sun creeping closer to the line of the ocean and the place where light decides to go to fade into nothing. Jakub's mind dissolved into a place without thought. It was unusual for him, and the clear moment of emptiness shattered with a voice.

A woman's voice.

"Nice scenery you have here. Mind if I join you?"

His brain tried to grasp what was happening. There was an accent. It wasn't British, a little more relaxed, and he understood she'd asked him a question, the pinprick that jolted him back into reality.

The first milliseconds of processing hit him with an electric shock. For someone who was an expert at losing himself in a crowd, he wasn't prepared for the girl that was speaking to him.

"I'm sorry, I didn't mean to disturb you," she said, flashing a toothy smile. After the teeth, her ice blue eyes caught him as the tsunami of endorphins let him know he should respond quick, before she got away.

"No, no please. Have a seat. I was just watching the sunset."

She maintained the smile and seemed to glide onto the bench beside him like a dove coming in for a landing. She sat mostly perched on one leg, her body facing him, head pointed to the fading sun.

"What a beautiful front row seat you have heah," she said.

Aussie. She was Australian.

Jakub looked her in the eyes, which she seemed to engage immediately, "We," he said, "We have a front row seat." She smiled and returned her gaze to the setting sun.

They watched in silence, observing the disc in the sky fade down to dull rust and disappear. It was a moment in which there was really nothing worth saying that could add to anything, and the art of being quiet seemed to make it all more potent. After dusk had affixed itself, something needed to be said before things got awkward.

Deep in his brain, an acronym popped into his brain that made him choke down a short laugh: WWAD? *What Would Aiden Do*? The thought crossed his mind that he had a pretty good example, as well as a pretty good idea, but he was going to at least amend the cardinal rule for tonight.

"I'm Jakub. Sorry I didn't introduce myself earlier. Guess I was just in the moment."

"Completely understand. Name's Ellie. I'm in town for a conference for the next day or so. I've actually been here most of the week, but they're finishing everything up tomorrow, so I thought I might see the beach at least one more time before I left. I mean, we have beaches back home, but all of the ones near me face the East, so..." Ellie paused, seeming cautious, calculating, "There's certainly nothing like *this* that I ever get to see."

"Hey, if you aren't doing anything tonight..." he paused. She was looking him straight in the eyes, and the anticipation he was praying for was there. "I have reservations just up the street there at Ye Olde King's Head at 7:30, which is just a few minutes from now. Of course, they're for one, but I doubt they'll object to a *plus guest*. It would be my pleasure."

Ellie gave a demure smile and answered, "I think that would be lovely."

He stood, and escorted her to the crossing, across Ocean and down Santa Monica Boulevard to the restaurant a block away.

"I really like this place," Ellie said as they approached the door.

"You've been here before?"

"Two nights ago. We've heard about this place back home. I saw it in a travel magazine and had to visit. My reservation was for one, too." She locked eyes with him for a moment, and he felt like the world was stopping.

The reservation wasn't a problem at all. They were quickly seated in a nice little four-top, caddy-corner to the front door as a gentleman with a thick Irish accent popped in to greet them and ask for their drinks.

"Af-n-af," Jakub said, as Ellie fiddled with something in her bag. It looked like she was turning her cell phone off. She looked up to let the man know she was ready.

"And for you, miss?"

"I'll have a pint of the local, please."

"King's Head. I'll get that for you now," and he sauntered off.

A few moments later the drinks arrived, and Jakub discovered that maybe he hadn't given beer a fair enough chance.

Fish and Chips was precisely the star of the place, Aiden had been perfect on his suggestion, and Ellie seemed pleased as well. They kept the conversation light and tried to avoid getting too personal with their information. Something in him said that she wanted it that way, and he detected that this evening was going to go much more in the direction he'd fantasized instead of the one he had planned.

"Can I interest you in dessert?" He asked, feeling enough liquid confidence that he thought he could function well but not be out of control of himself. This was the least he'd drank by this point in the evening for some time.

The wicked glint in her eyes made his heart skip a beat.

"Depends on what you mean by dessert. If you're referring to something sweet, I'd suggest the trifle. Never a bad time for that. If you're looking for something *sweeter*, that's not gonna be here," she purred across the table.

"I have all night," Jakub responded.

"Then I would suggest you use it to your maximum advantage." She gave him a knowing smile, and a slow deliberate wink.

"It seems to me that a nightcap might be in order," Jakub proposed, his heartbeat moving into overdrive, "Would my place be acceptable?"

"Your place would be preferable, actually. Maybe we should just... get out of here."

"Uh... check, please!," Jakub blurted. She giggled.

When the gentleman came by a few moments later, Jakub cleared the tab and they left.

As they stepped out onto the sidewalk Jakub happened to glance left, over into the street side seating area of Plan Check when a shock of bright platinum and aqua hair caught his eye.

That was his first mistake.

The second was when he realized he was looking over the back of his friend Sarah's head directly into the emerald green eyes of Lindsey Barber. Sarah's girlfriend, his dream. Or nightmare, depending on who you asked. She wasn't mean to him, just didn't like him. It popped up front and center in his mind every time they crossed paths. Frankly, it irked the piss out of him, because he still couldn't figure out what the hell he had ever done to make her that way.

Other than be so damned attracted to her it hurt. Of course, Willie was the only other person on Earth to know that fact.

Lindsey solved the problem by pretending that she hadn't seen him after all, looking away, giving a bright laughing smile that was more for show than anything else. But the electric arrow that had ripped through him let him know she had. She was fingering the edges of the shaved left side of her head, as if she were combing locks that weren't there.

Jakub recovered by turning to Ellie and asking, "Where did you park at?"

"I didn't," she said, "I took an Uber in."

"I guess you're riding with me then, if you'd like, of course."

"I think I would prefer that," she answered, reaching down and softly grabbing his hand, "Now the question is, where did *you* park?"

He gestured towards the parking garage down the block and said, "Over there, where your chariot awaits." She kept her arm neatly linked with his, making sure to maintain her closeness, to the point of making him want to swallow her alive.

Jakub led her to his car and unlocked the passenger's side first, allowing Ellie to take her seat.

I am so glad I cleaned this thing out yesterday, he thought.

They pulled out of the parking garage and onto Santa Monica Boulevard. A few moments later, he felt Ellie's hand reach across the center console and rest on his thigh. He sucked in his breath. "Gettin' a little dangerous, doncha think?" He asked her. She moved her hand closer to home and sent a rush up his spine and throughout his body.

"I like danger," she said.

And I like women that are forward.

"You won't when I wreck this car," he answered. She didn't move her hand. In fact, she doubled down and kept it there, gently massaging after they had turned onto Overland. It took everything within him to keep the car from jumping onto the sidewalk. So he returned the favor. God bless automatic transmissions. If he'd had to shift gears, they'd have been dead.

Ellie made a purr and ground herself against his fingers. He tried to remember every breath control mechanism he had ever heard of to focus on the road. He was almost home.

"We're gonna be parking in just a few minutes," he told her.

"I hope to god so," she said breathlessly.

And this is why I love Los Angeles, Jakub thought.

After he pulled into the parking garage under his building, they wasted the minimal amount of time getting to his apartment. Naturally, he did the decent thing. He offered her a bourbon and Ellie happily accepted. "On the rocks," she requested.

The small talk almost didn't seem to be existent, because they both had the same end goal in mind, and they were just trying to get there with a minimum of interference. Ellie took a sip of the bourbon, savored it for a moment, and then took a mouthful of ice and began crunching it between her teeth, eyeing him like a cat that had just trapped a mouse. As she slipped down to the edge of the loveseat with cat-like movement between his legs and engulfed him, it was clear why she chose to chew ice.

From that moment on, they connected and intertwined like feral cats fighting to the death. Soon they were dripping with sweat, exhausted, and floating on the moonlit night-time clouds over the Pacific.

Jakub woke to the sound of his alarm clock. He had a blissful residual feeling of the night before, a soft scent of recollection in the air.

She had left during the night, some time between the moment he'd fallen asleep and the time his alarm had gone off. He felt for the warmth under the cover, and the faint detection of it led him to believe she'd taken off about an hour before. That's the beauty of having the right duvet, the insulation was great.

As he lumbered into the kitchen to grab his morning coffee and get ready for the day, his eyes landed on a small note positioned on the bar. From the look of it, the paper came from a specially designed note pad, embossed with a little golden butterfly on the lower right corner. He'd seen small pads like it for sale at that shop in Century City.

Just a few simple words, thanking him for the 'incredible' evening the night before. She signed with a scripted cursive letter E.

This was one time when he wished he had his own card. Like Aiden. Not that it would ever be used again. He was sure with about 99.99% accuracy that he would never again lay eyes on Ellie in this lifetime.

It was specifically the recent tan lines on her ring finger that he'd spent the bulk of the night ignoring that had tipped him off to the fact that there would be no repeats. The fact that they were so recent told him that she was a married woman. Most certainly in town on either business or vacation, more than likely on business, and she wasn't in sales or an executive because she didn't have a rental car.

Perhaps she did, and the driver services were simply to cover tracks. Either way, he was sure she wasn't going to be back around anytime soon, and he figured there was a good chance her name wasn't even Ellie.

The other thing he was certain of was that last night was in his top three nights, ever.

won't fall asleep

"I'm gonna go home, get loaded, and then get out on the water," Jakub announced. He was saying it loudly over the cubicle wall to be a prick. He heard his buddy's voice reply, "You're doin' what?"

"I *said*, I'm gonna take it back to the shack, knock down some brown stuff and go sailing," he repeated.

"That's illegal in most states," Cliff answered, "In fact, I think that's an international thing."

"I'm not a law-abiding citizen."

"This much is obvious. Hey, can I have your hockey stick over there when you don't come back?" Jakub looked over at the hockey stick standing in the corner. It was a Mike Modano stick that he had been given on his birthday when his brother-in-law Carl had scored them Stanley Cup Playoffs tickets. He had no idea what strings Carl pulled, since they passed the stick over the glass after the second period, but it was the last time he saw Modano in the flesh. Dallas beat the San Jose Sharks that night in overtime, 2-1. Happy Birthday.

No getting another one of those.

"Better not fuck with my stick," Jakub growled.

"Dude, if you aren't here in three days, and I find out you're having a vacation in a county cage, I'm

87

sacrificing it to the hockey gods. My Kings need to win another one."

"Ain't gonna happen."

"I'm not kidding. That's a choice specimen."

"Nawp."

Cliff peeked over the partition, "Are *you* kidding?"

"Nah, I'm sailing in VR. Nobody gets hurt, and I can pass out on the boat without getting arrested. So the stick's safe. The worst that could happen would be that the power dies. Or I get mad and break it off in your ass. But I'd need to be *really* mad."

Cliff grinned and nodded, slapping a grubby paw on the top of the partition. "I'll get right to work on that. It still counts as a sacrifice."

He probably would, too. Cliff liked being a nuisance and ensuring that it was almost to the line of not getting any help at work without actually crossing the said line. Actually, that wasn't completely fair. Jakub had to admit that they had a prank battle from the moment he got to the building on the first day. Jakub first found his chair anchored to the desk with what seemed almost an illegal amount of strapping tape. "So that's how it's gonna be..." Jakub had said. Cliff was unaware that Texans have a bad habit of carrying pocket knives in their front pocket.

It's a thing.

From Big Spring to Marshall to Refugio and beyond, almost any male native Texan to be seen will have one. Or two, or three. Maybe it came from Jim Bowie, no one really knew.

Jakub exacted revenge on Easter Sunday. He invested $300 dollars and took 12 hours to line the expenditure of marshmallow candy Peeps into a standing army. They awaited instructions from General Cliff on his arrival to work Monday morning.

For Jakub's birthday, Cliff had taken more strapping tape and roughly sealed the entrance into Jakub's cubicle. With the help of the office staff they filled his cubicle overnight with about 500 balloons.

Their boss was less than enthused when he began popping them with the knife, *pop-pop-pop*, causing a racket that could be heard all over the floor. He came and admonished Cliff for his prank.

"Sounds like you're gonna get it for this one," Jakub had said.

"I doubt it," Cliff answered, "he helped blow about half of them up."

Cliff's summer vacation was answered with every single item, manual, and piece of equipment in his cubicle being wrapped in children's wrapping paper. He took it in good stride, impressed by the Sesame Street paper Jakub had chosen for a few select items. Cliff wasn't the only one that could enlist the manpower of the office.

So when Jakub went to Vegas for a vacation with Willie, he knew there would be hell to pay when he returned.

And so it was.

He returned to yet another sealed-off cubicle, this time filled to the brim with bright pink styrofoam packing peanuts. As far as Jakub knew, there was still a garbage bag or two sitting full in the warehouse being used for outbound packages.

As many threats as Cliff made, Jakub knew he would never lay a hostile hand on the Modano stick. There were just some things you didn't do, some pranks that were beyond the pale, and to mess with that hockey stick would be an action that angered the hockey gods. If hockey players and their fans are anything, it's superstitious.

The pranks had continued. The end of summer had brought for Cliff a surfboard that had been cut to resemble a shark bite, and a medical skeleton in his chair that had been taped by the spine to the back seat post. A message was taped to the monitor with a picture of the ocean and the words "Well, that sucked." The skeleton was spirited away after being properly named Robert by the passerby in the company that had snickered and giggled during the two working days Cliff had been off.

Halloween brought a re-visitation of Robert as he appeared in Jakub's chair, zip-tied with about 42 hard plastic zip ties. It was a bitch cutting him out of there. That was after he had circumvented the mass stringy sheets of faux cobwebs, with tiny spiders that Cliff had added for effect. The screen read, "Waiting for a raise."

This time, the boss was not amused. He had no issue with the spectacle, but rather the quaint message Cliff had added to the screen. More so because *his* boss had seen it first, and having the sense of humor of a concrete cinder block, *lost his shit* to put it lightly. Robert spent the next two weeks riding in the backseat of Jakub's car, looking out the window with a hand carefully extended against the glass as if he were testing it with a fingertip. The riding trip for Robert ended when Jakub drove north to visit a friend in Calabasas and the local Homeowners Association chairwoman got her cranky little drawers in a wad and took the spectacle way too seriously. She even called the police on him.

They were so angry that she'd called them to investigate a homicide, since she had some weird delusion that Jakub was a serial killer. They wanted to charge her with false report and take her to jail. She *really* pissed off the wrong people. He begged hard to get them to just drop it with the crazy lady.

Pick your battles.

Robert had been cooling his heels in the living room on a spare chair watching television ever since.

Medical skeletons are not cheap. Especially when they're legit.

It was the glitter that ended their fun. Once Jakub had the box of glitter shipped to Cliff, who had the natural stability of a chihuahua in a freezer, it was all over. The high powers that were disallowed future pranks in the office. No exceptions.

The cellphone lightly vibrating caught his attention and Jakub flipped it over to look at it. Aiden was actually calling back. *Will wonders never cease?*

"How you doin' today?" Jakub answered.

"Magical, buddy," he responded, "I told you I'd call in and check on ya. How did the night go?"

"All in all, I'd say it went rather well. Getting used to being by myself a little more now."

"That's a good start. Soon you'll feel more like exploring new things, and that's when the fun really begins."

"Dammit. I can't bullshit. I broke the cardinal rule."

"Oh? Do tell." He heard a chuckle on the other end of the line.

"Her name was Ellie."

"Hmm." It went up in pitch at the end, more like a *please tell me more*, rather than a *you're an asshole for breaking the rules.*

"She was damned near perfect, blonde, Australian, visiting for work. We had dinner, I brought her home, amazingly at her direct request, and I'll never see her again. Doesn't live here, obviously."

He laughed out loud. "But you had a wonderful time, yeah?"

"Oh, that's putting it *very* mildly." It was hard not to purr.

"Then you've learned a very important lesson that's gonna take you far, and I'm very happy to hear it."

"I have?" Jakub asked, slightly confused.

"Sure have. All rules have their *exceptions*."

"Is that a fact?" Jakub mused.

"In fact, my brother, it is. You'll come to the realization soon enough that everything that's going on in your life is something you should have a say in. Ya can't let the world control you, you need to control *it*. At least the best way you can, because ya never know what's comin' around the corner, and if you aren't in control, it will hit you in the face with absolutely nothing you can do about it. So be fluid, be liquid, my man. Let life flow *around* you."

"How did you come to know so much about all this stuff?"

"Honestly?" Aiden paused a moment, "Experience. I been there. Been through all this crap, know where the journey starts. One day you'll be doing the same for someone else. That's just the way it works, y'know? You go through a bunch of crap in life, see someone else going through the exact same thing, so you just give 'em a few shortcuts. Make no mistake, there's a part of this journey you're gonna hafta make yourself. I can't do it all for you. But it'll be easier because you get to avoid a few 'banging your head against a wall' moments. So what are ya doing tonight?"

"I got a virtual reality set from a friend of mine that's kinda like a crack dealer for hardware. He says it's pretty much the best thing since sliced bread. I'm a bit partial to sliced bread, so we'll see about that. So far, it's a really cool thing, so we'll see what happens with that. You?"

"Well, I'm at a truck stop just outside Lancaster. Friend of mine named Shelby dropped me off. Got another friend of mine that drives tractor trailers and I'm riding with him to Vegas where I'll cool my heels for a few days and then maybe to Colorado. It's a pretty neat thing once you get your little networks all set up. Doesn't hurt him, adds a person to his log books, even though I can't drive the thing, and it doesn't hurt his fuel since that's paid by the company. I just gotta pretty much pay for whatever I need or want. Once I get done with Colorado, I'll probably head back in to LA. We'll see. I've really been liking Vegas lately, though."

"You mean the Strip?" Jakub asked.

"Well, the Strip isn't that bad, I have a couple friends that live there, so I can crash out in the real city where the humans and non-tourists live. Maybe go learn a few new skills, try my hand at a few things I've never done before. New things are always good. I think the more things you can learn, the better. You never know when that off the wall talent you picked up in some small city somewhere will come in handy. Guess the moral to that story is to learn everything you can everywhere you can."

"What exactly do you do, anyway?"

Aiden laughed, "Damn near anything or everything I can get paid to do. I'll probably do some temp work there in Vegas."

"What's that like?"

"Your usual manual labor. Moving things around, cleaning up yards and buildings at offices and warehouses, junk like that. It's good for you. You don't have to worry about any real career goals, you do what people need in the moment, so that's fulfilling. I like helping people. Makes me feel useful. Pay isn't great, but if you bust your ass right, sometimes the folks in charge of whatever project it is take care of you. I've done a one hour project and been paid for eight. I've moved car parts around, swept parking lots with heavy equipment in 'em, built things. Sometimes it's unloading trucks. You meet all kinds of people doing that crap. Good people, bad people, broken people. Some really high jokers..."

"How does it stack up against when you were here working full time?"

"Mixed bag. You have to figure out what it is you actually want. Some folks need that stable thing, with the rent and the predictability. I'm just not after that, I prefer my leisure. So it doesn't really take a lot for me to live. I basically take what I need from LA, then head wherever I'm going and experience it. If things get stupid, I tap into the trucking network or whatever and get back. You also have to really do your homework and be prepared for mass stupidity. I normally run around with a backpack that I have organized for most of what I think I'd need."

Jakub was taking in this idea. How do you just run around without any real place to call home? But more importantly, he knew Aiden had planted a seed in his head, because one of the next thoughts he had was *what the hell am I wasting my money and my life for? What am I actually gonna get out of all this?*

"Once you spend a night on the BLM in Arizona looking up at the stars, you're well fed, you don't have anywhere to be the next day, and you're not lost, you'll realize why this is such an awesome way to live. And it really reduces your impact on everyone else, which is also cool. You should try it sometime. Take it in small doses and build up. You'll be an expert in no time."

"You're convincing me. I don't know when, but I'm going to hafta try that once."

"I've done West Texas. Been out there near the oil rigs. I didn't actually work on the rigs, mind you. There are limits to the amount of work I'm going to apply to any particular purpose, but it was worthwhile and enjoyable. Plus, Texas is good for steak and barbecue. I don't have to tell *you* that, you already know. But you'll wanna hit Odessa and Big

Spring before the summer really takes over. Spring or Fall. I know guys that spend all year chasing seventy degrees. Up and down, up and down. There's a lot more people out there livin' it than you'd think. We haven't even talked about the RV people and the Snowbirds yet. It's a whole different world out here, and it's international."

"I'll look at that when I get home and have a little more time and space. It might not be bad to change up things a little. I think I've just fallen into a great big rut, and I can't get out of it."

"Exactly, brotha. That's what I'm talking about. I know where you're at because I had to make the same decision, but you don't have to make the decision all at once, and that's the wonderful thing about it. You just hafta be willing to live life a little more. Welp, there's my chariot, pullin' in. We're probably gonna eat, I'll head off. Might catch up with ya next week or so. I'll be out of cell range, so if you need to, leave me a voicemail and I'll get back to you when I drift to a good signal space."

As they ended the call, Jakub felt excitement building. It was a good idea for him, but he didn't feel like he belonged anywhere. At least he now had the VR to play around with and see some stuff before he visited in person.

Fortunately for him, they had created an app for that.

y tu eres las mas bonita

There was a new app on his Library screen that he hadn't noticed before. It was called *Luna*. Probably another one of those space programs. He'd seen several of them already, and they were pretty cool. Then again, with a name like Luna it probably had to do with the moon somehow. He figured if it was bad enough, he'd take a break and howl at it.

Jakub clicked on the app button to see what was behind the logo. What the heck was "Luna"?

A Latina woman appeared talking in a casual setting. The beige sofa she reclined against appeared to be suede, with fluffy pillows and a colorful Saltillo blanket over the top. It struck him as California.

The girl he watched looked familiar for some strange reason that he couldn't place, but what he *did* know was that she was *utterly* beautiful. It was like seeing a work of art, or a scientific law of physics. No absolutes, because its existence *was* the absolute in itself. She was like that.

There are people that fit you for this reason or that one. You can't really explain it, and for some reason just seeing them fills you up. She rolled over him like a windy gust at the top of a mountain peak on a beautiful sunny day.

She was talking, and he wasn't listening. What he knew was the sound of her voice was absolutely soothing, and she had doe eyes that he stopped to take a swim in.

The girl wasn't an idiot. She talked with authority, but with a calmness and sweetness that put him at ease. He was trying to focus on what she was saying, but he also knew that he was glad to hear that accent, and it screamed to him that he was home.

The exhilarating and refreshing accent hit him immediately.

She was a Texan.

That's one thing about Texans. They can find each other in a crowded room, a crowded park, bar, building, or even in the middle of the desert. It's almost like natural radar that paints an invisible Lone Star right on their foreheads.

When Jakub was a kid, his father used to take him out in the woods to shoot at things. He got pretty good with that BB gun. Then he graduated to pellet guns. One day he didn't have Dad to watch over him, and he saw that beautiful blue jay and took a perfect aim. He didn't know any better back then. He didn't understand the permanence of things. Every tiny action can have repercussions that roll on seemingly forever.

He remembered how the bird jerked, fell straight down some twenty feet to the ground, blocked by the padding of the wooded floor of leaves. He had killed it instantly. He remembered thinking he should have been proud, but he wasn't. In doing the thing he loved and had excited him, he hurt the object of his attention permanently. The look on his father's face when he presented the dead bird to him. He had done something he didn't know how to fix. And for once, his father hadn't known how to fix it either. There were tears. There was a hard lesson learned. It was not the last time he used a rifle, but it was the last time he took a life and let it go to waste.

It wasn't the death that made him think of this event. It was the recall of that simple straightening jerk as the pellet entered the chest of the bird. He felt that now. His uncle made him read something out of the Bible once when he was trying to help "turn him into a man", something about a woman and a dart striking a man in the liver or some garbage. Right now, he knew one thing more clearly than anything else he had ever witnessed or conceived.

He had now laid eyes on a woman he could never unsee. In an instant she seemed to take over everything, and now she was etched in the back of his brain.

It burned like fire. It was a different fire than the one burning down the back of his throat.

I'd better not be in love again, he thought, *I thought I just got over that.*

There she was, and he wanted to know who she was. He hit replay and watched again.

She was stroking a black rabbit that was relaxing on the tabletop in front of her as she talked.

"I'm Veronica," she said with a shy smile, "And this is Luna. We suck at cameras, don't we Luna?" Veronica paused, smiling down at the rabbit like an angel. "My papa gave Luna to me as a baby, and Luna's been with me through high school, college, and now is a happy California bunny." It was nibbling some vegetables she was hand-feeding it as she talked. He caught himself looking at her rouge-brown hair and drifting off again.

"I guess I need to get used to the whole video idea if I ever want to start dating again. I don't really get out that much. Most of my friends are all couple-ized, so the future is not bright for me on that front." She laughed, and it rang in his ears like a soft wind-chime.

Dating.

He heard the word, but hadn't realized what the context of it was. From the sadness in her eyes, it probably wasn't good. He felt his heart racing, because the virtual reality video made it appear like he was sitting across the table from her, and he had the sudden thought he'd give away everything he owned for that chance.

Jakub rewound again.

She was saying that this was a video test, and she was working more on these projects because for all intents and purposes she'd *given up* on dating. He felt like cold water had been poured on him, and the chill went straight up his spine.

Jakub studied her lips, the shape of her face, even the baggy shirt she wore looked spectacular on her. The major problem he faced was the emotions welling up in him were different than what he had felt in the past.

With Mitzi, and admittedly with Janet, it had been very sexual. He saw everything was in the right place, and Junior down below made all of the tactical decisions from there on out.

This was different. This girl certainly had a sexual pull to her that was like an Imperial tractor beam from *Star Wars*. But there was an extra layer in there that he couldn't identify, and he knew it was what he had been looking for. He was drinking her soul in through his eyes. Every word she said was like a drug to float on. The thing of it was that for the most part, there was no showmanship or anything else going on, she was simply talking to a camera, very possibly with the intent of another human being never seeing it. It was candid, and seemed almost like a form of therapy to him.

They way that she talked was intelligent, and he wondered what it was that she did for a living. He knew that she was a college graduate, she liked rabbits, or at least one rabbit anyway, and that rabbit was a lucky little bastard. He wished he could be that close to her. She had mentioned that she planned to do more videos, and he was going to wait and see when the next one was. It would probably show up here, since this was her app anyway.

For some reason he thought that maybe he had saw her when he was lit, but she didn't fit the mold for any of Jermaine's parties, so it couldn't have been there. It was somewhere else. He had seen her before, somewhere in real life and that was the thing that kept entering his mind as he scoured it trying to figure out where.

Jakub checked for useful or identifiable information. There were no credits attached to the video, nothing he could extract or look at. He tried to think of what he could use to reverse engineer the data and get clues from it. Nothing was listed in the catalogs on the goggles, or in the application database. Just a graphic buried in the system applications, hidden, like it was meant to be found, but not by just anyone.

Perhaps it had been added and then forgotten.

That didn't make sense, either. Supposedly this device had been wiped not once, but twice. No logical reason why it would still be here for him to find.

Maybe it was like finding a $100 bill on the street. Sometimes you don't ask questions and just enjoy the fact that it *is*.

Darkness was stretched out like a blanket. She could sense it, and something was different. It was like those times when you know you've forgotten something, it's right there in front of you, but you can't remember for the life of you what it is. Nothing else. No wind. No pain. No sound.

Where the hell am I? She asked herself, as she tried to remember for a moment who she was.

She tried to think about the things that she knew up front as the pressure of the haze in her brain seemed to subside. It was dark. She was there. She was aware. She was a girl. But what was her name?

Identity.

Being unique from everything else that was there in the darkness. It was more of a feeling than anything else. Feelings were really what she had in the moment. She needed to get things together, get a handle on what exactly was going on. Perhaps it was time for another checklist.

She was not kidnapped, there was nothing restraining her, there were no sounds.

Wait. There was a very faint whirring sound. Minute. Not industrial like a building, more like electronics. Nothing organic, though.

She felt beneath her to nothing. *No floor?* She felt a moment of incredulous shock as she spun her hand around herself. *I am actually floating, like suspended animation.* This didn't even seem possible. She couldn't feel her hand either, but there was no numbness.

What can I remember? She asked herself. She remembered the events of the morning, the coffee shop, and she'd worked in the office at her desk all day.

She came home after picking up dinner to go because she was working on a new interface for an application that was supposed to go out in two weeks. Getting all of the kinks and bugs out of it so none of the team looked silly. Of course there would be a few things come up that were out of whack, but nothing too bad if she could help it. The application itself was by design pretty solid and she was quite pleased with her design.

Empanadas. From that little Argentinean mom and pop shop. *Empanada's Place,* that was it. On Sawtelle. They always had the best. She had a glass of rollo mojo with them from the liquor shop next door. The taste was coming back like a ghost. Thankfully a pleasant ghost. *I'd about kill for another empanada about right now.*

All of the checklists she had worked through. Loaded the application package into the VR headset through the development kit. Everything was in working order.

The flash.

There was a flash, and the feeling that she had been sucked away in a moment, like a whirlwind. A piece of paper into a fan.

But what happened next?

This. This was apparently happening next. *So now it's down to brass tacks,* she thought, *I have to figure out what this is. Am I in a coma, maybe?*

Where do I live?

She could see in her mind's eye the red brick apartments she lived in. She had to live there because the building looked like Texas to her. They were off of Centinela. This was her second year of living in that building. She had originally moved in the first year with that nice girl, but couldn't remember her name. She knew that they were really close, which made her inability to recall even more annoying to her. It would come back to her. She moved next door with that other pretty Jewish girl with the dyed hair. They had become an item.

The second year was with the new girl that worked as a production assistant for a smaller film company. She was a sweet girl named Marta. She was from the Czech Republic. Had that nice guy for a boyfriend...

Everything she could detect came down to feelings and sensations. She still had conscious thought.

This has to be a coma.

While pondering that thought, she heard a voice. Not so much *heard* it as felt it.

Perhaps both.

It seemed to have an echo. It was her grandmother, speaking Portuguese. She'd never bothered to learn the language, but she recognized it when she heard it. But Avo had been dead for years. She could actually feel the words as they settled into her chest, then they translated into a single thought.

Baby Girl, find the light.

nobody's asking anymore

The spectacle grabbed him enough where he had to find out more about it. Where did this come from? Was it something that Jefco had put on the system or was it a part of the VR goggle manufacturer testing? There was only one way to find out, which was to call Jefco and ask him.

Jakub picked up the phone and looked at it for a second, trying to visualize exactly how he was going to bring this up. Sometimes Occam's Razor was the best policy. He'd call and spit it out.

Punching the numbers, he heard the gruff but peppy voice on the other end of the line.

"Sup, Jakie?"

"How did you know it was me? Do you actually have me saved in your phone?"

"You're either sleepy or stupid. I think it's the first one. You need coffee. What is so important that you would call me first thing in your morning? Are the goggles still working okay?" Jefco's voice took on a hint of concern. He had a thing about being the best and most stable in the business, so he got miffed when things weren't working as advertised. Personal pride.

"Yeah, the goggles are awesome. What makes you think I'm sleepy?"

"You called an office phone, dipshit. You're also the only person I know with a Dallas number that would be calling the shop."

"Good point. I'd forgot about that."

"Which one?"

"Both. Listen, I have this app on the set I wanna ask you about."

"Okay, which one? One of them going wonky? You know you can delete it and re-install it from the database."

"Nothing like that. It's called Luna."

"Never heard of it. What does it do? Moon cycles or something?"

"No. It has this girl…"

"Menstrual cycles."

"Nah, nothing like that. It has this girl…" Jakub proceeded to describe the girl in the video and what little he could remember of it. Jefco listened without comment until he was finished, and then said the words Jakub hadn't wanted to hear.

"I have no idea what that is. I didn't put it on there. Did you look to see who the developer was?"

"Dude, I don't know how to do that. I wanted to see if you knew where it came from and who the girl is."

"Love in VR. What are ya gonna do? Marry her when you find her?" He laughed aloud. "I didn't sell that as part of the package. Maybe I should think about it. Put dating apps on these things and sell them as *get yourself some ass* machines. You're full of great ideas, Jakie. I should talk to you more often."

"You probably should, but this isn't helping me. How do I find out more about this girl I'm looking at?"

"Get a name. Run it through a search engine. Snap a screenshot, run *that* through a search engine. Look up the damned developer. Not call and ask me about it. I just load things. I don't create the things. As a general rule of course. Now, if you don't mind, since I can't help you, I'm gonna run along. I have this porn marathon thing going on. I like to dedicate my off time to strokin' and pokin'. I'm gonna put on a bunch of movies and..."

"Don't wanna know," Jakub blurted. "Don't... have to know."

"I'm grilling steaks. Jeezus, you have a dirty mind."

"Um, porn festival at your house and *I* have a dirty mind."

"Hey, you called me. Not the other way around."

"I was calling for advice and information. Now I want a drink."

"And I can help with all of that. My advice would be to look online, where assholes like myself will not take the time to make your life a living hell when they don't know the answer. The Internet doesn't apologize, and I don't either. As for the drink, I understand that grain alcohol goes best with cornflakes. Haven't tried it yet, heard from a friend. You have a wonderful, skippy day, y'hear?"

"Aight. Thanks, Jefco."

"You're very welcome. Call back again soon, preferably later in the day when I might give a shit. I appreciate a good chance to be salty among friends for no reason at all."

The line disconnected. Jefco really needed a therapist.

He didn't have any more answers than he had when he placed the damned call, other than the fact that no one seemed to know where this app came from.

Loneliness hurts. Those hermits he'd seen on the internet could handle it, but something about it wasn't working with him in the least. It was a dull throb, always looking around for someone to talk to, to help validate you were alive to begin with. That was why Aiden's adventures were appealing. Scary, perhaps, but still appealing. No worries about whether you'd gotten up on time or not, but still being able to feed oneself and remain productive.

He wondered how many women lived like this, if any?

There had to be somebody doing it. Right now he was a bit concerned about whether he could find a girl that looked like the one in his goggles right now. More to the point, would they put up with him if he didn't have tons of money or a career?

Time to stop and take a breath. This was the wrong rabbit hole. Whether the pun was intended or not was still a matter of debate. After all, he'd been down this one several times before, and every time it ended the same. Time to get on the boat.

Jakub checked the charge on the goggles and saw that it was almost full. That sailing app would be the best for this, because he needed to think and it would be a pretty good place to do it. Jefco was right on that choice, even though it hadn't sounded great to begin with.

Perhaps sailing was the best idea, get out on the hardly realistic ocean with the typical cubic waters and ride in a slightly better designed sailboat. The app was relaxing because of the sound the water made when he rushed through it, the very thing that he needed in the moment.

So back to the problem at hand. Part of this was patience. Aiden had a good bit of that, and Jakub figured that since he was the best put together person he knew, he was a good person to emulate. But how had he gotten that way? From what had been said in their conversations before, they had a lot in common in the past.

Jakub sailed the boat up to an island to think. More precisely, he sailed the boat into the island at full speed, with the simulated jolt of the impact startling him. It was how most people parked when they were drunk.

Close enough for government work.

He clicked his way up to the bow of the ship, turned around and surveyed the open water down towards the stern. The main sail above him flipped and waved back and forth as he listened to the water crashing against the hull beneath him. The audio was incredibly good on this app.

One more party, and he was going to have to make some decisions. Being led by the nose was not doing him any favors. He had about two reasons for helping Jermaine with his presence, and neither benefited him. Let the guy hang himself, or let him blow up. Either way, it should never interfere with Jakub's schedule.

The loneliness thing was a self-enforced cop out, too. There were what, four million people in Los Angeles? Aiden could not be the only person to know. Maybe it was possible to build something like a little black book that was just friends and acquaintances, people different from those he knew right now.

The daytime of the app abruptly shifting to night without warning. A large pale yellow moon aloft in a charcoal sky, with the rings in the heavens lined out like a failing wide tipped marker in the hands of a child that wanted a black rainbow. The stars were scattered around the clouds in an afterthought, tossed there just to see if some of them would digitally stick.

He wasn't feeling quite so lonely anymore, actually, a little calmer. The answers weren't there, but at least a few of the questions weren't so pressing and didn't hurt so bad. They weren't worth dwelling on, so he tried to turn his focus to more important things. Not so much on how to get this fake sailboat off the island, and more on how to enjoy this virtual world he was in, at least right now, in the moment.

Of course, curiosity killed the cat. He knew he'd never let himself out of researching who the girl in the video was, at the very least he could do it without getting all emotionally caught up, just in the hopes of feeling something. That was pretty dangerous in and of itself.

There was a bit of fun and solace in researching, too. Sometimes that was the only point of it. The thrill of a chase, and even if you caught it, you weren't really out anything.

Floating Girl was grasping at straws. The silence was the worst part, because it left her with thoughts that she couldn't identify, the ultimate form of confusion. They floated in like soft, mismatched blankets. Like the flannel blankets you buy in a box store that are always gentle and comfortable, but never the right size for any bed you could possibly ever have, smaller on one side or the other. Not even big enough to hide under unless you were a child.

And Avo, she hadn't heard that voice in years, well over a decade, but that was grandma, and there was no mistaking her voice. She had lived with them until she died. She had practically raised her. She knew the woman speaking was Avo, but she couldn't remember her actual name. What was her name? And who else was in the house?

It was still. She didn't like stillness. She needed motion, things going on and constant action. It was like the motion of an atom or the reality of physics. Things needed to keep moving, and if they weren't it became maddening. Once, a professor had told her to slow down, tried to teach her about meditation.

The problem was, now she couldn't even remember where she went to school, or what she went for. Something geeky. Something she wasn't doing anymore, and might have never done and gotten paid for it.

The grey around her didn't seem to make sense, either. There was nothing really definite about it, no normal wall or border, just the color and a sort of wireframe. It felt like being inside three dimensional space, but not like the real world as much as if she were inside a game.

She wanted to take a moment and soak the nothingness in before she had to begin figuring out things.

There was no smell. Usually there is an odor of some sort, good or bad, wherever you are. The air freshener in the house, the smell of industrial cleaners, grease and exhaust outside, the salty beach air when you were lucky. But there was nothing here. Not even the smell of electronics.

Somehow she still knew what electronics were, and for some reason that was bugging her. How can you know about something tangible and not even know anything about yourself or your own life? It just didn't make any sense.

There was a sense of relationship with this space, but she simply couldn't put together how they related. It was familiar, something she had been connected to but the *how* of the equation was missing.

Figuring out what this place was seemed to be as difficult as trying to recall any memories at all. She knew she needed to be patient. Somehow she knew that it would come back to her, no matter slowly things seemed to be trying to come into focus, but when they did, maybe it would all come in a rush.

She tried doing basic math, multiplication tables, square roots. That would let her know she still had the capacity for quantitative analysis. She recited the alphabet, and that seemed to be there, too.

When she closed her eyes, she saw was seemed to be almost like a pale green cloud shaped like a four-leaf clover. It had what looked like train tracks running through it. Trains were familiar. Train tracks were familiar. She knew somebody that was connected to the railroad. Someone close. Someone she had a deep affection for, and that was verified by the feeling sweeping over her when she thought about it. They had lived in the same place together.

She felt the need to get quiet, to crawl into that cocoon of nothingness and float in it for a while. That might help. There was something right there under the surface, trying to get to the top where she could see it. A thought, an explanation. Facts and figures were the things she liked best. They were the least trouble to deal with.

And there was that thought trying to come to the top, almost like a blurry mass that had been hidden under that cold stuff. What was the cold stuff?

Ice.

One more word. One more thing she could visualize. What was ice made from? Water. She tried to see them both in the palm of her hand, tried to see them change forms. Maybe that was the next part of the process, re-teaching her brain to make the right connections again.

Who was that person she loved?

you've got to manage

"Parties are so stupid," Jakub said with a huge grin to the blonde next to him, the pounding music washing out every other sound or conscious thought. She smiled, nodded, lifted her drink and meandered further into the crowd. She hadn't heard a single word he had said to her.

For once, he didn't care. In fact, he could not give less of a shit. He was nailing down his alcohol, having the unheard conversation here and there. This was all a favor to his friend Jermaine who thought he would hook Jakub up with a new girl. And on the other, improve his repertoire as a promoter by having one more body at the party, Jakub felt the need to just troll the populace.

They couldn't hear him anyway. Nobody could. Getting anyone to listen to a fucking word he had to say was maddening. In fact, it was making him mad, period. He was also feeling depressed on top of the alcohol. He couldn't get that señorita from the VR set out of his head because she was stuck there, the scene playing over and over, developing, imprinting.

"I have an angry raccoon in a bag outside," he said to another brunette as she made eye contact, scanned him for his earning potential, gave the same toothy grin with the obligatory nod and headed in another direction with her cup. She hadn't understood a word of it, either.

This was so obnoxiously fun it was getting downright boring.

He wondered how long he had to stay to fulfill his *I came to your party* quota. Sure, the entry was free for him, Jermaine had covered that, but he wasn't a VIP. Jermaine had put more money into that little select group. It involved illegal activities that cost a *lot* more money and were reserved for the people Jermaine thought could really help him become rich and famous. Jakub was only a half-assed wingman on this venture. As usual.

And here this clown wants to be Bulldog, Pitbull, whoever.

Jakub didn't know anything about the guy, other than he was famous, did things with music, and Jermaine wouldn't shut up about him. He sounded cool. Cooler than Jermaine, anyway. He should probably go to that guy's parties instead.

Usually Jakub went into deep thought or performed math equations in his head to check out when Jermaine talked. Besides, renting out an entire venue and hiring the talent to put on a show alone costs money.

That's math.

If the math finally worked out, Jakub wouldn't need to be involved any more, and that would certainly be welcome.

Maybe about ten more minutes, and he could bail on this mess and go back to his normal life where all of the real human beings were. He felt a tap on his shoulder and a tug on his sleeve. His heart skipped a beat. She was another cute little party girl.

"Do you know where the bathroom is?" She asked with a slight slurring.

He pointed over to the corner hallway. "Over there."

She looked at him blankly. She could have been talking to a wall, or a video game.

"Do you know where the *bathroom* is?" She asked again, acting irritated.

"Manson knows," he replied.

"Ohmigod, is he *here*?" She squealed, squirming excitedly.

"I meant Charlie, not Marilyn. And no, I think he's tied up at the moment. Probably literally."

"Oh, fuck you. I gotta pee," she hissed, and wandered off.

"I can pencil you in when you're finished!" he shouted after her, his voice lost in the crowd.

He was feeling retribution for all of this nonsense he was putting up with. He wasn't into the party scene, but people kept insisting to drag him there. In the past month he had been to two of Jermaine's other parties, a drag improv, a comedy show, and a Lakers game. It was against the 76ers, and he'd wished both teams could lose.

He shoved his hands up in the air and shouted, "And you spoiled brats are why daddy drinks!" The music and alcohol swirled around him as whooping erupted and some drunk college boy gave a war cry. Or a cackle. Nobody had a clue. It was noise, they assumed something good just happened, and they reacted. It was like he had joined a party for coked up lab rats.

The liquor hadn't hit yet. *And now comes the part where I debate if I'm an alcoholic,* Jakub thought to himself. Then the bursting push of an exhalation.

There we go. Now I'm feeling it. That's what I was looking for.

The official drunk stage had now entered the building. And it was interrupted by a forceful clap on his back.

"Isn't this party *awesome!*" He heard, way too loudly in his right ear.

Jermaine had found him. *Good. Now I can get over the schpiel and get outta here.*

"Yeah, looks like ya got a lotta folks here."

Jermaine had a big grin on his face. He was the party guy, actually. It was like these things made him come alive. He was into all of this booming, not being able to hear each other, and all of the annoying superficial crap that went along with his festivities. He was babbling something, but Jakub decided to play along with Mr. Everything like he knew what the hell he was saying.

"Yeah," babble babble babble "Uh-huh" mumble mumble "Right on..."

He gave Jakub an excited cup clink and disappeared again. The next thing Jakub chose to lay his eyes on was the damned exit sign.

Mission accomplished, mofo.

I am free.

The warm exhaust air on Sunset hit him as he exited from the venue. He shuffled out of the doorway towards the parking lot. There were two or three ways to handle this. Jakub never drove to these things because he knew he would automatically become impelled to drink too much. Pulling out his phone, he fingered up his favorite ride application. Keeping money stored in that thing was a wise foresight. He could hit a couple of buttons and the system would use his location to send a car right to him, with directions sent to the driver. The driver was paid on pickup. One less problem to deal with.

Pretty foolproof setup. Especially when you're so lit you can't read.

He exhaled again. A cropped blonde wearing 80s neon at entirely the wrong function seemed to think she was at a rave. Considering it, that might be exactly what Jermaine had set up, which meant she might actually be dressed right, and he might be the one with the wrong crap on. All he knew was that it was electronic dance music at a volume so loud the deaf could feel it. She looked him up and down, smiled, and pulled the cigarette from her lips and stuck it firmly in his mouth. She locked eyes with him, exhaled the smoke, and with another smile strolled up to the doorman.

He kept the cigarette and strolled in the other direction.

Not today, Satan. I just got rid of one exactly like you.

About to tap the transaction button, he looked out to the parking lot where Sarah was getting into her Nissan with her partner Lindsey. He waved and headed in their direction. The couple were two more bodies that Jermaine had somehow befriended and connived into coming to his functions as well. It was pretty obvious they had the same idea he'd had and were making their escape while they could.

He had met Sarah two jobs ago, where she worked as a paralegal in a firm so large they forgot their employees even existed. Okay, so maybe it wasn't that bad, but one of the partners there didn't recognize him after a year and called security when he had come up to service the lawyer's computer. It started out embarrassing for Jakub, but the partner was the one that ended up with egg on his face. He was the guy who signed Jakub's initial hiring forms.

Business in the City of Angels. Gotta love it.

Sarah looked like your typical Jersey Jewish girl, she was cute and kept a constant dye of red in her hair that seemed to work for some reason. She was very smart and easy to work with, but at first glance appeared to be an airhead.

He waved a five dollar bill between his fingers at Sarah and asked, "Headed my way?"

"Whatever way you're headed, I'm headed the other way," she answered, her face spreading into a flashy grin surrounded by bright red lipstick. She had a moral obligation to give him shit at every turn. And she took that obligation religiously.

"Trying to get home," he looked over at Lindsey who gave him her usual pseudo-friendly but cool once-over and said, "You ladies are lookin' hot tonight!"

"Bullshit," Sarah answered, "That won't work. Get in, Tex." She popped the back lock for him and he slid into the rear seat. "And keep your money. You know it's no good with me."

"You hungry?" She asked as she placed the car into reverse, "We're probably gonna grab something on the way home."

"Nah, I'll sit this one out. I got no problem riding with you guys, though. I can use the break."

"I bet. It feels like you're on another planet coming outta J's shindigs. You *wanna* be hungry?"

He thought about it and the señorita flashed in his mind again. He was going to need to sober up. "Not tonight," he answered. "I have some stuff I need to handle before tomorrow, and I should probably sober up a little before that."

"Kay. It's all the same." They passed through a late night fast food shop while Jakub kept his head back against the seat in hopes of the fuzzies clearing.

Lindsey looked back to check on him as she rolled a joint between her fingers. "Rough night,

Tex?" He cocked his head in response. It hadn't been too bad, just depressing in a way, given the fact that nobody was paying any real attention to anything and that seemed to be a total waste of time to him. He tried to surf the wave of the fact she'd spoken to him directly. It was like having your favorite starlet address you directly. He actually existed in a good way now. Jakub could work with that. One less person hated him tonight.

"Not rough anymore," Jakub answered, providing a slight smile. "Y'all made things much better, and I thank you."

Lindsey was a completely different matter in herself. She had short blonde hair with a shock normally folded over an eye, and a thin strip that always seemed to be tinted some various pastel. Her cool aloofness was solidly joined with the fact she was heart-stoppingly gorgeous, which made Jakub feel conflicted and nervous anytime he was near them. He'd learned to shove any other thoughts out of his head as they arose quite some time ago. It wasn't right, and it wasn't going to happen. Those two were just a *thing*. You learned to accept them as a pair, because they were rarely apart when they weren't working. Janet had called them *whina bifida*. It explained why no love was lost when she'd left.

The worse part for any straight males within her purview was she could stroll in and out of the covers of any fashion magazine she desired. He did not know what to make of why she did everything *except* become a model.

Today's flavor seemed to be a strawberry of some sort.

By the time they had reached his doorstep, his head seemed to be clearing.

"Thanks for the ride, ladies," Jakub said, "I appreciate ya gettin' me out of that one."

"No problem. We completely understand the need to escape a Jermaine party," Sarah called out as he stepped out of the car.

He entered the doorway and headed to the kitchen bar, where he placed the phone from his pocket and noticed a voicemail indicator. Not sure how he missed that, probably happened at the party. Equally predictable, it was Mom.

"Honey," her voice came erupting silky smooth out of the speaker, "I've went ahead and found some resources that can help you." She then gave a Los Angeles number. It was to the Los Angeles LGBT Center.

She is just not going to quit, he thought. He considered changing his number. His eyes moved to the desk, to the goggles. It was almost like going on a date you weren't invited to. Something about the señorita still had his attention, but he couldn't remember what she said her name was, or even if she did.

He walked over and lifted the goggles off the desk and tried to turn them on.

Nothing.

At first, he panicked. Then he realized that the problem was simply he had left them unplugged. Because the goggles still drew power in any position, it ran out of power. He should have turned the power off and plugged them into the cable, but he was new at this whole virtual reality thing.

Lindsey. That was her name. The other girl that had become her partner... The one with the dyed hair... Sarah. Right. The S&L Express, they used to call them. Sarah was in the legal field but was never in courtrooms, so that's why she got away with the dyed hair. Something with entertainment. Everyone in Los Angeles seemed to be connected with entertainment some way.

Including herself.

She had lived with Lindsey. They were different but got along very well, she was almost like a big sister even though she really wasn't much older.

Floating Girl didn't know what had happened exactly, or where she was. She wondered if she had missed work or how much of it. This was a bit freaky, this place.

She could still hear the whirring. But something was coming, floating in. It was a thought, one that she knew she had to have, had to accept. It seemed to hit her in the face like a bolt of lightning wrapped in a soft blanket.

My name is Veronica Luz Salazar. I am from San Antonio, Texas. I am 27 years old. I work for a company called MetroTech.

A feeling of calm began to settle on her. *Things are starting to come back,* she thought. If things were beginning to come back to her, then everything wasn't lost. It was improvement. You can solve problems with improvement. New information helps to create progress.

Now that she knew who she was, she could begin to work on figuring out where she was, exactly.

The pitch black was beginning to ease into a soft gray. Something didn't seem right with her sight. Everything seemed pixelated, blocky, and nothing was perfectly clear. Her senses were on high alert, however, she was feeling things more potently. Possibly because of being in the dark. It had very likely heightened everything else in the absence of the light.

Maybe if it was a coma, she was beginning to come out of it. Perhaps it would only be a matter of time before things got straightened out. She was trying to figure out if maybe she was in a hospital or a facility somewhere.

This couldn't be a dream, because dreams were usually uncontrollable, and she felt very much in control, even if limited by what she could actually do. She'd wanted the master challenge, and apparently this was going to be one. The first step was to try and understand what the parameters were of this place.

First things first.

How long have I been here? I don't remember coming here.

guilty by design

The video girl was beautiful.

Not like just the pretty faces on TV or in the movies, this was something different. He didn't know if anyone else would think the same way as he did, and it made him feel a little creepy, but everything about her to him was perfect. She wasn't beautiful in the same way Lindsey was. She was beautiful in some completely different way, like those times when you have a face in your mind, and that's the face you want to see when you walk in the door.

He'd paused her mid-sentence, hung in a smile so he could just study her.

Her attire was homey and modest, a UTSA Roadrunners hoodie in a steel gray with the expected orange lettering. He could see the deep navy of the inside of the hood poking around her neck. The sweatpants had seen better days, frayed a bit at the ankle cuffs. They weren't the same gray, a lighter shade. The socks didn't match the ensemble, either, a girl after his own heart. This girl was not planning on going anywhere out in public when she filmed that video. She was just happy being seated on that futon going on about who knows what with eyes like fresh chocolate drops from the Ghirardelli factory.

Jakub had been there once on a trip with Janet. He was a secret sucker for chocolate, and since she was allergic to anything Jakub liked, he ended up touring by himself.

The factory was gone, anyway, but he'd saw the chocolate swirling around in a vat, and the deep, dark brown just looked sweet and wonderful. He had paid more than he should have, but hey, Ghirardelli Square is a thing you have to see in San Francisco, and this girl's eyes were very much the same.

She hadn't talked like a ditz or a typical college girl, she was plainly intelligent, to the point of making him nervous at himself.

No ring.

It was a habit, something guys just naturally do, whether they are interested or not, Ye Olde Ring Check. Find out if there is a guy you're going to have to worry about, or has been everywhere you wanna be first. She didn't have one, so there was a chance. If he could just figure out who she was.

He figured he could easily stare at her all day. She was incredible exactly the way she was. Jakub found himself obsessed with studying her like one might examine a work of art in a museum. He looked at every little detail in the scene, every component of her face as if he'd never see her again, completely lost in time and memory.

The shape of her nose, how the end was slightly rounded, the angle of her jawbone and cheek he followed with his eyes like a caress, that little tuft of hair just beside her ear. It was almost naturally combed over from her left to her right, as if she had laid her head sideways first and swept her hand through. Her hair was natural, she didn't have anything in it that most self-conscious girls would coat their mane in. Mitzi was horrible at that kind of thing. She'd used so many chemicals in hers that sometimes it crunched.

The girl's lips were full, and not in that grotesque plastic surgery way he'd seen so many times in Los Angeles. Everything about hcr was exactly as God had given it to her. If she had makeup on, it was so light as to be almost undetectable. She had the gift of simply being naturally beautiful.

I might be a creep for this, but I can't help myself.

He took a sip from his glass, cracked a piece of ice in his teeth, sucking the flavor of the bourbon off that had coated it.

He selected the Play button, just to hear her voice again. The way she enunciated everything flawlessly, casual, but with a voice that just made him fuzzy.

I wish I could just find this girl, he thought, exhaling hopelessly, *but she'd probably hate me just like Lindsey does.*

Because I suck.

Jakub turned the device off, and went to bed. Sleep took him almost as soon as his head hit the pillow.

He knew he was dreaming, but couldn't seem to wake up. Like he was knee deep in an invisible mud and couldn't move. Glancing around, it seemed both familiar and unfamiliar at the same time and he didn't quite recognize where he was. It was warm, hot actually, and dusty, so it wasn't California, at least not anywhere Jakub identified.

The suit. He was in a suit. That was highly unusual. He heard himself murmur, "But I'm not Catholic," as he realized he was in front of a priest. Everything was coming together so slowly, pieces flittering in to form the complete puzzle, and as he heard the priest's next words, he saw that he was holding a woman's hands, a woman shorter than him, dressed in white.

"... take Jakub to be your lawfully wedded husband, to have and to hold from this day forward, for better, for worse, for richer, for poorer, in sickness and in health, to love and to cherish, till death do you part, according to God's holy law..."

"I do," she said, "And *death* will not part us." She looked deep into Jakub's eyes with a soft, but powerful smile that felt like it was stopping his heart, and he realized he was looking into the eyes of the woman from the VR he'd spent so much time staring at earlier.

He woke with a start. It was the same old bedroom on Juniper that it had always been.

Wishful thinking, I suppose.

Jakub closed his eyes and slipped into another dream, it was smooth and without effort, as if he had strolled into his own movie theater and taken a place on the front row.

He was near an ocean, walking towards it, the feel of a hand in his, pulling him closer to the crashing waves he could hear in the distance. Long green scrubby grass danced back and forth in a breeze that seemed to smell of salt. This hand was different, slender, long fingers.

Feminine. But certainly not the woman in white.

He felt rings under his fingers, and realized he was wearing one, too. They were moving, almost gliding towards the ocean on a sandy natural pathway that appeared to push upwards and forwards to an outcropping ahead. As the woman guiding him became more focused to him, he saw her shoulder and neckline. It was familiar with an elegance he knew he had admired before.

She was happy, almost ecstatic in a way, with a smile that covered her face and eyes that shone like stars. The girl was talking to him, but he couldn't hear what she was saying, he just saw her lips moving, and she was very impassioned about whatever she was trying to tell him. The lavender and aqua streaks registered as he came to the full recognition of who was leading him.

Lindsey.

She rarely spoke to him in real life, barely talked to him, and constantly had a look on her face as if he'd just killed her new kitten with his bare hands any time he was within slingshot distance. This was a dream worth having, just to feel like she didn't despise his existence for once.

The beautiful scene dissipated in the beach air and was replaced by a completely different scene, the smell of smoke and gasoline swirling, and although he had an impression that he should be very afraid, he wasn't. It was a feeling of relief. A strange, vague feeling of relief, like when you've waited months studying for a major test that you have completed and have the idea that you passed it with flying colors. Everything else seemed so warm and *electric*. The feelings he had didn't match the situation he was in, but he couldn't clearly see where the smoke and the gasoline smell were coming from. He just knew that he had something soft and round in his right hand. It felt fuzzy, but Jakub was unable to look down at it to see what exactly it was.

He felt his left hand held in another hand. He looked up to see his Latina VR girl again. She was wearing a dark denim pantsuit with jean jacket, which seemed a bit odd to him, but she seemed to be pulling him from a seated position with a gentle smile on her face like she should see into the very depths of his soul. He felt as if her gaze cut completely through him, and as her lips moved, he understood that he couldn't hear what she was saying, either.

The lady pulled him close to her, wrapped her arms around his neck, and pulled him gently down to her. It was one of those moments that you have as a teenager when you want to go for that first kiss, but it's awkward, uncertain, shy. Everything in you is screaming for it, but you aren't sure that's what the other person is after.

But Jakub was. As he slid his arm around her, he leaned in for a moment that he wanted every time he'd laid eyes on her as she melted out of his arms to sunshine warming his face.

She diminished, replaced by a heavy smell of lavender. He stood in a purple field of it, watching a young girl with dark auburn hair about ten years old swirling and dancing among the rows. She wore a gigantic smile on her face of pleasure as she appeared to take in the moment for everything it was worth. She scattered butterflies everywhere she moved. He loved her immediately, passionately, to the point of tears, and had no idea why.

A voice behind him, a woman, laughed with glee and said, "Isobel, where's Daddy?"

The little girl beamed, held her hands up as if she were holding the clouds, spun in a circle with her pale purple colored sundress twirling and announced proudly, "Daddy's *everywhere!*"

"Do you talk to Daddy?"

"From time to time," she answered happily.

"When is 'time to time'?"

She beamed a grin that was missing a tooth, "When I need him. Sometimes when I don't."

Jakub ached to go to the little girl because he felt like his heart was going to burst, and stood to step forward.

And slid immediately out of the dream into the pale light in his bedroom.

You've got to be kidding me. What the hell are these dreams?

Looking over at the clock on his bed stand, he saw the time, and something just felt weird.

5:55AM.

Jakub was exhausted. Which defeated the purpose of going to sleep in the first place. He decided to break the early morning protocol and plodded out to the kitchen. He rinsed out his favorite crystal glass and dropped a round ball ice cube into it, letting the cracking of the ice under the bourbon wake him up. Coffee could come later.

Right now, he needed a drink. No more dealing with women, goggles, or steamy dreams until after work.

There was a calmness that had spread throughout the area, though the area itself was hard to quantify on its own. When you look at a wall, and a floor, you can see where they meet, but here, there seemed to be no wall, seemed to be no floor. It appeared to be a gigantic sheet of nothingness. Perhaps she was in the middle of creating her own existence or something. For this place, it was hard to tell what was real, and what wasn't. Right now, it seemed to be none of it.

She felt something, like dripping water, as if it were hitting her between the eyes, but there was no moisture, and from what she could tell, there was only the sensation of it.

I haven't even tried to move, she thought. Veronica wondered why she hadn't even attempted it before. Maybe it was the sensation of suspended animation that kept her from even trying. It was an instance of being at absolute peace, no cravings, no desires, and for a while, no memory of who or what she actually was. That was starting to come back, at the very least.

Hope remained.

She willed herself into an upright position and discovered that it was easier than she figured it might be. It was like walking had been outside, but her legs didn't seem to feel weight or have the same muscular impacts that were normal in other circumstances. It was a lot like being inside of the 3D programming platforms she had once programmed on.

That's what I do. I'm a programmer!

Unlike her work before, she seemed to have little to no control over this arena at all. It was like the controls had all been taken away, and she was left to explore her own creation from the inside. Something was ahead of her, in the distance. Not too close, but not too far, either. Looked almost like a door!

She moved towards it and discovered as she was getting closer it was a large piece of plate glass, like bulletproof glass. The kind you'd see in a bank or a corner store. The edges were smooth, almost polished, and she could move all the way around it where it stood suspended in mid-air with nothing to support it.

How weird.

Veronica moved completely around it, checking for any kind of support structures, strings, cabling, anything. It was literally floating about a foot off of the ground. Or what served as ground, anyway.

It could have been a worse gray. Darker would have been too night-like and drab. Too light, well that would be better lit, for sure. Color would have been nice, whatever this place was. Maybe some of those cool lights like they had in that science-fiction movie, the one where everybody rode around on weird electric scooter looking things that had the lights on them. She remembered watching it with her papa when she was young, and then someone did a remake of it, which for once didn't suck.

Why does everybody feel the need to remake things, anyway? It's not like anyone seriously thought the Mona Lisa needed a remake. She did have a poster of a Mona Lisa Chewbacca, but that doesn't really count. It wasn't considered a priceless piece of art. A really cool rendition, maybe, but nothing you'd be selling at a Beverly Hills auction.

Although stranger things have happened.

There was a new sensation, a prickly feeling that seemed to cling to the back of her neck, like warm needle pads being applied just under her hair. What was that? And it came with what felt like a more intuitive emotion.

It was the notion of being watched. At first, she felt fear, but that state dissipated. The feeling seemed to be more like someone watching her doing a menial task out of sheer boredom rather than the sensation that it was devious in any way.

Who are you? She thought. The response came into her head almost like it was spoken, but there was a difference. The sound seemed to be in her head, close in but not like headphones.

I am Jakub.

The sensations arrived into her mind clean but confused.

She tried communicating again. Telepathic?

Who are you?

I told you, I'm Jakub.

Veronica thought about it for a few more moments. She couldn't see anyone, or any cameras. There were no windows, but she was connecting with someone she didn't know. She couldn't remember anyone she knew named Jakub.

The gray in the room felt like a cave. It also seemed to be endless as far as she could see, knocking her perception off. She decided to play with the voice a little more.

What are you doing, Jakub?

I'm watching a beautiful girl with a rabbit.

A girl with a rabbit... Wait a minute. Veronica recalled that she used to have a rabbit. A black one with long floppy ears. Named after the moon in that kid's show she used to watch growing up. Then she felt like she'd been tossed into an ocean, dark, wet, the clouds hovering low and the rain feeling torrential. It was emotional more than it was literal, like the waves of despair flowed in and lapped around her, and her arms, her body, her head.

She was feeling him firsthand.

Why are you so sad, Jakub?

Because I'm lonely, and I'd never be able to get a girl like that to save my life.

Veronica felt bad for this Jakub guy, whoever he was. She'd had the same kinds of feelings before. She had crushes that were spoken for, crushes that turned out to be complete assholes, and then the occasional horrible date. If it was a bad date, she'd probably had it at least once.

Why would you say that, Jakub?

Because it never happens. I dream about it, but it never happens.

He sounded kinda mopey. But she had to admit that she'd had the exact same thoughts before, so if he sucked, then she did, too.

What if she came to you?

They never come to me.

Challenge accepted.

into the core

Jakub.

Hearing his name completely threw him off guard. He watched the girl Veronica's mouth.

Jakub!

Her mouth was moving. She was talking to him, but how? He didn't feel his crystal glass leave his hand, rather he heard in a faint reaction the sound as it hit the stone kitchen tile and shatter.

Jakub stayed on the bar stool he was sitting on. He wasn't going to step blindly into the glass, but he wasn't taking his eyes off her.

"Yes?" He asked cautiously.

"Omigod," she exhaled with what sounded like relief, "You can actually hear me!"

"Uh, yeah?" This was getting to be too much like one of those hidden camera shows. He was feeling strange, waiting for the punchline to hit.

"Where are you?"

"Here?"

"Where's here?"

"Los Angeles. Off of Jasmine."

"I know where that is! Where am I?"

"Is this a joke?" This had to be a hidden camera thing.

"I wish it was." Her excitement faded and her face became somber. "Can you see me?"

"Oh, god, yes."

"This is humiliating. Do I even wanna know? How are you seeing me?"

"I'm watching you in virtual reality. This better not be a joke, or you owe me."

"Virtual reality," she was getting excited again, "It wouldn't happen to be a black pair of Anteryx GS689s would it? It'll be written on the bottom, near the nose."

Jakub pulled the goggles off briefly and looked at the bottom. Might as well play along with this crap. *If it gets me to the girl, I'm gonna do it.*

"Yes, that's exactly what they are. Good guess."

"Okay, listen carefully. I have two more questions. First, the serial number. It should end with 1494. 'Columbus plus two' is how I remember it. Does it?" He checked again. That was precisely what was engraved, next to the model number.

"Yes."

"Last thing. Might as well confirm my fears while I'm at it. The foam pad that is against your face right now... Pull it up towards the middle and look under the left eye against the base. You *should* see a little taco sticker, no, I'm not kidding, you should see a little taco sticker there."

It was precisely where she said it would be. This *had* to be a joke.

"Why the taco?" He asked.

"I'm from San Antonio. It's a Texas thing. Nobody else was from Texas, so that way nobody could run off with my headset without me being able to identify them."

"I don't believe you. Name three major things in San Antonio."

"Why do you have my headset?"

"I bought it. Three things."

"Really? The Missions, Fort Sam Houston, and Lackland Air Force Base."

"Not the Alamo?"

"The Alamo is the fifth Mission. Who doesn't know their geography now? Next you're gonna tell me *you're* from Texas."

"Actually, I grew up in La Grange."

"Like the ZZ Top song?"

"Exactly like the ZZ Top song. And you look familiar, by the way. So why don't you come out from behind the curtain or wherever you're at. I wanna meet you." Might as well put some pressure on it.

The smile fell.

"I'm not behind a curtain," she said, "Actually, I don't know where I am."

"Seriously?" He snorted, "You don't know where you're at, but you're talking to me."

"Seriously. All I know is that it's dark where I'm at, and I'm supposed to get my project out before Labor Day, so I don't have a lot of time to jerk around. You're gonna hafta play nice and gimme those back. It's gotta get done."

"What's your name?"

"Veronica. Veronica Salazar. I work for MetroTech. It's a production company. We create virtual reality and Internet graphics. Off of Sepulveda. We're near all the special effects folks."

"Mind if I check your story?" He was going to call this girl's bluff. Either she was full of crap, or he was going to get to the bottom of this. Make it as bad TV as possible, because he didn't want to be on television anyway.

"Be my guest," Veronica answered.

Jakub removed the goggles and stepped wide to avoid the shattered glass on the floor. Then he walked to his bedroom where he had placed his phone. It was certainly out of voice range, so he was going to find out what was going on. He did an internet search and came up with the main phone number rather quickly. So at least the company was a real thing. It was also located roughly where she'd said it was.

He punched out the number to a delightful girl's voice on the phone.

"Thank you for calling MetroTech, how may I direct your call?"

"Veronica Salazar, please."

He heard her breathing come to a complete stop.

"Could you repeat that?" She asked with weakness in her voice.

"Veronica Salazar," Jakub confirmed.

"She's not... *available*, sir."

"Might I ask when you think she will be available?"

"Could I get your name, sir?" She asked cautiously.

"Jakub Riser. I was told she worked here, and I could reach her here."

Deep breath on the other end.

"Can you tell me roughly when she might be available?" He asked again.

"I'm not sure how to tell you this, sir... Veronica passed away in 2017. Right after I started working here, like around Labor Day. You might want to check who you're speaking with. I'm afraid you might be dealing with identity theft. If you'd like, I could connect you with our HR department."

"No, that's fine. I'll start looking into this right away from my end. Thank you."

He disconnected the call, plopping on the bed. This chick was going to have to wait until he figured out what the hell was going on. And he still had glass to clean up from when she'd first talked to him. He knew one thing for certain.

You don't call into work *dead.*

So she wants to get her work done, and work says she's been deceased for over a year. There's only one way to figure this out.

Jakub went to the laptop on his computer desk and woke the screen up. Opening a new browser window, he entered into a search engine

Veronica Salazar San Antonio Los Angeles MetroTech

145

You should be able to catch something with that. After all, the Internet knows more than it should ever have been allowed to know about people. He was presented with a results explosion and glanced at the first page.

Three obituaries.

One in the *LA Times*, another in the *San Antonio Express-News*, and a third on a trade site. He felt the hairs on his neck stand up as he pulled up the first article and saw the posted picture.

It was the first time Jakub had been forced to brutally accept the possibility of life after death.

He was looking at the smiling face of Veronica, an almost perfect headshot, and she was in his VR headset at this very moment. It was technically *her* VR headset, but she had no idea she was dead. And now he had to decide whether to tell her or not.

There was no closed circuit camera television show. No one could possibly know about what was happening in his apartment, and this wasn't a case of identity theft. He was either talking to the most advanced artificial intelligence about fifty years ahead of its time, or he was talking to a dead girl. One that he was so attracted to that it hurt.

This is not a drill.

He also needed to think this out before he put the headset back on. She still thought she was misplaced somewhere. He hadn't considered *where* she would think she actually was. He didn't know her well enough yet to understand what her thought processes and belief systems were, what exactly she meant by "darkness" and if she was blind or anything else. He just didn't know. Perhaps it would be best to just get her talking, learn more about her, and then figure out where to go from there.

It was obvious that she was alive in some shape or form, but not in her physical body. According to the obituaries, her body had been shipped to San Antonio and buried there. He couldn't help wondering where she actually was. Could he reach her?

Jakub went back into the kitchen and looked over the mess in the floor. The first order of business would certainly be to get all of that glass off the floor, and he wasn't even upset that it broke. At least he'd had the foresight to steal more than one glass when Jermaine had hosted that party at that club on Sunset. They were even engraved.

His mind was more on the wonder of the fact that he could still interact with this woman. She was a bit of a captive audience, and he really didn't have to worry about folks getting in the middle. In some ways, it was a stroke of good fortune.

Grabbing the whisk broom that he kept near the refrigerator, he gently swept up the shards and deposited them into the trashcan. He wanted a drink, but he had just broken one glass, and couldn't seem to motivate himself to pour another.

How strange.

He returned to the goggles and put them on again. Veronica looked up as he breathed.

"What did they say?" She asked.

"They confirmed that you did in fact work there," he said, trying to make sure the details remained as vague as possible, at least for now.

"I told you so," she said, and flashed a grin.

"Veronica," He asked, "Tell me about what you can see."

The conversation she was having with Jakub seemed different than any other she could remember having. She couldn't see anything, but the voice seemed to be coming from in front of her, and slightly to the left. What she actually *could* see was in a deep, dark grey with a geometrical design embedded in it. Almost like a development whitespace. It was like being in VR, with no ground, no real top, 360 degrees of grey.

No, I can't be. This has to be a dream or something.

She was still hearing the gentle whirring of electronics. He had asked her what she could see, and as she described what was around her, the grayness and the geometry, she noticed more to the conversation. Every time that he spoke, she felt sensations, like when someone is too close into your space and you feel the gentle shock waves of every word as it comes out of their mouths.

She could *feel* him. She realized that he felt sad. Almost depressed. It wasn't like that when he had left before. Everything felt normal in as reasonable of a way as could be expected. The sound also felt organic, like it was being spoken inside the room, rather than through a speaker. That ruled out several things, but didn't quite explain how they were connecting in the first place.

He was wearing her VR goggles, so that meant she was somehow connected to virtual reality. But virtual reality was for the most part an optical illusion that used the eye and perception to create an alternate reality. You weren't actually *in* that environment, it was simply the one presented to you, and your brain took it and ran with it.

"Tell me, Jakub," she asked, "How do I look to you?"

The vibrations changed on a dime, and he didn't speak. She felt the shift, warm, almost soft. He was quiet, and all she could hear was his breathing.

He is actually trying to think of how to answer me. Why?

The field that the vibrations seem to arrive on began to increase in speed. It felt luxurious, like when she used to sit on the beach in the sunshine, listening to the waves and there was just ocean air with a fine mist and a California sun shining down. She heard him choke as he began to speak, and he croaked slightly.

"I feel like such a creep saying this," he started, "I've been staring at you in this app for four days, and you are just so beautiful that I could stare at you for 400,000 more."

"I'm not going to even do the math on that," she said, as she felt herself smile. Maybe it was a blush, she wasn't sure of herself anymore.

He laughed nervously, "Don't. Just know it's a lot."

"You know," she said, "I don't believe anyone's ever said that to me. Like, *ever*."

"On what planet is that even *possible*?" He asked. She picked up on the vibrational shift. It was a real question.

"This one, apparently," she answered, "I'm serious. I've never had a boyfriend say anything quite like that to me. Of course, I'm not asking you to stop, please don't," she laughed, "It's just... wow."

"So you have a boyfriend?" She felt a slow down in the waves.

"No. I mean, I *had* one, but he really wasn't what I was looking for. No connection. He was some guy that my roommate's boyfriend knew and tried to set us up. She's from the Czech Republic, and so is her guy, and so was this guy. He was all about working out and trying to be a star at *something*, I really never figured out what. Had that whole woman-belongs-in-the-kitchen mentality. I'm a fucking engineer. I've forgotten more than that dipshit would ever know." She cringed, "Oops, sorry. That just came flying outta there."

"It's okay. I tend to drop F-bombs like a World War II bombing raid. I was trying hard to not offend *you*."

"So what do *you* do?"

"I'm an IT guy," he said. "Not quite like you, I work with desktop and software support, play with servers, networks, things like that. General support monkey."

"But you understand technology. See, you're easier to talk to. You actually know what the hell I'm talking about. Even if I were to get into the guts of things and talk over your head, it's really just out of your wheelhouse, not above your comprehension. That's different. That's *compatible*. I wanna meet you if I can ever get the hell out of here."

A new sensation began. It was like when Avo spoke to her, words that were simply floating and becoming embedded into her and the meanings presenting themselves like bubbles in the flow of a stream. The vibration slowed down even more, and felt depressed again.

"What's wrong?" She asked. He exhaled. It wasn't a good one, either.

Shit.

He probably had a girlfriend, maybe even a wife. That was historically her luck. All the good ones were always taken by the time she got to them. Now she looked like an idiot.

"Veronica, what is the last thing you remember? What's your last real memory? When you could see everything."

"Well, I was working on getting the project together, because we have to have it ready by Labor Day. Everything looks pretty good, and they're planning to release in October so I have to do the final run-through, I validate and sign off on it, and then it goes to my boss Jordan, and he signs off on it."

"Yes, but what's *your* last memory?"

"I had the headset on that you are wearing right now, there was a flash of light, and I felt like I was being sucked through a fan. When I woke up, everything was black. I'm still not sure where I am."

"I'm certainly not an expert, and I'm gonna sound like the biggest moron on planet Earth, but I think you are literally *inside* your own VR goggles." He told her.

"Now, that's nuts."

"The date... what's the date, at least the last one you remember?"

"It's August 31st. I just got paid last night, because I get paid on the 15th and the last day of the month. Bill pay took care of a bunch of my bills, and I killed off the rest this morning."

"Have you ever heard of ventricular fibrillation?"

"Yes. It's when the heart vibrates instead of pumping blood. Like a heart attack."

"Do you have a history of heart problems in your family?"

"My father died of a heart attack."

More words floated in. She wasn't prepared for them, and they hit her in the chest like a brick. It was Jakub.

How the hell do I tell a beautiful woman she's dead?

Veronica realized that she was literally hearing his thoughts. The more powerful and emotional they were, the more accessible to her they were. And then she truly digested what he had thought.

She was dead.

That was what was wrong. But she could think, analyze, interpret. It was on a different scale, though, which meant that life after death was a thing. She was still alive, but not in the normal and conventional sense. So what was that? That meant that Einstein was right. Energy cannot be created or destroyed, only transferred.

Transferred! The word flashed through her mind like a lightning bolt.

"Holy fuck, I know what happened!" She exclaimed without thinking. She had forgotten she was being actively observed. "You're telling me about the fibrillation because I *had* one, right? The human body carries an electrical impulse. It's low, but it carries one. When we're alive, the body maintains the electrical system, and then when the body dies, it releases the hold on the system. Like gravity."

Silence.

"So I was wearing the headset when that happened, and I can tell you officially those headsets conduct. If they had been on the table, I would have went into the wild yonder, or wherever the hell that is you are supposed to go. But since they were on my face, I literally went into the headset instead. Jakub, you're a fucking genius!" Then she stopped to think again.

Then she giggled. She was actually *living* science fiction. Now she felt like a Time Lord. Or perhaps a Time *Lady* in her case.

"So the bullshitting's over," Veronica announced, "Neither of us have a damned thing to lose now. Well, I don't, anyway. What's today's date?"

She heard him suck in his breath and exhale slowly.

"April 23, 2019. You've been in there about a year and a half," he said, "I'm still trying to figure out what to do with all of this."

"You? I'm the one stuck in here!"

"True. I'd give anything to get you out of there, too. I guess you're sort of a captive audience, so I might as well be cheesy and say it." She felt the warmth coming back and couldn't help but smile. The happy waves were good things. They just felt blissful. Might as well put the boy in a corner while she still could.

"What is it you're so chicken to say," she asked coyly.

"That I *finally* have the woman of my dreams in front of me, but she's in virtual reality. I really suck at this game. I was ready to hunt you down to the ends of the earth. I wasn't expecting all of *this*."

"And that's the line you're sticking with?" She wished she could take it back the moment she said it because she felt him deflate almost immediately. Not what she'd planned at all. "I'm joking. I'm only playing with you."

"I'm not."

i become a sea

"You know how to make a girl all weak in the knees, don't you?" She knew she was baiting him, but this was getting to be fun. If you're going to sit somewhere that you can't really tell what's going on, you might as well have fun with it, right? Especially once you're blessed with the highly unusual attracted audience.

"I don't know about all that," Jakub answered. She could sense a twinge of something in his voice, but she wasn't sure if it was embarrassment or shyness.

"I bet you try that one with all the girls," she tried again, not completely sure what she was even fishing for in the first place. The warmth came through again.

"N-No,' He said, shaken, "Just you."

It came in like a blanket, wrapping her gently. Apparently these emotive responses were only tangible to her where she was. She couldn't watch his face for a reaction, but she *could* feel him out.

I wonder what this guy looks like?

She thought it out of curiosity initially, but she really did want to know. It would be disappointing to discover that this guy she'd been chatting up was some 300 pound guy in momma's basement. She'd been down that road before.

The information floated in to her as effortlessly as the name had before.

The face.

Dammit. Not him. Anybody but him.

It was almost a mind's eye sort of thing, so it was probably wrong, and in this case, she was hoping so, for her own well-being and self-preservation. Like some people you just don't want to ever see you with a hair out of place or in the middle of a fashion faux pas. He was one of those people.

She had seen that face before. He was that cute hockey guy she'd crushed on once. Green. Veronica had made a comment in passing because he had on the Dallas Stars. It had seemed to slide off of him like Teflon. Hockey wasn't her thing, but you just know every sports logo in professional Texas sports if you live there. Where exactly had she met him?

"Hey..." She spit out at him, "You a hockey guy?"

"Oh, hell yes." He said. It came through with a bravado, a sense of pride, not quite as soft as the emotion it replaced.

"Who's your team? Not that I'd really know, I'm not *that* into sports."

"Oh, Dallas Stars. Since I was a kid. Any self-respecting Texan knows who they are even if they don't like them. They're in the Playoffs again, by the way. Your Spurs and the Houston Rockets are both in the NBA Playoffs."

"Not *my* Spurs, but I get it. My brother on the other hand, Pablo was *all* about the Spurs. Everything he wore was black and silver. My dad was the same way. I was pretty much raised on the Spurs. I brought it up because I think I remember seeing you, and I seem to remember you wearing a Stars jersey. It was the black one with green letters. Modano."

She felt the skip as soon as she'd said the name. She knew she'd just mispronounced the name of his favorite player.

"Mo-DAH-no."

Oh, who cares?

"To-may-to, to-mah-to. He's not gonna give a shit."

"He's retired. But he won't answer to it, either." She heard the slight laugh. "But the fact that you remember me, plus you actually remember the name on the back of my jersey, that's a million-to-one shot right there... that's what I'm astounded by."

"Some things are just memorable. Some faces you just remember."

"Is that a good thing?"

"Well, usually I would think so. Not if you're in a police lineup, I guess. Ever been in one of those?"

"Uh, no. No, I have not had the pleasure."

"Good. Me, either."

"I did however see a Krispy Kreme truck parked outside the police station on Venice, near Highland."

"Bullshit. I'm calling bullshit on that one, " she answered. Things like that just don't happen in real life.

"Have a picture to prove it," he answered with a victorious huff, "You don't see that on your way to work and *not* take a picture. That's why they put cameras into phones to begin with."

He was feeling happy. She could tell from the warm vibrations she was feeling. Maybe that's what is going on when people are said to have a magnetic personality. Could be that they're just vibrating in a way everyone can feel, so it attracts them. She knew that she felt good with the way he was right now, and it made her comfortable.

"So, were they unloading the truck?" she asked him, curious what his response would be. After all, a story about a doughnut truck in front of a police station was so horribly stereotypical that it generated both a laugh and a need for a good story to go with it.

"You're probably going to be disappointed. I think it was unfortunately broke down in front of the precinct, because the hood was up. But I made sure to get the picture from the back corner so you couldn't see that little fact. Besides, framing is everything, right?"

"Unfortunately, for the driver?"

"Oh, no. Unfortunately for me. If they had been carting doughnuts in the place by the rackful, I'd have gotten a Pulitzer for that shot or something. That's the sneaky stuff I doubt anyone would ever see. The LAPD would never live that one down. Still not sure where that stereotype came from, either. Y'know, the whole cops-and-donuts thing."

"So, Mr. Jakub, we haven't talked about you much. Tell me about yourself. La Grange, right? So what was it like there, tell me about you, who else is in your family, all of that. Inquiring minds want to know."

"If inquiring minds wanna know, then I guess I'd better make it good. I need aliens and crap in there, but I really don't have it. Everything was pretty simple. I was in La Grange until about seventh grade. I think I was about 13 when Dad died."

She immediately felt the vibration plunge. It dipped low, and knew that this was a big deal the second it escaped his lips.

"I'm sorry," she said, "If you don't mind me asking, what did he die of?"

"Self-inflicted gunshot wound. In my opinion, temporary insanity. We left La Grange and moved to Houston."

"I would imagine so."

"Not quite by my choice, not that I had a say in it at all. I had to move with the person that was the reason for the temporary insanity. She's permanently insane. I didn't exactly win on that one."

"Just you?"

"Me and my sister Willow. She was about 17 at the time. We moved just a little north of Houston. Willie got married, and right after that I moved in with her."

"Willie?" As soon as she said it, the nickname clicked, "Oh, Willow, Willie... I get it. Did she ever get any shit for that nickname?"

"Not from anyone that valued their general health and well-being. She's someone you don't want to mess with. She's like a white, redneck chola. For a while there, she was even doing the makeup and everything. Seemed a bit much to me, but I was a kid, too. I think that part started when we first moved south. We were on the south side of Houston for a little while when Mom was trying to get everything together for the house we moved into. We were *broke* for a while, so we were staying where Vera came from."

Veronica waited. No sense in asking, he wasn't done with his train of thought that he seemed to be carefully putting together, probably for her benefit. There were parts of this story she could feel that he wasn't telling, and it would be a bad idea to press for them before he wanted to share.

"Vera," he continued, "Is my mother's girlfriend."

There it is.

She felt him switch gears.

"Mom was the love of my Dad's life. You know how there's so much Czech stuff in Texas? Like down to Kolaches and all of that? I understand that's big in your area, too. I know for a fact it is when you go south from La Grange towards the 10 Freeway. My great-grandfather was a Bohemian, so they came over in the 1800s and moved to Texas with all the other folks of their kind. Same with Mom's family, although I hear it that they came just a little later.

Everything seemed to be pretty insular, and most of the folks were marryin' in and out of the various communities, y'know. Not sure what kind of wonders that does for genetics, but by the time it got down to us, we don't really recognize a lot of it or care. We're just Texan now. But that's where Riser comes from."

"Do you like Vera?" She asked.

"I reckon I like her all right. She's *very* pretty, sweet, loyal, all of that. I just think she can do a lot better than Mom, and easily, too. Mom is just a fast talker and seems to be slick as snot, to be perfectly honest with you. Vera was Mom's nurse at the time my Dad did his thing."

"You mean..."

"Eating the business end of a firearm by himself, all in one sitting? Yeah. Vera really wasn't at fault. She seemed to be the prize they both wanted, and I don't even know if she was fully aware of it at the time. I mean, if I had to give you an image to work off of, she looks like she could be Madeleine Stowe's sister. So it's easy to see why they'd *both* be after her, poor thing. As far as I'm concerned, my mother is just an equal opportunity grifter."

"Willie calls her The Grifter Queen, and Grifter Martha Stewart. Because like Martha Stewart, she wants to be at the top of her game in lifestyle, culture, design, and all of that. The difference is that Martha runs real businesses and does real things, and Mom just robs people blind while trying to look good doing it." He paused, as if he was trying to remember something, "Ah, a grifter is someone who basically scams the piss outta people. Sure you already figured that out, though. I forget that I use language differently than most folks."

"Yeah, I did. But it's not a term you hear that much."

"Blame Texas. And me constantly hanging out with older people."

"Are you the only one in California then?"

"Yeah. Just me. Kinda like it that way, actually. I do miss my sister, but she has enough on her plate with the kids and her own family. We see each other every year when they come to Vegas. How about you? Did you ever go to Vegas?"

"I went a few times. Once for a wedding. Ran from the bouquet. Bride threw it right at me, too. You know those scenes when someone's trying to stage dive at a concert and then the second they leave the stage, the crowd clears and they faceplant on the hard floor? It looked about like that. Nobody was touching that shit. It was like, 'We see what you got, bitch, and we want none of it.' But Vegas itself was fun, I guess. I'm not really a gambler type, so I just tried to enjoy everything else. You know how the Strip is, though. If you really wanna enjoy it, you either need to come with a piggy bank, or put enough of your piggy bank in the machines that the casinos will help you out."

"Exactly. That's how I help them get out here. I take a weekend about every three or four months, sit around, drink, enjoy a suite, sink a few hundred into the slots with no intention of actually winning anything, and that along with greasing up the slot host, are just about enough to get them out here for a few days or a week. We get to enjoy ourselves without *her* around. You learn the game after a while and get to play it well enough that it works out the way you want it to. That's pretty much the reality with everything, I guess. How about you? Any brothers or sisters?"

"I had an older brother. He died in an accident at work. I guess he was a typical older brother. Kept the boys off of me when I was younger, extremely over protective. After he died, I pretty much went to college after that. I picked UTSA because it was easy for me to get to, and it was right down the street. I could stay at home and not have to venture out that far. I wasn't the wild type, pretty much a homebody."

"That's the way I try to be now, when I can get away with it."

"You don't go anywhere much? Explains why you're here with me," she said.

"Nothing quite like that. Or maybe. I basically go where I'm voluntold to go. See some things I don't care about seeing, go to places I'd never go on my own, usually with people I would never normally want to meet."

"Friends?"

"Overbearing acquaintances, more like it. I'm not always alone, I have friend who's in the same boat. She and her girlfriend end up being dragged to the same things." He paused again, as if he was going into another sore subject. She could tell when he was hitting those because the energy would shift, and she could feel a spike in the tension.

"Sounds like this person has a lot of power."

"More like a lot of personal pity. We're basically going to his little parties to help him out. To give him credit, he does comp our entry and drinks, so we basically go to be seen, not that I'm anything in particular to look at, but I'm a number on his sheet which seems to help him some way. They're the lookers. I'm more hooked into this because we work together."

"Well, I'm sure you're likable, it doesn't seem like it would be that..." She let the sentence trail so he could finish it.

"No, nothing like that. I guess I always feel like I'm in a little box and I can't get out of it. Been that way for years, so I don't connect with too many people. Either I get pissed off, I'm pissed off already, or I just don't warm up too well unless someone is in a similar situation to me, and I haven't found too many of those. Especially out here. Haven't really looked, either. Everyone's so superficial out here. It's the Soul-Sucking Capital of the World. Everybody on every street corner and restaurant is an actor, and they want me to know about it. I just don't have the time or patience to really care."

"So, no close friends, no full time family around, no girlfriend, obviously, or you wouldn't be sitting here talking to me."

"There *could* be a girlfriend..." he poked.

"No, there's not."

"How do you know?"

"Because no girl in her right mind is gonna let a guy she really gives a damn about sit and talk to another girl online for hours on end."

"But you're not online."

"She wouldn't know that."

"Still..."

"No girlfriend. Admit it."

rip it out

Veronica had a way of cutting through all of the subtext and getting to the root of just about any conversation, it seemed. She always appeared to know what to say next, how to steer a topic without coming off as an ass. It was refreshing. He hadn't had any conversations this good while sober in recent memory, and he wasn't sure he'd had any this good while lit, either.

So she was beautiful, talking to him, and doing it in a way that was fulfilling and awesome, as if there was any other way to put it. Maybe he'd just been lonely all this time. It was hard to tell what the real factors were here other than she was a captive audience, and he, for that matter, was a *captivated* audience.

"You're staring at me again," she said softly from the corner of her mouth.

"I'm looking into a pair of VR goggles. What do you expect?"

"No, you're staring at *me*."

"How do you know?" He asked.

"I *feel* you. We've covered this. Every emotion you have comes in here like a gust of wind. I've told you, it's like waves rolling in, almost like standing in the surf at Santa Monica, you know, when your feet are in the sand and the water is rushing over your feet. Except picture it rolling over your whole body. I used to go there from time to time, usually by myself. Other times I would go with a couple of friends of mine. They were actually a couple, though. The S&L Express."

The bolt of shock went through him at full force. *S&L Express*! That was Sarah and Lindsey!

They had adopted the nickname for themselves because Lindsey's father was a railway man that had worked for a major railroad in his younger days. He had apparently retired, was going to retire, Jakub didn't know. What he did know was that Lindsey's father called them that after they had been together about six months and it was obvious they weren't going to be split up any time soon.

Lindsey's dad had taken her coming out better than would have been expected, and Sarah... who the hell couldn't love *Sarah*?

"You *know* them?" Veronica gasped. There were gears turning in her head, he could pretty much see that on her face, but unlike her he didn't have a good tap on her emotions.

"How in the *fuck* do you possibly know that?" He exclaimed, astonished.

"You felt surprise. There would be no reason to feel that way unless you actually *knew* who I was referring to firsthand. It was the shock wave that gave you away. It came through here like a bomb.

I'm getting some of this figured out. I didn't take Biomedical Engineering for nothing."

"But I thought you were an interface designer," Jakub countered.

"Yeah, but I got caught up in the technology. You know the drill. Once that happens, it's over. You're a geek, and you're not getting out."

"You know, I have a friend that basically wanders everywhere. We've been talking off and on since I broke up with my ex last month."

"You get dumped?" Veronica asked.

"Uh, no. I kicked her out."

"How mean of you!"

"Mean? She was screwing the lost fragments of the Pearl Jam Fan Club in my apartment while I was at work!"

"Oh. Good boy, then."

"Anyway... I met this guy, and he basically goes all over the place and travels the world. Really nice guy, easy to get along with. Does temp work to get by and just floats around."

"Sounds like a globetrotter."

"A what?" Jakub asked.

"Globetrotter. Backpacker. Traveler kinda guy. I've met folks like that. Sounds kinda cool to me too, actually. They were starting to hire people like programmers and whatnot to do that in tech now. Then. Whatever. Point is, like I said, it really sounded cool to me too back then, and I'd considered doing it since I didn't really have much in LA other than work."

"What kept you in LA, then?"

"Work. I was down the street from all of the major special effects companies, so that was a dream come true for me. But dreams last a while and then you get another one, I guess."

"I've always had a dream of finally getting away from my mother."

"And did you?"

"I moved to California!" Jakub blurted, exasperated.

"Apparently still didn't work. That seems like a bit of a problem to me. You might just end up getting lost. At least you can get yourself in a position where she can't continually harass you. Sounds to me like you need some real breathing room, and while ya got geography on your side, you're letting her overcome that. Control freaks are the worst. I dated one for a a while and then my Mama decided he just needed to go. Took us a while to get it through his head that he wasn't welcome in any shape, form, or capacity. Some folks are just thick."

"Money has a sliding scale in opposition to intelligence."

"You think so?" Veronica asked.

"Sure. Go out on the 405 and tell me I'm wrong. If you get cut off or have to avoid someone trying to accidentally kill you, I'd give it about 99 percent that you'll either see a luxury symbol or a Jesus fish on the back."

"Sometimes both."

"True, sometimes both."

"What does that have to do with the price of rice in China?"

"What?"

"Have you ever had a relationship that actually worked? That was exactly what you wanted or expected it to be?"

Jakub stopped and thought about it. She didn't give him too much of a chance.

"No."

"But…"

"Your answer is *no*. Every relationship you've had has been a settling act in some form or another. You've had to give up one thing to get another, or you had to have just a passable amount to stay in it, but none of them gave you everything you wanted out of 'em. You've never really held a winning hand, so to speak. It's okay. I've had the same problem."

"How the hell do you do this? It's almost like you're reading my mind."

"Honey, I *am* reading your mind. And it's a hell of a lot cleaner this way, believe you me. I know what you actually want, and you don't have to bullshit about it. Life is so much easier. Well, life as *you* know it, anyway."

"Would now be a bad time to ask about the meaning of life?"

171

"42."

"What? What's that supposed to mean?"

"You asked the meaning of life," Veronica said, "And any self-respecting geek that claims the title has read Douglas Adams at least once in their life. So don't sit there and act like you don't know what the hell '42' is. It's the meaning of life. C'mon, man!"

Jakub laughed. He'd managed to walk her right into one. At least there was a tick in the Jakub column for a change.

"Honestly, I'm just having fun talking to you."

"You should, I'm a very interesting person once you get to know me," She answered.

"Well, that one is obvious. And we have opportunity and time."

"And motive. What are we doing, robbing a bank here?"

"Wow, what got under your collar?" Jakub asked.

"I'm playing rough. I thought you liked it when girls played rough."

"Well, I do."

"See? Then I'm doing it right then. Stick around me, kid. I'll show ya a thing or two."

"*Wow*," Jakub laughed, "And I thought I was the one with the best shots at one-liners."

"Nope," she answered sweetly, "You're just the *cutest* one with the best shots at one-liners."

"We're back to the question about the meaning of life."

"I don't know that it has any particular meaning, *per se*."

"None?"

"Well, I mean, we're there, then we're not. Maybe we make an impact, maybe we just steal air for a while. Who really knows?"

"But how did you feel about it. I mean, you're at the end, now, and neither of us know what comes after this, but we do know that the whole 'assuming room temperature' part doesn't end it, so how do you feel about it?"

"If I took the whole romance thing out of the equation, pretty good. Could have been better. I could have spent more time outdoors. But then again, I was lucky enough to not be born where you actually have to stay outside most if not all of the time. There are still a bunch of aboriginal colonies out there, y'know. I had fun. I got to do a lot of cool stuff. Had a job I really liked. So I guess I did well, all things considered. How about you?"

"I think I need to get my shit together," Jakub said, "I have a job I'm not too crazy about, one friend that lives life much more extensively than I *ever* have, romance hasn't been what I'd signed up for, not counting this, of course. But still, there is more to do."

"You need to get outside and go do some things. Like, go find that guy you keep thinking about."

"Isn't that a little invasive?"

"What? Find a guy you already know?"

"No, you reading my thoughts to *know* there was a guy there."

"Sweetie," Veronica said, "I didn't make this connection, you did. Don't blame me for it. I'm just reporting the news, not making it."

"What else are you picking out of my brain?"

"That other girl you've been crazy about. Can't see her, don't have a name, but I can feel her there. Don't worry, I'm not mad. A little jealous, maybe. I guess I don't have any right to be at this point. Old habits die hard, they say. Does she know?"

"More like she doesn't care. Hates my guts."

"What did you do?"

"Nothing, that I know of. That's what's so infuriating. I don't think we've actually ever even spoke."

"Whose fault is that?"

He had to stop and think about it. Jakub had never pushed the issue. He consistently wussed out at the points when everything in his gut was telling him to say something. Sarah was always the junkyard bulldog, making sure he didn't get too close, so he'd kept his distance rather than push the friendship beyond its stretchable limits.

Hiding this felt like an exercise in itself. Jakub didn't want Veronica to pick up that there had been another woman he had his eye on for what seemed like ages. It felt like cheating, but he knew in his head it wasn't.

"Why haven't you said anything to her?"

"I told you. She hates me."

"Wait, so you've never talked to her, and yet you assume she doesn't like you at all. Like, not even in a human context?"

"It doesn't seem so to me."

"Holy shit, dude, what did you do, kill her cat? Are you a stalker?"

The thought had crossed my mind.

"Which one," Veronica inquired, "Killing her cat, or stalking her? What'd her cat ever do to you?"

He exhaled. This was too damned close in to the skin here.

"Stalking her. I don't think they own a cat."

"I'd like to think that there are healthy levels of stalking. Harmless levels, like before the point where you start tapping somebody's phone and digging through the trash to read their mail."

Jakub laughed, "What? Are you serious?"

"Well, yeah. You just want to see that person again, and it doesn't really matter how. I had a roommate once that was stalking a guy. She was working as a courier, and wanted to hook up with some guy she was interested in at one of the offices she delivered at. She was all about this dude. She'd know when he got to work, roughly when he went to lunch, and when he went home. But she never would say anything to him. It was pretty fucking sad, to be honest. I really felt for her. Very nice girl."

"What happened?"

"Well, she never made her move that I know of. Sucked. She had guys falling all over her, but no, she wanted *this* dude. Stubborn, but not stubborn enough, I guess. Somewhere in all of that, she ended up with a girlfriend, which settled that whole thing. I think she'd have been better off opening her fucking mouth, to be honest with ya. Never did tell me what his name was, always called him Hot Guy. Spent a lot of time literally crying about him. Pretty heartbreaking. He was her little secret, and I got to hear about what nonsense she was doing, but not specifically who she was doing it *to*. But see, that's harmless stalking. I doubt he even knew. I can't think of a red-blooded male that could avoid being on her like white on rice. And as for her, she was really put together on the outside, but inside she was an absolute fricking hot mess. Fucked up position. She got into this relationship with this other girl, and I guess it got really serious, but there she was still in love with that mystery guy. Don't know what happened with that. I wonder if she ever got the guy?"

"How about you? Did you ever stalk anyone?"

She giggled, and her eyes grew wicked, "Why yes, as a matter of fact, I did."

"Who?"

"You."

"When was this? How the hell did I not know this?" Jakub felt flabbergasted. He'd have choked a small animal to get close to Veronica when he first saw her.

"After I saw you at the housewarming party, I had your name. There's only one Jakub Riser in Los Angeles, if you can believe that. There's a Jason Riser, but I knew it wasn't the same guy."

"How?"

"I called him. He's like 65 or something. Nice fellow. You can do a lot when you fake a wrong number and throw the accent at them."

"Why the fuck didn't you just call me? I woulda dumped pretty much anybody for *you*, especially back then. Mom had already tried to hit on her. That didn't go well at all."

"As they say in high government, *mistakes were made*. Ya can't go back once the moment's gone. But for what it's worth, here we are."

"Was it just the phone call? You don't seem like the type to do anything half-assed."

"There's a reason I knew where Juniper was," She said, with a knowing, almost embarrassed half-grin on her face, "I drove by your apartment once. It was a Saturday morning. You were with *her*. You guys were drinking your morning coffee or something on your balcony. I kept driving. What the hell was I gonna do? Come up the stairs and engage in Mortal Kombat with her? I knew I didn't really have a good way in there. I just wanted to look at you that day. I know it sounds corny, but an itch needs to be scratched. Besides, I ain't fuckin' with a bitch before her morning coffee. It's a rule or something."

"You coulda stormed the gates."

"You still can. Especially if that girl's still out there."

"So you're suggesting I chase another woman."

"Not willingly, but yeah. I guess I am. Nothing's gonna happen here but conversation, and that's totally against my hopes and dreams, lemme tell ya." Her smile had dropped. It seemed this had become a sore topic for her. She thought a moment and continued, "Something happens here, and if I get out of this, I won't be here. I won't have any kind of a say in the equation. If that's the case, you need to grow a pair."

"Wow, that's pretty harsh, there."

"That's pretty true, there. At least go get a yes or no and put that shit to bed. It's what I shoulda done. Don't make my mistake. It doesn't win you any awards in the end."

"Nice talk, Coach."

"I'm serious. You gotta quit with the things you don't know, and not gettin' an answer for 'em. That's probably my biggest shortcoming. I thought that 'right now' equalled 'forever', so I never made a move."

"You *do* know that guys with any sense don't make the first move anymore, right?"

"Not any that I wanted to be associated with. All the losers were the ones gettin' up in my grill."

"And there you have it."

"Have what?"

"Why I've kept my mouth shut."

"Yeah, I guess you have a bit of a predicament there. Can't say anything or you're a pushy prick, and if you keep quiet, they never know how ya feel or what you think."

"Exactly. It's a shit-ton of suffering with no reward. If you guess wrong, you get a boyfriend you didn't ask for that's waiting for you to pick up the shower soap. Or you get on a list somewhere when all you did was ask a grown adult woman out for ice cream. I can eat my own damned ice cream."

"Why does this crap have to be so damned hard?"

"I don't know. I just know it *is*," Jakub answered with finality.

don't trust machines

"That got heavy real fast, didn't it?" She appeared to be looking straight into his eyes. "We can get into a lot of hard topics now, and you don't have to worry about any consequences. I'm not sure there's really much of anything else but heavy topics. Once you're here, you can't hide from them anymore." Jakub had noticed that anytime she wanted to appear serious, Veronica had this little action where she would place her thumb just under her chin and prop it there, an index circle wrapped under her lower lip. Almost like she was grabbing the tip of her jawbone.

Which was exactly what she was doing now.

"So what are you thinking about? I don't have the advantage of reading your mind."

"This. All of this. Being in the machine, what I am, what happens next, a whole mishmash of thoughts and emotions that I now get to sort out. It's like when you're handed a ball of yarn that's in a bunch of knots, and then you hafta take all the knots out of it. Sometimes I don't enjoy the time and effort I have to put into it, but I was always into puzzles, I guess. This just seems to be another one."

"You're good at puzzles. I'm sure you'll figure it out. I'll do whatever you need me to do to help, you know that by now. Including cutting your Gordian Knot."

"Empanadas."

"What?"

"I want another empanada from Empanada's Place. You ever been there?"

"Um, no. Aren't we shifting topic just a bit?"

"Helps me think. If you ever go, and you should, you'll know it. White building, blue sign. Right between a blue store and the liquor shop. Off of Sawtelle. Really can't miss it if you're looking for it."

"Wait," he realized that he'd seen the place before, "You mean on the corner of Venice and Sawtelle?"

"Yeah."

"That's right across from my burger shack."

"Burger shack? Oh. I know that one. But I promise the empanadas are better. You won't regret it."

"Where else have you been that we might have almost crossed paths at?"

"Anywhere, really. You know, you come out here and then start looking for anything that might remind you of home. It's funny."

"I know. I came out here to escape Texas and live what I thought was the 'good life', primarily because of my mother, and the first thing I hunted down was a Texas barbecue place out in the Valley. Ain't no HEB out here."

"Boy, don't you start talkin' dirty to me now. You'll get me all hot and bothered."

"Do taquerias turn you on?"

"Shut up, boy."

"And what are ya gonna do if I don't?" He asked slyly.

"Math. Lots and lots of math. Until you cry."

"I give up. You win. I am *not* a math person."

"Me either. But I can bluff like a motherfucker, huh?"

"You certainly got me there."

"So, I can't see any end to this room I'm in. It's a wireframe, now I know what it is, I can expect that. I would think that's what you see when you look in the headset, but for me, I didn't think I'd have the same view. Sometimes we miscalculate. But if I remember correctly, the simulation will keep adding real estate the further you move around, so it's really like there's no end to it all." She paused and looked around. "It's actually a bit maddening. Scenery, dammit! I need some scenery."

"What kind of scenery did you have in mind?"

"I don't know. I know this sounds odd, but for some reason I'd really like the Mission San Jose. They have this window there, doesn't look like much. It's called the Rose Window. When I was a little girl, I always imagined I'd get married there, right there in the yard in front of it. You ever heard of it?"

"I don't think so. Haven't really ever toured San Antonio."

"Shame on you. Shame on you! What are you thinking? San Antonio *is* Texas! C'mon, man!"

"So tell me about this window."

"Okay, so back in the 1700s, there was this Spanish guy that was hired to make an ornate window for the Mission church. It's a really pretty window, by the way, but he spent a lot of time carving it, because while they thought he was doing it for God and the Church, he was really doing it for the love of his life, Rosa. When he finally finished, he sent for her to come to America." She waited. It was pretty clear that Veronica was baiting him to get her to continue.

"Well? What happened?"

"She died. Shipwreck."

"That's no way to end a love story. Really?"

"Nah, the whole story's bullshit. But when you're a little girl, you don't care. You'll take it. It really is a beautiful window and a beautiful place. I was always drawn to it. Mama was a member of that parish when I was really little. I barely remember moving to the North side."

"They actually have a church there?"

She acted as if he uttered the dumbest question known to man.

"Uh, yeah. Mission San Jose Church... remember that stupid little thing you used to do with your hands as a kid?" She interlocked her fingers and touched her index fingers and thumbs to each other. "Here's the church, and here's the steeple, open the doors, and there's the people?"

She waited and laughed. "Okay, so I stole that from a Protestant kid, but whatever. Point remains. Yes, it's a church. Mama went to the graveyard a few times. Wasn't sure who she was going to see, I figured it was my Avo."

"Avo?"

"Grandmother. Mama's Brazilian. Roundabout. Grandma was always Avo. Spoke Portuguese and Spanish. Avoided English like the plague, even though I know she understood it. She practically raised me, at least in the moments Mama wasn't working. But I remember the graveyard because it was the first time I ever smelled real lavender. What about you? Any special places?"

He stopped to think. "No, not like that, I don't think. I mean, I've went to monuments and stuff, but nothing that really spoke to me like that. I'm pretty boring when it gets down to it."

"Nah, you just haven't seen enough for anything to stick, that's all. You'll hafta get out more, see more new things. Something will grab you, I promise. It's the way the world works."

"You grabbed me."

"Something different. Something you can actually touch."

"I count this as a special place. I can see you here. And you have the next fifty years to stop looking at me with those eyes."

"You don't have that much battery life, son." She smiled. He knew he'd made a mark. That was what he was going for at this point. It didn't much matter that they could never meet, he could see her, and she could hear and feel him, and right now that was as close as it was going to get, but it was close enough.

"I have a power cable."

"Then I guess I have fifty years to spare."

"Which brings up another point."

"Yeah?"

"What happens when I plug this thing in? Anything you can see from your side?"

"Dunno. Why don't we try it? I know that when you step away, it gets a little darker, but not completely black like it was in the beginning."

"What do you mean in the beginning?"

"Well, when I first woke up, I didn't know where I was, and it was pitch black. Apparently you turned the Anteryx on and things became gray. So when there's no power at all, and the battery systems are drained, everything goes black. You've had it on or plugged in ever since, so it's been gray ever since. I guess you could plug it in now and see what happens."

He reached for the plug, and still wearing the goggles plugged the cable in.

"Oh, wow!" She said, "It's brighter in here. I have a wall! Or at least something to my right that looks like a wall. I guess that's the backplane of the device."

"It has a backplane?"

"Not like you're thinking. Everything that plugs into the Anteryx plugs from the backside, the part that's facing out and gets hot. That must be what I'm looking at. You were thinking backplane like on a motherboard, right?"

"Well, yeah. That's the only one I really know."

"This is similar, but a little different. I mean the plugging in part internally, of course. All your external plugs are on the side. But you already know that, or you wouldn't be here talkin' to me."

Jakub sunk into her voice, like he seemed to normally do. It was a medium timbre, didn't have too much twang to it. She'd merged it into a California mode of speaking which meant that she had a fast pace to her speech, to the point of chattering. It was like listening to an acid jazz piece, with syllables that drug out, and the end of every sentence sounded like a question.

It was cute.

Listening to her speak was like music to him, and he found himself as entertained by the sound and speech pattern as what she was saying. When

Veronica got hooked into a technical train of thought, she went off like a spinning top.

"I like talking to you. I like hearing *you* talk, though."

She put a hand up to cover her face and looked through her fingers. "Oh, gawd, what did I say?"

He couldn't help but smile, though he knew she couldn't see it. "Everything. I just like hearing you talk. It's *adorable*."

"Ugh. You're gonna make me self-conscious. Am I whithping or something?"

"No," Jakub answered, "No lisp. I just like hearing you speak. I like the sound of your voice. It's cute."

"We'll see how cute you think it is in fifty years. After all, you're the one that brought that up."

"Can I get that in writing?"

"Hell no, you can't get that in writing! What would I write on anyway? I'm in here!"

"I'm sure we can figure something out. You're good at figuring things out, right? Didn't you make a career outta that or something?"

"Partially. I don't think I got all of my money's worth out of life, to be honest."

"I guess some don't. But you get the extra bonus round, and I don't think that many folks get that. Wait. Lemme go check my toaster and make sure there's not a girl in *there* that I missed."

"Very funny. Personally, I'd wonder about the chick in the blender. She's the part of your harem you should be most concerned about."

"Who said I had a harem?"

"Multiple machines, multiple women, I'd think that would be the textbook definition of a harem. Not sure how the authorities would feel about that, though. Seems to me that polygamy is illegal in most states."

"Well, I know know *I'm* not feeling the benefits of it."

"Well, now."

"I promise you're the only electronic girl I'm seeing."

"Does that include DVDs?"

"We're not going there."

"Aha!" She giggled, "I knew I'd eventually catch that little tiger in there somewhere."

"I have *Fast Times at Ridgemont High*, I think I might have a few unrated flicks... *Showgirls*?"

"Those aren't the movies I mean, and you know it."

"I mean, I did try *Aliens* and *Apocalypse Now*, but I just couldn't get in the right mood for it. Just couldn't rub me the right way."

She was grinning, trying to visualize it, knowing her. It was nice to find someone that at least had a similar twisted sense of humor to his own.

"So you don't have a stash *anywhere*? I find that quite hard to believe," Veronica asked knowingly, a sly look in her eye.

"Even if I did, keep in mind that I'm here talking to *you*, so, there's that."

He immediately saw the edge of her lower lip suck in between her teeth. Jakub felt his smile grow wider.

I think we just brought this line of questioning to a screeching halt.

perfect pretenders

"I wanna see you," Veronica said. It was true, she did. If she could figure out how to get to where the holographic nature of everything was more visible to her, then she would have power of access.

And she wanted to make certain that Jakub was the guy she had in mind. It's one thing to feel someone, but that's like dating while blind. For her, it might sound neat on paper but functionally it made her crazy.

"Are you sure about that?" Jakub replied.

"Why? Are you a 300 pound momma's boy in the basement?" She heard him laugh out loud.

"No, I'm not 300 pounds, I hate my mother, and I don't have a basement. Well, we *do*, I just park in it. I told you, I live in an apartment on Jasmine."

"Just checking. Still want to see you. And you're not supposed to hate your momma. Why ya hate your momma? Isn't that a rather strong word?"

Warmth. A single word.

Ronni...

"I have a nickname now?" She heard a soft gasp. "Yes, I guess I should have warned you. If your thoughts have enough emotion in them, I can hear them. And I like the nickname. You should keep it.

It's cute. Besides, nobody's really had a cute nickname for me before."

"Really? Never?"

"I was a pretty boring girl."

"I can do boring, if it's you." He felt more at ease. Higher levels of vibration meant tension, slower ones were when he was at ease.

"So let's think this one out. I am guessing that I am part of a hologram. I'm real, trust me, but I'm still part of the hologram. I read some weird book somewhere once that said we basically live in a video game. I thought it was just a load of crap at the time, but we're here, so let's test the theory."

"What's the theory, and is there anything I need to look up? I have the goggles on my face with a browser, and I have a laptop I can get to."

"Fair enough. The theory would have me inside the hologram. Now thinking scientifically, if I'm inside the hologram, I will see the guts of it, which is probably why everything from my side right now looks like a grey wire meshing. That's almost like the view when you first start the headset up. Remember that?"

"Yeah, they're like octagons or something."

"Exactly. So I'm inside that, but you are viewing me in living color." She paused. Gave a slight chuckle. He wasn't responding. "See what I did there?"

Dammit, at least have the decency to laugh at a girl's jokes.

"Oh, yeah. Got it. *Living*. I'm just making sure I'm on the same page with you. So if you're in it, then I am watching you from the outside."

"Righty-o. The question now becomes how do I get to where I see your side of the hologram. All of that happens inside here, because you are viewing passively."

If everything was active here, what powered it? If she was visible to Jakub, that meant somehow she was diverting her own energy into it. She existed in a form she wasn't familiar with, one that was pure energy. She didn't have organs of perception.

How did it work in The Matrix?

So this would be what consciousness meant. From here it was a matter of perception. How could she get to that point where she could be an observer on the outside of the projection?

"Let's think this out," she said to him while zoning out slightly, "You're not stupid, you can help." She could feel that he was uncertain of himself. "You know that I can feel when you're full of shit and doubting yourself, right?"

"Yep, Ronni, I kinda picked that up, and I don't know how comfortable I am with it, y'know?" He sounded more insecure than irritated, which was a plus somewhere.

"Are you more afraid that someone can know and feel everything about you, or are you nervous that it's specifically *me*?" He stopped to think. Veronica could tell that he was stopping in a full internal system halt to consider the question she posed to him. Of course it had implications. That was why she'd asked it the way that she had.

If he answered that his answer was the first option, then that would make him shy and self-conscious, perhaps even guilty. Guilt sucks. It's a lot like those dreams where you are in front of a large crowd naked. Everybody sees the bits you don't want them to, and as usual everyone has an opinion.

If it was the second option, then she was dealing with someone who happened to be enamored with her specifically. She had no idea why she was pushing this given the situation between them, since there wasn't a hell of a lot they could do about it.

But that was a bullshit excuse on her part, too. She knew exactly what the facts were, and though it was entirely unfair, Veronica was a little glad she had a wall that Jakub couldn't see through. She was definitely as about Jakub as he was about her, and she just wanted to hear him say it.

"Both," he answered. He held a moment before continuing.

"It's good that you have that kind of access into me that no one else has, and honestly, I'm happier that it's you specifically. I've kinda gotten a little attached to you."

"A lot." She felt herself smiling a wicked grin.

"Okay. A *lot*. Your timing sucks ass, though. Anyway, it's hard to just be understood in life as it is. Nobody really knows what I'm thinking, and generally, they don't seem to give a shit, either. The only time anyone cares what I have to say is when it brings them dollar signs."

"You like green."

"What?"

"You like green," Veronica repeated, "And not just because it's the Stars colors, you've always liked green. Since you were a little kid. And not that pistachio pudding nuclear green, either. You like those deep ones, forest green and hunter green, stuff like that."

"I don't know the difference," he lied. She knew he was lying because the response felt prickly.

"Well, I'm a girl, so I guess it's in my genes or something. Knowing a color wheel has nothing to do with your sexuality, anyway. You were so close. It could have been your birthstone. Emeralds. I like the blues and purples, personally. Like amethysts. They have that gorgeous purple to them. I like blue topaz, and sapphires after that, just in case you're ever out shopping for me. Oh, wait..." She giggled. He snickered in response.

There ya go, now you're getting the hang of this.

Somewhere in the mirth of it was that sore piece, the one that wondered aloud exactly where this could possibly go. That was the thing about being dead, you aren't really. You apparently get to simply sit on the sidelines and watch a game you were supposed to still be playing in.

It was nice to know there was consciousness beyond everything. It was a possibility she hadn't considered, and to have a vehicle to speak to another living person afterwards was icing on the cake that she hoped wouldn't come with an end. But everything has an end, doesn't it?

"Hey, I have a silly question," she asked him.

"Shoot."

"When you are looking at me, what are you seeing, exactly? I mean, do I look like high quality video, am I black and white, on a screen, what is the exact context?"

"Well, you seem to be separate from everything else. Like, if I were to pull up the browser or look at a video, I think you'd be inside it."

"Let's do that. I want to see what it looks like from my side. For example, what am I doing right now?" She waved her arm up and down.

"You're waving your arm."

"Okay, so you can actually see me in real time. Pull up a browser and tell me what you see."

The grid work of gray brightened as she realized she was looking at the new screen from the back, almost like a see-through tapestry of text. As the browser had appeared, she realized that she was in something that appeared like a small hallway. A gray wall to her right, the bright browser in reverse to her left. The plate of glass that had been glowing before appeared straight ahead of her.

I get it! I'm inside the LCD display.

Veronica excitedly pieced everything together again.

"I'm inside the display," she said aloud, "I think I'm beginning to figure out what happened. Here where I am, I can see the back of the display to my right, and the browser screen you're looking at to my left, except it's reversed. I'm looking at the back of it, so all of the letters are backwards."

"I can't see you as well anymore," Jakub said. "It was much clearer before I brought this browser up."

"Good. I can hide now," she quipped.

"Try it. I'll turn the damned browser off."

"If it means that much to you. But in the meantime, try selecting something. I want to see how this works, and if I can interact with it at all."

She saw the beam of light float in and point into the URL block like an arrow, a flash as he pulled the trigger on the controller. Veronica reached out to the middle of the screen as it came up and discovered her hand easily moved through it.

The browser itself was a projection. And given the light that appeared when she moved her hand through it, the good news was that it could be manipulated. She had just enough electrical impulse inside her to be able to mimic the controller.

"Well, that escalated quickly," she said.

"What did?" Jakub asked.

"Well, I can use this thing from inside here, apparently. Let's play a little bit. I want to see exactly what I can do here. Bring up a search engine and search for something," she paused as she felt his impulse come through, "Don't be a dick about it, either. I already sense you trying to pull something goofy on me."

"Okay. I'll pick a topic we both love, then. How about technology?"

"That works for me. Let's see what we got."

As the results filled the browser, Veronica surveyed them and said, "Wait a minute, don't touch anything. If my idea is correct, I should generate just enough electricity to affect it. I'm thinking it'll be a micro amount, if I remember the hardware correctly."

Veronica looked at the blue lined result closest to her and attempted to reach through the projection to it. As her hand moved to the link, she saw it brighten and then the page disappeared entirely. After a few seconds, it re-appeared with the web page she had selected, an article on technology from an online encyclopedia.

"Oh, Mommy, look what Baby Girl can do!" She said aloud as Jakub gave a laugh, mostly in surprise. "This is kinda a big deal. If I can do this, then that means there are other things and other directions we can go in. I just gotta figure out what I wanna do with it now."

The accounts. She needed to find a way to get into all of her social media accounts, provided they weren't all locked down. Usually those things became memorial accounts, left to honor the person that used to own them. Veronica was thinking that she probably wouldn't disturb them, but the act of logging in alone would possibly turn a head or two if anyone was still paying attention. She doubted that they were.

One or two other accounts she needed to get into, and her email. Those things last damned near forever. Some of the free providers had so much space they'd clean forgotten about. An account could sit for years relatively untouched until the right person with the proper credentials remembered how to get it.

She remembered how to get into hers.

There was one person she knew that had a little secret not many people were aware of. That secret was a perfect commodity about right now, because all of this would make sense to them. Maybe then she could figure out what was possible and what might be next.

Right now, Jakub was really growing on her in a way she didn't want to admit, but it was true. Nothing could come of this, her being locked into the headset the way that she was. And him living outside in the real world, breathing air. She knew from what she had felt of him, no matter what he seemed to show the world, he was the type that would hang in for the long haul if she was just selfish enough to push the issue. Veronica wasn't comfortable with the thought. Neither was she too enthused with the idea of being locked away alone.

As for how she got there to begin with, the prevailing theory that she had seemed to indicate that she came in through the microphone as she breathed out her last breath. It was situated at her head and flowed directing into a processor that would be sucking in the electrical charge, and thus, her. From there, the signal was processed, with her as part of it, where the sequencing chip sent her to outbound audio and thus, the screen. Which seemed the most logical way to be in the LCD screen.

But what was that glass door thing across from her?

The more she watched it and thought about it, the more it seemed like a portal that wasn't part of the hardware. Something that was extra, and very probably meant for her. Veronica had heard the talk of things like this. The whole going to the light thing, and the accounts she'd read when she was younger about how people just go to another place, another realm when they died, and a bright light was involved. She'd been interested in the thought for a while after her father had passed, and it seemed like a good idea.

Every so often, there were shadows near it. But it just felt like hard bulletproof glass. It clunked, it wasn't easily malleable like the screen to her left.

"What am I going to tell him?" She'd asked, not realizing she was speaking aloud.

"Pardon me?" Jakub responded quickly. Apparently he'd been off in his own slipstream of thought as well, and she'd forgotten to keep a bearing on it.

"Nothing, sorry. I was thinking aloud. So I noticed you don't actually do anything else with this headset. Don't you usually buy them for other functions? Games and things like that?"

"I did."

"Well, what happened? Why aren't you actually using them for what they were designed to do?"

"You're in there," Jakub answered, "So I don't really care about anything else now."

no scenario

"Pony up. Since we were talkin' about it, let's just say that you could have a completely lust-filled vacation anywhere in the world, where would it be?" Jakub figured that it was time to put Ronni in the hot seat for a minute.

"Bora Bora." She said it matter-of-factly, without hesitation. Like she'd been waiting for the question to pop up and get asked.

"Why there?"

"Well, I've seen pictures of it, and I figured that if I ever got married, maybe we'd be lucky enough to have the money to go. It's a perfect place for a honeymoon. Clothing's optional, weather's perfect, a good bit less populated than the Bahamas, and I don't have to worry about some local trying to sell me fruit while I'm trying to get mine, y'know?"

"Is that a thing?"

"I don't know. I never made it there, either. But a girl's heard stories."

"About buying fruit, or getting laid? Who's telling you these stories?"

She looked like she was having a bit of a blush and tightened up. "Okay, sometimes I read reviews in my spare time."

"Reviews to what? Who the hell is buying guavas and papayas from street vendors while getting head? Isn't that a bit out of bounds?" She began laughing loud, and he continued, "Do we need referees? Is this being televised?"

"No, nothin' like that. I saw something where there were complaints because a couple were doing their thing on the beach, and supposedly some old island guy strolled up with some local fruit and tried to sell it to them. Maybe he just thought they were wrestling."

"Wrestling? Naked, on the beach. Wrestling. I'm gonna remember that. Especially if I ever get caught in public with my pants down being attended to and the police decide they wanna inquire as to the nature of my activities."

"Not sure that'll work," she said spluttering, trying to catch her breath, though he knew well she wasn't actually breathing anything. Seems like habits die hard. She held a hand up. "Shut up a minute..."

"Wasn't *that* funny," Jakub teased.

"Would we ever have sex on the beach?"

"With these things on? I'm not sure how the local police would handle me jerkin' it on the beach with VR goggles on. I bet there'd be a jail cell and a shrink with my name all over 'em."

She burst out giggling again. "I'd pay good money to hear you try and explain your way outta *that* one."

"Yeah, that ain't happening in this lifetime. Sorry."

"Never count your chickens before they hatch. I do have a lot to learn about all this."

"Still not jerkin' on the beach. I have my pride. So you'd better come up with something good."

"Well," she snorted, "You *could* just buy a papaya from a villager and poke a hole in the end. On the beach. With a VR headset."

"Oh, yeah, fuck just breaking the law, let's *create* a reason for new ones! You know that every strange-ass law out there is because someone did that stupid shit in the first place."

"You'd have a place in history."

"But I'm not lookin' for a place in history."

"You could be the reason it's illegal to have sexual congress with a papaya while wearing a virtual reality headset on a beach in The Bahamas."

"They might drug test me for that."

"But you'd be clean."

"But I'd have a court-appointed shrink. I don't think that justifies the experience."

"Are you sure? I'd think it would have the right amount of moisture and, um, material inside. How do ya not know that it's nature's sex toy for men?"

"If you don't shut up, we're gonna start talkin' about cucumbers and bananas. You're startin' to make me swear off fruit salads for the rest of my natural life because I won't know where they've been."

"I think we might have gone off the deep end here," Ronni said, still laughing.

"And I think this conversation might be illegal in most states."

"Betcha I could get you to kiss me now."

"You would need a pack of starving Rottweilers to stop me. Or be stuck in a VR. That works, too."

"I don't know how I get out of here," Ronni said, the grin falling.

"I don't either. And we don't know where you go."

"What hurts is that I know I eventually will have to, but I don't want to. I don't want to leave being with you, and it seems to me that maybe by getting out of this, I can find a way to get back to you. That's what I want to try to do. Get back to you."

She felt the way her words resonated in him, but she wasn't sure that he understood what she was saying.

There had to be something 'out there' that was bigger and closer than being inside this contraption. The fact that she had visitors at the glass thing made that part perfectly clear. It was too bad that she hadn't paid as much attention to Lindsey when she had the opportunity. She knew all of that stuff, could tell her what she was dealing with, how to get out of it, and what she was getting out to.

Veronica had fallen for Jakub some time ago. It wasn't the fact that he was good-looking, at least to her, he gave off a vibe that was like a homing beacon, and she hadn't gone after him as hard as maybe she should have. It was a regret she got to take beyond the grave, and even though she seemed to have him now, there wasn't a lot she could do with him. That wasn't exactly great for either of them.

She wondered what she would do once she did go to wherever was next. What would that mean for them? Jakub would probably do what most guys would do, and just go on to the next girl. There really wasn't any reason to pursue or hang onto her, unless he really did hold to the idea now that there was more beyond death. It was a deep topic, and they had scratched the surface pretty well, or at least as well as one could with a bare minimum of information on the topic.

"What is love going to mean for us?" It kinda slipped out. She had screwed up and let the words just run.

"I don't know. I *do* know that you've taken my world and turned it upside down. I'm having a hard time understanding what the world around me is anymore. I thought I knew. I thought I had this all down, and this whole situation has put a complete corkscrew on all of that. I couldn't explain it to anyone else if I wanted to. I'm not sure I could even explain this to my sister, though she'd trust anything I said, even if she thought I was a little touched in the head."

"What are you gonna do when this ends? It'll have to end someway, sometime. You and I both know I can't live in these things forever, even if I wanted to."

"I'd rather cross that bridge when I get to it, to be perfectly honest. I can't make plans like this. I can't build a house on river mud, I can't drive a car when I don't know the tires work. I'm at a loss, babe. I just know that I'm gonna hold on to what I have here and what's going on until we actually know what the hell's up."

"Then don't take this outside or let a tree fall on your apartment, because I really don't know what would happen if the headset broke, or if it got so damaged it couldn't turn on."

He was thinking. That possibility had hit him hard. The idea that she could be trapped in a way that no one could help, could redeem her from her fate was proving to be almost too much for Jakub to even think about. She disliked feeling him in this much pain and confusion, but frankly, she was there too.

"I'm really not trying to make things all heavy and sad, I swear I'm not," Veronica said to him, "But if I don't think as logically as I can, I know I lose you forever, and I think we've gotten to the point where neither of us wanna gamble like that."

"No, we don't. But I do trust you, so if you make a call, I'm gonna go with it, even if it hurts. You know what the hell you're doing in there, much more than I do. I only get to watch you, admire you, and thank god I get to pester you."

She smiled. He always had something good to say. She never had to worry about that. He was just someone that made you feel better by being there. It didn't take much else.

"Is it too early in the game to use the L word on you?"

"I thought that was what we've been doing this whole time."

"Since you put it that way, I guess we can dig deeper where it hurts while we have a chance," Veronica said.

mercury morning

"I know I don't have to tell you what it's like to lose a father," she said. She was looking down, almost at the ground, and her face has shifted to pain. "But I also know what your sister went through. I was the one who found Papa."

He knew that this was the time to be quiet for a while. Sometimes it's just better to shut up when a woman is talking.

"It was just a normal day, he had the grill fired up in the back. Pablo was still alive then. That was my brother. We were all inside, doing our normal thing, and Papa had this deal where he would leave KXTN on and sing in the backyard at the top of his lungs. That's the Tejano station there in San Anto..." He saw her grin. "It wasn't always a good thing. But that was Papa. When he was happy, he was *happy*. When he sang to the radio, he was *happy*. He could straight up *kill* a carne asada. Got that recipe from Mama's side, I think."

"So he's singing along, and we aren't thinking anything about it. Figured he was taking a break. Not usual for him, because he normally had a little *concerto* of his own goin' on out there. A few minutes later, we still aren't hearing anything, and I can smell the meat on the grill burning. If you knew

Papa, that was an impossibility. For him, cooking on the grill was a Holy Sacrament. I went to see what he was up to, and I still remember rounding the corner, and there he was, on the ground." She stopped, her face was blank.

"Face first, had his hand bent up under him. He always used a pair of tongs, and I guessed I looked for them. They ended up being a few feet away, but all I really remember was feeling the scream come out of me. It's funny, I don't remember *hearing* it, just feeling it come out. Like everything moved in slow motion, and I wasn't really grasping what I was looking at, I just knew it was *bad*. Everyone came running out of the house, and I was pulled away as they called the paramedics."

"How old were you?"

"Fifteen. Pablo had just turned eighteen and had graduated high school. The way that kids look at you is just so weird for a while. You feel like you're all of a sudden less than them, you have less than they do, and it's true... you do. I've missed the hell out of Papa."

He watched her. Every delicate gesture, every shift of her face. As she spoke, he studied her lips, the angle of her nose, every strand of hair as if he were studying a Monet on his last day before leaving Earth.

"Then there was Pablo. I was at UTSA by then. It was about four years later. I said goodbye to him that morning before he went to work, and that was the last time I saw him."

Jakub could see the pain on her face. It had to be hard, losing your father, then your brother, and then riding the line to see who finished the trifecta of death. Only to discover that it was you.

"He worked at one of those places that makes those huge concrete pipes that they use for culverts and drainage, things like that. I don't know exactly how it happened, but he ended up under one, some, something. I just know he was crushed, and Mama had to identify him. She's never talked about that part again. It was closed casket. As bad as I think I've had it, Mama's had it worse. Everyone in her sweet little family is dead. She's the lone survivor. I worry about her. I hope she's alive and okay."

"I can imagine. If you ever want me to call and see if she answers, I can do that for you."

"I'll have to think about it. It seems to me that she'd freak out over all of this. And she doesn't know who you are. You calling to find out if she's still alive might be the wrong way to play it."

"Okay. So tell me more about Pablo."

"Well, I guess the good thing was that he got to see his Spurs win a championship. Oh my god, was he excited. I don't think he shut up about it for the next six months or so. He didn't talk about much else. He had a girlfriend that he'd put a ring on during Christmas. She was a cute little thing. Absolutely adored him, girl named Mili. Emilia

Martinez. His death rocked her world, I can tell ya that. Not sure exactly what happened to her. She hung around a lot for about a year, and then just kinda stopped. I dunno if she found someone else, or it all just got to be too much."

"I imagine it was pretty rough for her, too. Had they set a date yet?"

"Summer sometime. I don't think he really told any of us yet. But when I got home the day he died, she was at the house in a complete mess. That was when I knew that something was really wrong. I mean, she wouldn't be sitting there if they had broken up or something. I knew in my gut it was gonna be ugly. I don't think I was ready for it."

"It's a hard one to swallow, I bet. How did your mom handle it? I should say, what was the extent of the damage?"

"Well, I think it wrecked her. I know that when I was younger, and even when I was older, she would go get groceries on the South side, near the Missions. She was a member of Mission San Jose, but we didn't go with her much. I know she would always stop at the graveyard down the street from there. We would have to stay in the car. She'd never say why. Never say who she was going to see, but there was a grave she'd go to, and sit next to it and cry. That's what she did the day after Pablo died. She went there and cried. Felt like an hour or so. I remember it was like walking into a lavender shop.

You could smell it in the car. Day after that we went to Papa's grave, and she cried again."

"People were bringing food over and checking on us, people I'd never seen before. I think it's a little different when it's your kids instead of your mate, y'know? Your baby's dead. People kept saying to her, 'I'm so sorry you had to go through this again,' and she'd just cry. Something just struck me as off about all of that, but I never could put my finger on it. Still don't know. I assumed they were talking about Papa, but I didn't remember some of them ever being at Papa's funeral. Then again, it wasn't quite like today when you have social media and can hit a lot of people at once. I mean, that was '04 when Papa died. I don't even think social media like we know it was a thing yet."

"Did people ever say things to you, like 'so-and-so is watching over you, they're looking down on you and smiling, they're so proud of you' and all that crap?"

"Yeah," Ronni said, rubbing her eyes, "Back then I didn't believe it. But here I am in this situation, and I hafta admit that it's plausible. My roommate always swore up and down that it was a thing, so I guess I just held onto her hope. Now I know a little more of what she knew."

"If I wasn't talking to you now, I'd still say that it's all bullshit. I've had a hard time with all this. A good hard time, if that makes any sense."

"You mean that conceptually you've never accepted the idea of life after death, and now you let the dead girl wrap you around her little fingers?"

He took a deep breath and exhaled. "I think that's exactly what I'm saying."

"I can get used to that," Ronni said with a smile. "I do like that we can share stories here, and I mean, it's a little late for judgement, so we can say pretty much anything we want to and not have to worry about the other person thinking something bad."

"Yeah, it pretty much is what it is, isn't it?"

"I don't think I've had a depth of conversation with a guy like this before. It's refreshing. You're definitely not an automaton."

"I don't normally get this deep with guys *or* girls. Willie's about the only one I had had any deep conversations with. Maybe Carl a time or two. A lot in that guy that he doesn't advertise."

"So what's your story?" Veronica asked, figuring it was a good time to hear more about what he had gone through. After all, she'd spilled her piece, and it was his turn. There was so much she didn't know and wanted to learn, because who knew how long this situation would last.

She could easily be sucked away into nothingness, or get pulled through that glassy thing. Then all of the fun would be over.

"What part of the story do you mean?"

"All of it. We have time."

"You have time, you mean. I still have a job and bills."

"Okay, so when you're not working the job and paying the bills. I want to hear about all things Jakub."

"It's not that exciting."

"I'm pretty boring as hell, but you seem to be interested in me."

"True," Jakub said, drifting off.

"Wait a minute, jack hole! It's true that I'm boring as hell, or that you're interested in me?"

"Interested. I don't really care if you're boring or not. For the record, I don't find you boring at all."

Jakub was slowing down. He was probably getting tired. She could feel the flow of his vibrations begin to ebb when he got tired. Usually she'd have to send him to bed, force him off the VR headset like a mother correcting her teen aged boy.

"You should probably go get some sleep. I need you in good condition if you're gonna tell me some stories that'll make any sense. Right now, it feels like you're gonna get on a boat and sail away to Never-Never Land. Go to bed. We'll chat tomorrow."

"I don't wanna go," he mumbled.

"Go to bed."

Veronica knew that he had finally retreated off to bed when the lights dimmed. The headset was in rest mode, and she was hoping to get the browser to work since she knew that the low level of electricity could work as a pointer. Realizing however that the headset needed an actual wearer for that part of the programming to access anything made it difficult to pull off. She'd have to wait until he did his thing at the craft store. That would give her full-time live access to the programming.

Now there was little to do but wait. What else are you going to do in very dim light, with no one else to talk to and no other way to communicate? You're left with your own thoughts, your own questions that you still haven't figured out, or might never figure out.

She decided that meditation might not be a bad thing to do. It could help pass the time, even though she really couldn't feel time anyway. The irritations of needing constant motion had not been able to subside.

As the girl tried to center herself into a single point, she wanted to expand out into the quiet, fill all of the space that felt like it was there waiting for her. That place where everything needed to flatline. She found that place.

She stayed there.

It felt like mere moments when the light brightened again and she felt the warmth of Jakub returning.

"I've been thinking about your stories and where we left off last night. Sorry I had to go away like that. I just don't like leaving you here all alone. Makes me feel like I'm letting you down, somehow. You asked for my story, so I should probably get on my sharing cap."

"How did the thing with your dad go down?"

"Well, we'd went to school that day, and I remember Mom had been acting kinda weird that morning. Dad had already left to go to work. He normally left pretty early because he was working in Austin at the time, and that was about a hour away. Willie had to be in school first, and I was about a half hour later. I would normally bus in, and she'd pick me up, because she was driving at that point."

"Back in those days, Mom had been sick, and Vera was always around. Dad had moved her into the spare bedroom. At the time, we were in a four bedroom house. Willie and I had separate rooms to keep us from killing each other, and he had some study/hobby room thing going on that he cleared out so she could move in. I think it was easier on him, because he could then offer her room and board and that would cut down on the expense."

"We got home that day, and something just felt wrong in the house. We see the note on the table, Vera's room's cleared out, and Mom's stuff's gone. Willie was in shock. I think it took about an hour for her to get somewhat normal. It was like she was in a daze or something. I was young, I really didn't have it all in my head what it meant, and when you're that young, you don't have time to care at first. I was closer to Dad than Mom anyway."

He paused, and she could feel the prickly heat from his energy coming through. It was almost like he was trying to relive it, even though she knew he didn't want to, he'd packed it deep, buried it all below.

"It all changed that day. Everything between me and Willie changed. Any real successes I've had since then, I pretty much owe to Willie. I remember Dad got in, Willie made me go to my room, and I wasn't about to argue by then. He didn't say much. He just went and sat in his chair in the living room. Willie made sure I went to bed, and I remember her telling me that we'd get though this, and she would look out for me no matter what. I think that's when we were really getting close.

"I was asleep, I know it was after midnight when the loud crack woke me up. I didn't know what the hell was happenin'. I thought something might have hit the house. I got out in the hallway, and we lived in this ranch-style house, so everything had a common hallway. Willie was already in the bathroom, like I told you before. It was the look on her face that stopped me. She wouldn't let me where I could get a good look. I just remember there was blood on the ceiling and across the bathroom mirror. She forced me out like a linebacker and damned near tackled me. 'You don't need to see

Daddy like this,' she said to me. Guess I'm grateful now that I don't have that image in my head. I don't know how he looked. She does. I know for a fact it never left her, and she got *hard* that day. She's been a full on battle bitch ever since. "

"She's a bit protective, is she?"

"Oh, yeah. And her and Mom, that was oil and water. Still is. I think the only reason she didn't push harder to get Mom implicated was that she slipped down to Houston, and they just don't jail people for inciting suicide. We got packed up with her immediately. That *sucked*. I tried to stay around Vera more when Willie wasn't around, because during that time, Mom didn't want to have much to do with me. Used to say nasty shit to me, almost always had to do with how much I looked like Dad, and then she'd go into a whole diatribe on how sorry he was, and I was sittin' there thinking, 'He's dead, bitch. You can shut the fuck up about it now.'"

"When did you move in with Willie? I remember you mentioning that."

"Yeah, she met and married Carl. I don't know if she just hunted him, or what happened, but I don't think she was in Houston six months before that went down. He was a redneck godsend. Already had a lot of his shit together. They had a civil ceremony and up to Tyler they went. About three days later they came and got me. I finished school up there. I got a lot of my work ethic from Carl, I guess, because as soon as I was legal, he had me helping him."

"What did he do?"

"A lot of contracting kinda stuff. We built decks, poured concrete, mostly residential stuff. He had a few Mexican guys worked for him. That's how my sister got so good with cooking, hanging out with their wives and grandmas."

"Ah, the abuelita brigade. They don't fuck around with cookin' do they?"

"I swear to god anything they cook is a gift. Willie took to it like a duck to water. Carl kept us workin' hard so we wouldn't get fat. At least that's how I figure it. But that 's why I was ready to launch out on my own. By then they were trying to have kids of their own, and I didn't wanna be a burden or in the way. So I headed west to get a little school under my belt, then when I finally degreed, I headed out here to Cali."

sharing minutes of grey

She wasn't sure what it was she was searching for, if she was even searching for anything at all, but the question was gnawing at her because it wanted to be asked. Like it had sat there in some dark recess of her mind all of this time, waiting for her to ask it to the right person. She had no idea whether the answer would be silly or serious or what would happen.

"If you could do anything or be anywhere right now, what would it be? I know I just asked a strange question, but I'm curious."

"Anything or anywhere? That's too easy. I would have you here with me, and I don't mean inside these goggles."

"Seriously."

"I *am* being serious." He paused and she felt the drop in the vibrations. "I'm having to deal with several things right now that I never thought I'd have to handle like this. When I say you're the girl of my dreams, I mean that in a very literal sense. I have *literally* dreamed about you before. I have wanted to find you since I was 14 trying to figure out what love even was. We're both from Texas. I grew up 100 miles away from you. I went to college 50 miles away from you. We're here in LA, and this time, it sucks even harder because I've been less than 5 miles away from you this whole time. Now I find you, you're where I can finally talk to you, and I'm here alive, and you, the woman of my dreams, is deceased and stuck in a fucking machine. I don't think it's really fair, to be quite honest with ya. I don't know what to do with this."

The emotions were live, they burned like electricity as the tempo of his voice sped up and got intense, the searing heat and sadness coming through. He was getting worked up and upset, and it was more clear by the second.

"I wanted you the first time I met you," Veronica answered back, "I was ready to lose the jackass I was with. As a matter of fact, I was looking to get rid of the jackass I was with, if you'd like to get precise. Lindsey said no, that you weren't quite what I thought you were, that you were marrying that girl that she kept calling the 'shark' and that you drank too much. She really hated that chick for some reason. She knew I didn't really drink that much, and I don't. Well, I guess I don't drink at *all* now, but I thought that maybe if I just had a chance, I could do something with it. I ended up in here and never got that chance. We both got the shit sandwich on that deal."

"I don't know how to get you out of there." He said it almost with a note of finality. "I don't know how *any* of this works. I don't know where you would have went had you not been wearing this. I've wondered if I put a bullet in my head while wearing these, would I end up in there with you? Knowing my luck, I'd go into the TV and be stuck watching reruns of 60s shows for eternity."

She laughed. She didn't mean to, bless his heart, he was so emotional at the moment, but she saw in her mind's eye Jakub stuck as an extra on the *Andy Griffith Show*, and it was just *funny*.

"I'm sorry," she apologized, still snickering, "I caught a visual of that, and I just couldn't help it. Me, or Opie. You decide. I would *hope* I would win on that one." She felt him lighten up.

"Holy fuck, I would hafta to deal with Aunt Bea for the next gazillion years. I'd be *begging* someone to break the TV. I could just make the power go off at the climax of every playoff game so the next owner would get pissed enough to do it. Like in that French movie where the girl was mad at her neighbor so she kept moving the television antenna every time the dude's team was scoring a goal?" He paused. Everything came to a calm standstill. Perhaps he just spaced out, she wasn't sure.

"You okay?" Veronica asked. All she really had to go off of was his emotions and his voice. She really didn't have anything else, and it was almost like being blind.

"Yeah, I'm fine. As fine as I really can be, given the situation. I'll live. So what about you? Same question."

She wanted to take a little time before she answered him. Somehow she'd ended up behind the very eight ball she had designed for him. She hated doing that. You think you have a conversation mapped out, you know the responses and have all the comebacks, and then the script gets changed. She couldn't screw *this* answer up.

"Well, to start with, no bullets for you. However this works out, no bullets. No ropes, either. Get some self-control, man!" She paused again.

"I'm ripping off a band-aid here. I mean, you never think about what happened after you're no longer alive. I really wasn't too much on the whole Heaven and angels thing with harps and all of that crap. The scientific mind in me has always said that this spin is all you get, and once it's over, it's over and you go into basically nothing. I guess I kinda forced myself to believe that I would never die before I got everything I wanted to get done, done. Didn't happen quite as planned."

"Did you ever think about the normal things I assume all women think about? Like getting married, having, kids, all of that?"

"I don't really know what I thought. I hadn't dwelled on it much. Maybe deep in my gut I knew I wouldn't have any kids. I didn't think I would be alone forever. I'm glad you're here. I'm glad to find out it doesn't really end. I know I'm a unique case, but at the same time I'm scared shitless to be honest. I can't come back there, I don't know how long I get to stay here, and I don't know what, if anything, is ahead of me. I'm still actively trying to figure all this shit out."

"You mean inside there, not like the meaning of life or anything?"

"Well, yeah. The meaning of life for me is kinda a moot point now, doncha think? I'm trying to figure out exactly where I am at in this system, and how I can move around in here. Also trying to figure out how you can see me, what I am, all of that. I have some good ideas, but nothing I've really proven yet. If I could figure out how to actually interact, I could really do some damage."

"Damage?"

"Bad choice of word. I could actually figure out how to use this machine from this side. "

"You're not duckin' the question. Normal things. Women, which is you. Go."

"I said that I didn't think it would happen, so yeah, I did answer the question."

"Okay, so if you had a kid, assume. Play the game. So if I knocked you up, what would we name the kid."

"Whoa!" Veronica snorted in disbelief. "Slow down there, Sparky! You always talk to girls like that on the first date?"

"It's not the first date. Not at this point, anyway. And I'm not saying I can, we know I can't, but if we had met earlier, what would we have named her?"

"Angelica. And how do you know it would have been a *her*?"

"Because I beat my little swimmers like red-headed stepchildren."

The laugh exploded. She couldn't stop herself. "What? What the hell was that?"

"Seriously. I thought the whole bio thing was like, your degree program and shit. How would you not know this? Causes of low sperm count should fall under your biology studies, I'd think."

"I didn't study medicine. I'm not a doctor, or a sperm specialist, for that matter."

"Anyway. So I met these guys once when I was down in Catalina. They do some kind of diving for a commercial marine company, like deep underwater welding and crap. All daughters. Like seven daughters between them. Never could have a boy. Apparently the pressure messes things up, same with skydiving, hot tubs, alcohol, all that. So if only the strong survive, and those little survivors are all little girl swimmers, guess what we have?"

"A daughter."

"A never ending dress and Barbie bill. So yes, a daughter. Or three, because I don't know if I could stop myself."

"Where are we going?"

"What do you mean?"

"All of this. Where does it go? Where do I go? I mean, we've pretty much figured out where we stand, y'know? But there's not a lot we can do about it, and I can't come back. Everything in me tells me that I have a date with that glass door across from me, and when that happens, I won't be here, and I have no idea what that means. I'm good with the things I know, that I've put my hands on, but not so much about this 'Hey look, I'm a spirit now' shit." She felt him even out and the energy flatten. "And yes, I would eventually stop you, because there's a pill for that."

A girl appeared behind the glass plate. She looked to be in her early 20s, long dark hair. Latina. She looked a lot like Mama. The girl was peering in, like she was peeking at a saleswoman through a shop window. Flashing a bright toothy grin, she waved at Veronica. It was a confusing gesture, not a normal wave, more like a waggle of the fingers you'd make to a small child.

Who is that?

Veronica stopped the conversation to move to the glass where she was face to face with the girl, but with the talking the girl was attempting, no sound was coming out. She was mouthing words at Veronica, and finally understanding that she couldn't be heard, resorted to sign language of a strange sort.

She put her hands together and make something that looked like an explosion. Veronica must have had an utterly confused look her face, because the girl nodded, gave another wide grin. She pointed at

Veronica, then made a gesture with two fingers like walking. Then the explosion again. Waited.

Me, walk, boom. Am I going to explode or something?

Veronica remembered what she heard Avo say when she had first regained her consciousness, to walk towards the light.

The light!

As the young woman waited, still smiling, Veronica pointed at the plate glass, then herself, and then the plate glass again. A very excited nod. Yes, the glass. Veronica took a finger and tapped the glass, letting her know it was solid. The smile crumpled into confusion. She thought for a moment while appearing to study the glass, then held up a finger.

Wait.

And then she disappeared.

"That was bizarre," Veronica said aloud.

"What was?"

"There was a girl here on the other side of the plate glass, trying to get me to come through it. She didn't know it was solid."

"Do you know her?"

"Nope. Never seen her in my life, but she looked familiar, kinda like my mother. Same eyes."

"I guess we're talking about this now," he said. It wasn't upset, but more resigned. Like when you finally face something that you didn't want to, or you have to go home after a great day at the park where there was cloudless sunshine. Now the sun had set and the lightning bugs were out. Along with the Park Police that were letting you know like a tired bartender that you could go anywhere, but you couldn't stay there.

"I thought we already were. Anyway, we still have to face all of the crap that we don't wanna face. I guess that's the long and short of it, right? Probably no better time than right now. I mean, we got the time, that's not the issue."

"I'm not wanting to lose that time."

"Who said anything about losing time? Every minute's important. At least that's the way it seems now. I know every minute here with you is important to me, and it's not like we're saving the planet or anything."

two faces of a clown

"Why did you drink so much, anyway? And how much is *so much*? I don't think Lindsey ever really explained that to me." Veronica had asked the question he had been dodging and here it was to deal with.

"Maybe it was just that it was a lot for me. I had problems really dealing with people since I was a kid. Dealing with my mother, holy shit. She'd make a nun drink and punch kittens." He heard Veronica laugh and then reel herself in.

"Sorry, got a visual of that."

"I'm serious, she puts incredible stress on anyone within arm's reach, just to see how far she can push them and try to break them. She wants to be worshipped without reason, without any logical reason for it. She doesn't care who she injures, or how she does it, just so everyone else hurts and she's the queen bee."

"So she is why you drink?"

"Yeah, a large part of it."

"She flies out here and pushes the bottle into your mouth and you just drink. I thought that stopped after infancy." Ronni was being a little pushy. She wasn't quite getting it.

"Ha, no. But she does her thing, I drink to put up with her. So cause and effect. That's what I've pretty much seen since Dad died, and she was pretty goofy before that, if I remember correctly."

"We're both fatherless children, babe. And I've raised the pot a brother. Not that it really makes any sense to create a comparison list on dead kin. Push deeper, while you can. Once you get here, you have way too much time to think and chew over things, too much time to feel the regret and what you lost out on. Shit, I should be the one drinking at this point. I'm not claiming to be an expert or an addiction counselor or anything, I just get a feeling that you drink for more reasons than some cranky bitch in another state, no offense."

"None taken. I have better words for her."

"So hate is part of it."

"What?"

"Hate is part of the drinking. She's given you a good spin around the block, and it's one thing if it's someone you can cut off like a bad date, but she's *blood*. That always makes shit harder, I'd imagine."

"My mom sucks."

"As bad as this sounds, you can have mine. I'm not really using her anymore, and she's an absolute angel. God, that sounded bad."

"No, I get it. I just despise being hurt all of the time, always having to hide from her and her constant attacks. They serve absolutely no purpose at all, and the joy she seems to get out of it in her warped mind only benefits her and no one else. I wonder what happens when she finally gets to where you are."

"Better not come here. I'm ready to knock her ass out as it is."

"I mean, I hung onto the idea that there was judgement somewhere, like some big god creature was gonna tell her what a bitch she is and thump her on her ass. She makes ya want to believe in a Hell. People like her make you want to believe in that shit."

"Why else?"

"Why else, what?" Jakub asked.

"Why else do you drink? Why is it a thing with you, why are you drawn and compelled to it? I understand the idea of drinking at a party, having a drink with a meal, the whole concept of adult beverages. This is different. You're medicating. What are you medicating for? That's what I want to get to. You don't do things blindly, without an intention. It sounds to me like maybe we were both on autopilot until now." She was looking down towards her feet.

"You're not gonna let me out of this line of questioning, are you?"

"No chance in Hell."

"Why?"

"You're there. You have time. You can get things right, make them better, be whoever it was you were supposed to be."

"Not really, you're there."

"Besides that. Minor point."

"It's not a minor point to me. It's a major fucking point to me."

"Bottles won't fix it. Escaping reality won't fix it. Being bored won't fix it."

"Honestly, you're right. They don't. Drinking doesn't. It's almost like it helps me avoid the inevitable in some way. Or at least numb me for the impact, the other shoe that's always going to drop, and usually on me."

"So fear is your deal."

"What, fear? No. I wouldn't..."

"Yes. Fear is your deal. You've been smacked enough that you're chickenshit about what's going to happen. Maybe even with life itself. Not nearly as abnormal as you'd think."

"Then, yeah. I guess that's part of it. Makes me feel a little more like I can handle things. I don't think that's a bad thing."

"Hold your horses there, buck. I said I understood it, not that the reason was worth a shit."

"Still..."

"Yeah. So how much is too much? You still haven't answered that part of the question yet. What was so much that I shouldn't even know who you were? What were you doing, puking on everyones' shoes?"

He felt himself give a heavy exhalation. Embarrassment would have been the right word for the feeling. Humiliation didn't cover it, because he still felt justified. He hoped no one would observe it. More like smoking a cigarette at church, and less like getting caught jerking off in the gym shower.

"I guess I drank almost a fifth a day or two. Give or take, depending on how the day went or what I was doing. I don't think that's a lot. Not as much as I've seen others do. I drink enough to help me forget and to sleep."

"So now it's back to medication. A liquid sleeping pill."

"Well, yeah. Why is this so important?"

She gave a look like she wasn't sure if she wanted to slap him or say something else that would puncture him a little bit. It was appearing like she was speaking to a child that simply wasn't understanding what they were being told.

He didn't.

And didn't want to.

"It seems to me that no one ever talks to you about it, and if I had my guess, no one notices. You probably like it that way on one hand, and yet on the other you want someone to sit you down and bitch you out about it but in some ways you're still that kid thinking about his father on the bathroom floor. You need guidance. You ain't getting it. Except maybe from your sister. There's a lot of stuff even she can't set straight."

Jakub didn't know if he was irritated she could see into him like a cellophane package or relieved she'd said it.

"You're right, of course. And there isn't really much you can do at this point but talk from there. Maybe it's safer that way. For me, I mean. What are you really going to do there?"

"Don't get depressed about it. I can still feel everything you're saying and thinking, remember? I felt that drop. Look, I'm not saying I can solve any of your problems, but the good part is that I can feel them, and I kinda know how to handle some of that, so it's kinda like we're doing this together, right? I mean that's been part of this whole mess, being in the middle of something where you didn't have a bearing on things. Think of it as me being your navigator. Coping mechanisms, they are your friend."

"I'm still trying to get a good handle on the fact that someone else can get in my head like that. The fact that it's a girl in my VR is a bonus."

"Um, *my* VR."

"Not anymore. Mine now. I just get you inside it. So, Coach, let's get on with this shitshow."

"Don't look at it that way," Ronni said gently, "Look, when Papa died, I had to go talk to someone. I had to go to what they called grief counseling. Did you ever do that? What happened when your dad passed?"

"Exactly what I told you, and that fast. I think we were out of the house and in Houston within a week. Mom was already shacked up with the nurse, and I think she had already planned on making a play for us because the house they got had extra rooms. It wasn't like they got some cute little bungalow. I'll admit there's a lot about that whole situation I don't know, and most of my reactions to my mom are first that she did what she did and Dad did what he did, and then the tiny little fact that she has been a manipulative cunt to me ever since. So no, Willie was it. I didn't go to any counseling, and tiny towns in Texas don't give a shit about that either. At least they didn't back then."

"And somehow you still seemed to remain relatively normal?"

"Define normal. I'm always waiting to get screwed out of any good thing I get, I fight with her on a regular basis like clockwork, and the whole trying to use me to bury her guilt or whatever it was, is, makes me crazy. Vera's not hard on the eyes, either, even after twenty something years. She can do a whole lot better than my mother, that's for damned sure."

"So drinking helps soothe your nerves? Somehow I just don't think we're there yet."

"You're telling me you don't like to drink, that alcohol is bad, and somehow you want to come up with a magic cure to solve me."

"No, you're putting words in my mouth I haven't said. That's a defensive mechanism. So now you're protecting your little secret area. I didn't say anything about drinking being bad. I didn't say anything about you drinking being bad. But it isn't the same kind of drinking a brew master or a vintner or even a social connoisseur would drink. Yours has an ulterior motive. That's what I'm picking at, the motive. If you can fix the motive, hell, you might actually enjoy and be able to regulate your drinking a lot more. That's all."

"So you drink, too..."

"Uh, really? I was drinking the first time you saw me. I was drinking the night I died. Rojo, actually. More of a wine drinker. Maybe I had my own motives too. I was more into the California vibe of drinking, I guess. Never was much of a party girl. Remember, I lived at home the whole time I was in college, since it was pretty much down the street for me. I think I might have had one or two good tequila nights, and then that was pretty much all I wanted to do with that. Wine was a little different, it has a certain status and culture to it, I think. Maybe for guys it's whiskey, at least that's what I've noticed, anyway."

"Yeah, for me it's usually bourbon. Goes down easier on ice for me. I've done vodka before, went through that phase, but I kept coming back to whiskeys because they were easy."

"Do you drink when you're alone?"

"Yeah, of course."

"How do you feel about it when you're drinking alone? I mean, what makes it different than being out in a crowd and drinking, like at a party?"

"I actually prefer it. I hate crowds, and I get dragged into them at least once a month."

"Why is that?" Ronni asked.

"I have this stupid friend that thinks he's some budding party producer like that Pitbull guy he always jabbers about and puts on parties once a month or so."

"I know who that is. He's cool. Continue."

"Somehow I became the poster boy for one of the cool guys that has to be at his parties. I never get VIP status, I just wander around drinking mixed drinks usually, since that's cheaper on him, talking to people I wish I'd never actually met, daydreaming about shopping for socks."

"Socks?"

"I just needed to finish the thought. Point is, I probably could just drink a soda and fake it. But it occurred to me that maybe I want to be just drunk enough where the bill would hurt him for guilting me into coming there, and I wouldn't be in any shape to take anyone there seriously."

"Why don't you just tell this guy no? Isn't that a simpler way to go?"

"Simpler, yes. Much simpler. But I work with this guy, and he has been dipping his pen in the company ink, if you get what I'm saying."

"You mean he's sleeping with his secretary or something?"

"No," Jakub laughed, "He's the mail kid. He's screwing the Vice President of Marketing."

"Okay, so are they an item?"

"No. She's married to the Legal Counsel. The guy who wipes his ass with the loose hundreds from his paychecks."

Ronni snorted, "Got yourself on a powder keg there, doncha boy?"

"Something like that. If I cause any friction or say the wrong shit at the wrong time, everything blows up. His ego's way too much for his own good, and I guess maybe I'm protecting his stupid ass, because as long as he's doing this production crap, it's less time he's trying to hump the VP in other places. I'm guilt by association. He goes, I go too because they know we have a connection, whether I asked for that connection or not."

"You should just go first."

"What? Go where?"

"Where do you think? Get another job. It's Los Angeles. You can get another tech job pretty quick, I'm sure. Sounds like you're doubting yourself there. You know we're back to the alcoholic versus casual drinker part now, right?"

"They're both the same to me."

"Not to me. Quite different. You got real world problems to deal with. You should probably knock those out before you even *think* about the alcohol part. First, your mother. Like I said, take mine. Not sure how that would work, she's never even met you, and I guess you couldn't just pop up one day, but you definitely need to cut off Mom there. She's making you sick, givin' you an illness, really. So you gotta deal with that.

Then there's Cabana Boy. You're gonna need to dump all of that bullshit, too. Anyone endangering your job, or your right to enjoy it because they're busy screwing people that aren't you needs to go. That's a situation you get zero benefit from. Trust me, life is too short. I think you should dump that job and Cabana Boy and leave no forwarding address.

So that's two things that you drink about that are out of the way. Once you do 'em, you'll feel a whole lot lighter, I'm sure. Then, go take a tour, learn some more about drinking. Stop. I know how it sounds, but I once went to this place near Ojai that ran a small vineyard and did wine tastings. Hell, take a week off and tour Napa. Drink beer? Go make some beer. Then you're drinking because you like and respect alcohol, not because you hate life."

"Where were you ten years ago?"

"Trying to run into *you*," Veronica answered.

up from electrical

Jakub was certainly a boy for exhausting conversations. Granted there wasn't a whole lot else that could be done, but he was so damned addicting. Everything about him. Why he was the way that he was, how he had that jerky exterior but was nothing like that once you got him broken in good.

"So," he dragged the word out like it was on a string, "Since you're asking all the hard questions, you're there, you've hit the finish line, so to speak. Tell me, what is love? I mean, what is it really? To *you*, I mean."

Fuck. I walked right into that one.

"Ugh, are you serious?"

"Quid pro quo, Clarisse."

Veronica couldn't help but laugh. His one-liners were always on point.

"I'm shy. I've always been that way, played it off. Blamed all of my missed opportunities on it. Like you, for example. I should have just ignored a lot of what I've been told in my life, and things might have been different..."

"Ducking my question."

"No, I'm not ducking it, I've honestly tried very hard to not think about it. I realized early, like when

Papa died, that I wasn't going to get the fairy tale life I thought I'd have."

"And we're back to pain. Fear maybe? When it hit me, I drank. When it hit you, you shut down."

"I don't know that I'd call it shutting down, per se..."

"How do ya figure? From what I do know about you, school was the big thing that took up all of your time, then you move out here to LA and work seems to be the thing that took up the rest of your time. Okay, so you did some traveling and all of that, but with who? Who was the significant person that you went around with. I never really hear about anyone else than S&L, and I can tell you from experience how much third party hangers-on they put up with. Maybe they liked you more than me, but still. You're a workaholic. Admit it."

"And of course, you're not. You work, you go to places you don't want to go, do things you don't want to do, and then drink to be able to tolerate them. Not sayin' it's bad, just sayin' it is. And what does that got to do with me, anyway?" Veronica was feeling what it was like to squirm, and she wasn't enjoying it.

"I don't think you're understanding where we're at here," he said, the drawl coming out nice and milky, like home. He paused, either loading a proverbial shotgun or making sure he wasn't about to say something stupid. Whatever it was, she could feel the energy behind it.

"There was this guy once," he continued, "We had to read him in lit class when I was in college. For some reason out of all the bullshit I had run through one ear and out the other, this part stuck with me, and I've never been able to get it out. Kinda fits here.

> 'I am the monk of her love,
> Praying the prayers no others can hear,
> Feeling the solace no others can feel.
> She makes me complete.'

"I always wanted someone to say that to. I wanted someone to be *that person*. That is what I've wanted since the hormones came in and I woke up for the first time with a hard little pecker. You are that person for me. Right now. But back on topic of course, I'm not lettin' you off the hook that easy. You didn't let me, so I'm gonna give it right back. Tell me about love."

"What about it?"

"Everything, any kind of love, all kinds. Who did you love? What did it mean, How do you even *know* if you love someone? That's what I'm digging for here."

It was no mistake that Jakub intended on taking the bull by the balls, and he wasn't going to let go until he got something.

"Papa was the first. Maybe the strongest. I guess it's a thing that most little girls within reason love their daddies, and I certainly was a Daddy's Girl for what it was worth. He always had to have me close to him, like every day after work, I'd pretty much be wherever he was. I can't think of a day in my life where he didn't hug me or kiss me at least once. Probably what most parents do with their kids. At least I'd hope so. And he *loved* feeding people, especially me. I told you about the grill. He'd always take the best parts of whatever he made and give them to me. I mean, you could see it in his eyes that it was the piece of whatever he was eating that he really wanted, but I would end up with it anyway. I think I learned from that the meaning of the word *sacrifice*. When you love someone it always means giving them the things you wished you could keep for yourself, just to know that it made them happy, that they were getting the best thing you had to offer."

"So there is a part of you that associates love with giving? Even if it's something that in any other circumstance you wouldn't give up for life, love, or money?"

"I guess that sums it up."

She heard him rifling around, then he spoke again, "Do you like jazz?"

Veronica snorted, "What?"

"Do you like jazz? I figure that conversations like this either require jazz or marijuana, and I'm all fresh outta weed here."

"Where did that come from?" She laughed.

"I'm having a moment," he said with a soft chuckle, "Beautiful girl, captive audience, gotta make an impression."

"I think we might be a little bit beyond that now," she said, as soft sounds of horns began playing in the background.

"So, your dad. When you lost him, how did you feel? Did that have an effect on how you viewed love?"

"Maybe it was a little different for me because my Papa just had a heart attack doing what he loved for who he loved. I think you have a different scenario there, so I expect the result will be different. For me, I just lost the largest constant figure in my life. Now, as bad as it hurt me, I know it hurt Mama worse. They married young. They met when they were still practically kids. He was all she ever knew, and she wouldn't even consider dating after he died. I mean, from what I understand about you, your parents just weren't wound that tight, at least from one direction and I think that maybe that's what you've been looking and hoping for. I was in the middle of it, so that's also what I've always been hoping would fall in my lap. Like there would be a guy to love and adore me like he did. It makes you feel like you belong. Maybe we both miss the belonging part."

"That's fair," he said. "I never really felt like I belonged anywhere after Dad capped himself. I've wondered about the whole love thing, and maybe it got all warped for me because the very thing that he thought he was doing right was what bit him in the ass. Willy says that Mom was just bent to begin with, and with the exception of us being born, it was pretty much a wasted effort. I mean, my sis didn't wait too long to marry off. And she did well, don't misunderstand me, Carl is a fricking gem. He worships the ground she walks on and lets her damned near get away with murder," he gasped and laughed, "Here's what I mean, can you believe that she *actually cut* the TV power cable to get the fucking kids to go to bed? And he went out and bought a new TV in time to watch the Stars? Not a peep, no bitching, no nothing. Like it was the most normal shit in the world."

"Apparently he loves the Stars."

"Beside the point."

"What would you do if I had cut the power cable to your TV? Maybe smashed it real good? Like drove a tractor over it or something?"

"I would probably kiss you and buy a new TV." Veronica heard the pause, "Well, that makes sense now. You suck. Making me think." She couldn't help but snicker at him as he finished, "But's that not fair. It's different. I'd rather have you than the TV. Any day."

"Maybe he feels that way, too. He just knew he could get another TV anyway."

"Seems legit. So love is giving up shit and putting up with shit."

"Was this where you wanted the conversation to go?"

"No. And you still have lots of answering to do."

"Honestly," Veronica started, "I think love for me has been more about what I hoped would happen and less what actually did happen. No real connections, like everything was in some fairytale universe of being understood by another human being, and me being able to understand who they really were and what they wanted."

"A couple of my girlfriends were like house guests that I sometimes had sex with but just seemed to stay too long. Like, you just don't really know anything about them even after a few months."

"I saw that with a lot of my friends' parents. Guess I was lucky that my own were the way they were. I had one friend whose father didn't remember his wife's birthday or her middle name. I find that bizarre. I also figured it was a load of crap, but they just didn't get along, tried hard to stay away from each other, and had a lot of money. It was almost like they'd made it a point to forget each other, but they lived in the same damned house. My friends had nannies for as far back as they could remember."

"I didn't know San Antonio had rich people."

"You're jerking my chain here, right? Of course we have rich people. We have a basketball team and three military bases. *Somebody* has to be making money. You just haven't been on the north side much."

"Haven't really been on any side of that place much. Kind of a unfair question there," Jakub answered.

"Stop."

"What? What did I say?"

"Nothing about that. I just realized something." She was pausing to map this all out in her mind. Sometimes it's the simplest things that miss your radar, and then when they pop up, it's magical. "So, do you have a webcam, or anything like that? And where's your router? Do you have control of it?"

"Well, yes. What's this about?" Jakub asked.

"I'm thinking about how I can jury rig something."

"You mean jerry rig?"

"Shut up. So this thing is made to do something called casting. If I remember it right, you can cast to a television, which means that everything you're seeing here can be seen on the TV. Following me so far?"

"Yeah. And I can set up a webcam, stream it to a local webpage, and surf that webpage on the browser in there with you, in the goggles."

"That's exactly what I'm thinking about. Two way communication."

"But all you're gonna see besides my apartment is me with this thing on my face."

"I think I have a way around that, too. You'll

need to make a trip to the arts and crafts store. I actually did this before when I was testing the app on cast mode. You get one of those styrofoam heads, and put the goggles on it after you set in cast mode. It keeps the pressure on the sensor at the top of the nose so the goggles think they're still being worn."

"Cool! This might be easier for both of us. Then it's more like a video call!" She could feel his excitement building.

"Pretty much. So how much of the equipment do you actually have on hand?"

"Well, I have an external camera for my laptop when I video chat with Willie, and I have Bluetooth on my TV. So casting is a thing. I just need to go get the other piece tomorrow when I get off work."

beauty in the breakdown

"Why do you always spend so much time ducking the things that you really want to say?"

"Where did you get that from?"

"Well, it's what you do. You've got something on your mind you want to say, and everything in you wants to say it, but you won't. You just go off and say something completely different just to avoid it."

"That's completely crazy."

"Uh, no. It's not. Remember that I have an inside track on you, and I'm not bullshitting about that. You duck a lot of the things that you really want out there. Like you're afraid of getting smacked down for whatever it is you really want to say, and ya can't live like that."

Jakub took a breath in, deeply. *What is this shit?*

"Remember the old saying? *Be who you are and say what you feel, because those who mind don't matter, and those who matter don't mind.* You really need to internalize that or something."

He actually hadn't remembered ever hearing that one, but who's going to deny knowing Dr. Seuss?

"Yeah, I know it. I get what you're saying."

"You might get it, but you've never heard it. Interesting. And it's not Dr. Seuss, for the record. I'd hate for you to get out there and look stupid. I did that once."

Damn it! How does she do that? Who lets her just read my mind like that?

"I don't think it's a who, as much as a what."

"Shut up," Jakub said jokingly, but very much blushing.

"No," Veronica laughed, "It might not be the most fun in the world on your side of things, being wide ass open like that, but I'm having a blast. I get to know you so much better, like I get to be the glove around your hand. Do you realize how close you can be to someone if you get to flow with them, rather than be diametrically opposed to them? How the hell can you really embarrass yourself now? Think about it. Anything you come up with, I'm right there with you. I'm like an official guilty party in anything you come up with. I've never been able to be in cahoots with someone like this."

"We're not in cahoots."

"Aren't we? Are you sure about that? Every little fantasy you have that you don't think I know about, I have a front row seat to. I especially liked that beach scene you had in your head when you were in the shower the other night. You haven't heard me complain about it. I love 'em. I'm right there with you."

"Well, I guess that could be a bit reassuring."

"Is it? I guess it is."

"I like talking to people. I like talking to you. You know, like, have you ever driven that stretch from Barstow to Baker, just rolling with the windows down singing along with the radio and having those really deep conversations? Like the really abstract ones that are so intense and meaningful that you almost wanna break down and cry because they're just so beautiful?"

"Nope."

"Me either. I can't seem to get anybody into my fucking car. Especially for a ride to Vegas. You know I spent about a month driving around with a medical skeleton in the backseat of my car. His name was Robert. Don't ask. I had him positioned like he was trying to escape. Got told several times to use him and get in the HOV lane. I doubt the CHP woulda smiled brightly on that. They usually have the sense of humor of a brick."

"Did he manage to break free?"

"Who? Robert? Hell, no. He's sitting about 10 feet away right now. Wait... you wanted to do that sexy webcam trick. If we do that, I can show him to you. He's sitting in a chair watching the television screen right now."

"In your living room?"

"No, on the balcony. Yes, he's in my living room. Where do ya think I am?"

"I can't see you, jackass. You could be on the moon for all I know."

"I think it's about time that we fix that, don't you?"

"Well then... off with ya! Go do it!"

Jakub wasted no time getting to the crafts store. It wasn't that far away, the whole trip took about a half hour, and he returned with the thing he knew that he needed, the mannequin head.

He knew this was something Ronni needed, the ability to see who she was talking to. It must be like talking to someone on the phone, except they are on the other side of a two-way mirror. Seemed disrespectful to keep going that way. It would do her heart good, and that was all Jakub cared about at this point.

As he settled himself in the living room, he looked around making sure everything was in order. It was as good as a bachelor could expect. He had a better design touch than most bachelors he knew.

Leave Robert where he is. She wants to see him, anyway.

He got the head situated where it was sturdy, almost bomb-proof, and placed the goggles on his head.

"I think I have everything ready here. How do we do this?"

"You have the cables, and they're long enough?" Ronni asked.

"Yeah, I think so. I have the TV on, ready to cast, and my laptop's up with a higher quality webcam than came with it."

"I doubt that upgrade was hard."

"Right. The camera on the laptops usually suck. This one's high definition."

"Okay, so what you need to do is fire up the camera and serve it to a local web server. You have that already set up?"

"I do."

"Skippy."

He checked his settings one more time to make sure everything was how he wanted it. He'd perched the camera on top of the television so they would look as if they were viewing each other through a window.

"I want to get you set up first, get you on the TV so I can see you there. I'm not sure how this is gonna work yet, because you're behind the browser, remember?"

"Well, you get that figured out, and when it's up, we'll pull the browser up and point at your web server. When that drops down, I'll see if I can get around it, or to the front of it somehow. We won't know until you pull up the browser, though. I think you can reduce that size down, and that might just be enough."

"Sounds good to me. Here we go."

Ronni looked like she was in full on work mode, completely focused on what they were doing, and it was obvious why she'd been good at her job.

Jakub pulled the remote, made sure the television was ready to receive, then selected Screen Cast inside the VR goggles. Peeking out from under the edge, he saw that the casting was a success. Unfortunately, Ronni was no longer in 3D like she was in front of him, but he could see her clearly. "Okay, I have you on the television, now I need to connect my side. I'm giving the non-talking head the goggles." Placing the VR goggles firmly on the mannequin, he could see that everything operated like it had in virtual reality, just that he was now aiming at the television.

He fired up the web server and then launched his webcam software and went live. Writing down the device address, he picked up the controller and brought up a browser and surfed to the IP address.

Immediately a wide smile broke over Ronni's face, and she looked like a little girl at the tree on Christmas morning.

"Hey, you!" Ronni cooed.

moonlight on your face

The panorama of the room spread out in front of her, and she could finally see the man she had always hoped would be sitting there. Her intuition had been right all along. And there was Robert. She didn't bother to hold in the laugh. Jakub had dressed the medical skeleton in a Hawaiian shirt that was adorned with green palm trees to match the Dallas Stars t-shirt and hat. His skeleton feet were stacked, one on top of the other on the coffee table. Just kicked back, relaxing. He'd even taken the time to put him in olive drab cargo shorts.

It was a medical skeleton that screamed *I've been dressed by a complete geek.*

"Nice friend you've got there."

Jakub grinned. "Like 'im? He's very quiet, likes all the shows I like."

"You don't get to use your TV anymore. I'm taking it up."

"No show on the telly better than you, my dear."

"I have to admit, I do like this a lot better than doing things the other way."

"So do I. I really didn't think it was fair that you couldn't see me. I felt like a peeping tom. Which does have its perks, mind you. But you never got naked, so that was a bit of a let-down."

"Well, now. We gettin' a little cheeky there, aren't we?"

He put out a finger and thumb close together and replied, "Just a smidge, little lovely. Just a smidge. I'm sure you'll be okay."

"It'll take more than that to rattle me, young man."

"So I've noticed."

She heard the music in the background. It was familiar. "What's that you're playing in the background. I thought you were a jazz guy."

"Oh, I was just trying to turn you on," Jakub said as the smile spread over his face and emerged into a huge grin, "That's Stevie Ray. C'mon, girl! Gotta represent for the home country."

"Texas is a state."

"Texas is the *Republic* of Texas. That means it's its own goddamned country. And I'm representing my country. We should be in the Olympics. Not the winter ones, just the summer ones. We don't get enough snow and ice for Winter Olympics. We'd be like the Jamaican bobsledding team."

"Papa would kiss you right now. His mama was Tejano. Part of the reason why my Mama was always so tangled up in the Missions. She'd follow Papa anywhere. I swear bad things couldn't happen to a nicer person. Swear to me that if you get the chance, you'll look in on Mama and help take care of her. I know you don't owe me anything, in fact, I owe *you*, but please have a little mercy there."

His face sobered up. "I will help her anonymously, if I have to. I don't think there's a lot I wouldn't do for you now, and certainly nothing within reason."

She could still feel his emotions, even though she could also see him now. So, that ability wasn't sight related.

"I have a different question for you."

"Okay?"

"We've established everything's made of electrical impulses. And waves. Of some sort."

"Right..."

"So I can still feel you now, just like I could when I was unable to see you. I'm wondering if the human body doesn't act as some sort of insulation for our emotions and thoughts?"

"I think you're saying that before you figured that you had that ability because you didn't have a visual of me. Like when one sense is heightened because the others are deficient."

"Yeah, exactly."

"But you were able to see the inside of the VR there, so that wouldn't count. You still had visual, just not outside of the box there. That's different."

"So it is. Good job, there. That helps thin it out a bit, doesn't it?"

"I've been chewing on something, and I tried to not take it seriously, but maybe it's something you can work with. Do you know what happened on October 15, 2004?"

"You're kidding, right?"

"Nope. And it's a sports thing, so don't let your eyes glaze over, okay?"

"Ah, shit. Let's hear it."

"Okay. So the Boston Red Sox are down three games to nothing in the ALCS against the New York Yankees. There's been no love in the stadium, that's for sure. I'm rollin' around with Carl in the truck, don't remember why. I think we were traveling to pick something up, and it was after midnight. The game was already over, and we were listening to this spooky show, the talk show that talks about aliens, and the goat-staring people, and all that shit? So this lady called in, and was talking to the host. The premise had to do with mass amounts of people setting an intention and meditating on it, all at the same time. Could they change shit if they were thinking about it together. Apparently there had been some scientific studies done on this that said yes, but they weren't sure how."

"You got my attention. Continue..."

"So either she or the host points out, I think it mighta been the host, that the Sox haven't won a Series at that point in 90-something years. However long. Long fucking time, anyway. So they decided that they would take two minutes and everybody listening would stop and set an intention that the Sox would win the World Series. The reason they did it was that it was damned near impossible. The

Yankees were gonna put 'em out to pasture in the next game."

"What happened?"

"What? You don't know?"

"I don't do baseball."

"They won the next four games, knocked out the Yankees, then swept St. Louis. Understand this... they won *eight* consecutive games against two of the best teams in the country. Almost like they were standing still. Keep in mind that show had a listener base of millions. I mean, they're at about 3 million now, and I know it was probably triple that back then. Look, we even pulled the truck over to participate, and neither of us gave a damn at the time. We were just curious if it would work. And it did."

"So you're saying that the Red Sox won because a few million people willed it to happen."

"That's the prevailing theory."

"Then convince the country to will a Super Bowl for the Browns."

"They've already had four."

"What? No they haven't."

"Girl, yes they have. They won the first televised Super Bowl against the Colts. You're diluting the point."

"Which is?"

"I handed you pieces to a puzzle. You're supposed to put them together, not me. If you are truly feeling out my emotions and vibrations, then that has to be the same stuff that this story is based on, right? Those were all great teams. But the odds on any of them winning eight straight would've broken Vegas. They went into that Series as the underdog. No one I knew thought they could beat the Cardinals, but they swept them. So I'm inclined to think that the experiment at least had *some* effect on this deal."

"Okay," she exhaled, trying to put this together, "Gimme a minute to process this."

If what Jakub said, and what she experienced were made of the same stuff, then there was a platform on which it moved. Just like the idea of gravity in Einstein.

"Here's a thought," She said, "I don't know how familiar you are with Einstein's theories, particularly the ones involving gravity where he basically tried to take Newton's theories and elevate them. So think of this. Imagine you had the solar system, or a few marbles, if it makes it easier, and you put them on a piece of plastic wrap. Got that visual?"

"Mmm-hmm."

"Okay, so they press down on the sheet. So we're gonna skip that bullshit for a minute, because I want you to think about the sheet itself. The items on the sheet have free range to go where they want, right?"

"Yeah."

"But the sheet remains the same. Everything is connected to the sheet. Similar concept as radio waves or sound waves in air. What if these are waves, too. What if our brains are able, in the right condition to transmit and receive these signals?"

"I wonder if the color of blue to you is the same as the color of blue to me?"

"Dude, shut up."

"I get the point. That might be what I'm thinking. My point is that you will have that ability, at least in my uneducated mind I think you will, whether you are in the goggles or outside of them. That's really all I'm trying to say."

"Problem is, I'd hafta get outta here to test the theory. And we don't know how to safely pull that off."

"No," Jakub answered, "We don't. And that's where we're gonna be stuck for a while. You said there's a glass in there, and you have seen folks you know in it, which tells me that the glass you're seeing *has* to be the answer. The question we have now is how does it open?"

never tried to reach

"I *have* wondered something," Jakub pondered, "I know that you can hear or sense everything coming from me. But what would happen if there was someone else in the room? We really haven't thought about that one."

"Good point. I wonder too. Know anybody?"

"No."

"Well, there goes that idea."

"So you've been in there for a long time. But it seems that you don't get hungry and don't get thirsty either, which I naturally assume is because you don't have a physical body that requires it. Have you figured out what you actually need?"

"I've thought about that. I imagine the power just flows in, like I'm connected to something bigger than me. My first inclination would be to say it's the headset, but I don't think so. I think it's something else."

"Are you able to change your clothes?"

"I haven't tried that," Ronni said, "Why? You don't like them?"

"Oh, that's a loaded question right there. I like what you're wearing just fine, I didn't know if you had options or not. That's all."

"This is a completely different world I'm in here, and it seems to intersect with the one we came from. I'd really like to know more about what's going on, but at the same time it feels so safe knowing that you are right there. I mean, I realize there's nothing you could do, but I can see you and feel you, which makes things a little easier for me."

"You're afraid of what's coming."

She deflected the question. The pause told him she was somewhere between figuring out and understanding everything that had happened, and moving into an all-out hands-in-the-air screaming panic. They didn't know what could happen after this issue with the glass resolved itself one way or the other.

Jakub felt more at this point like a caretaker and guardian than the casual observer he had once been. That guy was just staring at the girl behind the glass, admiring and wishing, and not necessarily in the healthiest of ways.

He shook of a little of the shame that struck him about the initial voyeurism.

"You need to quit beating yourself up about that," Ronni said.

Dammit. I forgot. You can read me.

"I'm not just anyone, y'know. I spent a lot of my life doing my thing, not thinking anyone ever really saw me. Then here you come, acting like I'm some awesome star or something. It's been a lot to take in, especially feeling it from your side. Now I know what all of that is, I can relate to it. So look at it this way... you've given me a gift that I didn't have before. I get to really see myself from somebody else's eyes for a change, and I'm just glad it was you."

"I guess it ain't that bad once you put it that way. Still makes me feel like I was a peeping tom that got caught."

"But I *wanted* you to peep. That's the difference."

"I just had a weird shower thought," Jakub said.

"Yeah?"

"When you die, they say you're supposed to then be 'resting'. You know, the whole Rest In Peace, sleeping peacefully with the Lord, yada-yada. Do you feel rested? Do you get tired? I mean, what are they talking about, since you're there now."

"I haven't been tired since I woke up, now that you mention it. I guess it's because I'm all energy now, and I don't have a physical body that has any real limitations."

She examined the inside of her leg, missing the irony of the motion.

"Y'know, that just gave me another thought. This headset is covered in a protective layer that acts almost like a Faraday Cage, so everything stays locked in."

"I don't know what that is."

"Think about a microwave. It has a coating on the inside that keeps all the energy you're nuking your food with inside the appliance. Kinda the same concept here. Except these aren't microwaves that I know of. And 'nuking' is a bad word to use since you're just exciting water molecules. But they *would* contain energy. That's also why you have the heatsinks on the back that get hot."

"I get it. So the goggles keep you locked in there, and that's why you can't get out. Might also explain the glass door. But here's another question. How did the door get there? Who put it there?"

"Ain't that the question of the century. I have no clue. I don't know what it is, but it feels like it's the way out. That scares the piss outta me, though. Out to *what*?"

"It can't be that bad, since you're seeing people that you know in it. And they're people you wanna see. I think if it were me, and I saw my mother in there, I'd never go through it. But these are people that you love, and they loved you, so it should be okay."

"You think so?" She chewed her lip. It didn't seem like Ronni was overly convinced of the safety the glass would bring. She drew quiet, fiddling with her fingers in thought. She was chewing over everything and it was clear on her face that it was beginning to take its toll on her.

"I just don't know what's behind that," she said almost in a monotone, "The last thing on Earth that I need is to get the ability to go through that thing and fall off a cliff into nothingness or something.

I've just gotten accustomed to all of this, I don't know what the next new thing would be."

"But you're a scientist, and adventurer, right?"

"What are you trying to do, get me to leave?" She asked, cocking her eye with a slight grin.

"No, but I know you. You can't resist a good puzzle, something that needs to be explored. At least you're not completely by yourself. I'm kinda like your Houston here. Just think of it like being an astronaut."

"I never wanted to be an astronaut."

"And yet, here you are. So what are ya gonna do with it?"

He'd never seen that look on her face. It wasn't one of weariness as much as apprehension. Jakub tried to imagine what he would be feeling, what he would be thinking in her position, and unlike her, he couldn't get inside her brain to find out. The best he could do was to be there and support her, since she could certainly hear him.

Jakub felt a tingle and something almost like a new sense of confidence. If she needed a cheerleader, dammit, he was going to just do it.

"We're going to figure out what in the hell that glass is about, and we're going to figure out how to get you through it. Okay?"

"Okay."

"You just keep your eye out, and see who comes next. Try to get information from them, even if you have to play charades forever and a day. But you're gonna get through that glass, and everything is going to be better once you do. I know you can figure this out. Look at all the other things you've figured out, all the other things that you've been responsible for in your life. You pulled those off! You can pull this off, too. And it'll be a good thing. I promise."

"You can't promise, because you don't know."

"I can hope. If it were that bad, you'd be too afraid to get near it. But you keep going back to it, examining it. I can see you, remember? So it ain't a death trap or anything."

"What if I'm like a mouse, sniffing out cheese, and the damned thing's gunna snap on me?"

"You really think your dad and brother are gonna lead you into a trap?"

"How do I know they are really Papa and Pablo? What if they're figments of my subconscious imagination?"

"You're sitting here talking to me, taking up chunks of *my* day, which I assure you are very real. So I doubt that's the thing there. You just need to grab the next person you see and validate what's going on, what's on the other side of that glass. I think it's bizarre that you can walk around the whole thing, though. That's almost science fiction."

"This whole thing's science fiction, sweetie. I just keep telling myself that I'm some strange Time Lady that never knew who or what I was."

"If that works for you, then do it. Whatever it

takes, but I get the impression that you don't go through that thing without some trust and a bit of wild faith."

She exhaled deeply. The look of steel was in her eyes as Ronni tried to prepare herself for the possibility of something new, and something different. He thought that this was the same trepidation that people like John Glenn or Neil Armstrong felt their first time in space. The imaginations we have in our minds are always different from the reality. Like when you were a kid and you were afraid you'd go down the drain in the bathtub. It was common. It was scary.

It was wrong.

But reality is all we have, and the only way to know the truth is to experience the reality.

keep me hanging on

The glass plate was glowing again. She had her eye on it to see if anything was happening with it. Sometimes the whole thing was a waiting game, and nothing else would happen other than the glass lighting up. There wasn't a good way to figure out what was controlling that light that made the glass glow. It appeared to not have any visible source, nothing attached to the headset in any way she could see.

Veronica was torn because some things felt so right about this whole situation, others so horribly wrong. The guy she'd always wanted for her own was right here, and she was now The Girl In The Bubble. Sensing his emotions was second nature to her. She knew what he looked like, but would never be able to actually touch him, feel him against her skin, not one of the real dreams she'd ever had about a whirlwind romance could never happen. Not here, anyway.

Pablo.

He arrived with an excited smile, waving Veronica over to him. As she got closer to the glass, he grinned and with a wide mouth, leaned forward and blew a raspberry onto the glass so she could see the inside of his mouth and began laughing almost maniacally. She got it. It was something he used to do to her when they were younger, and he was going to get into the backseat of the car with her.

This would always start a session of sibling brawling and hi-jinx that would eventually get broken up by Papa or Mama. It depended on which one felt they were on kid duty that day, or were in the more irritated mood at the time. He still looked good, like he did right before he died, about 21. Pablo had taken on a more serious look and clasped his fingers together. She knew what he was going to do before he did it.

It was a brother/sister thing that they had. You would clasp the fingers of both hands and bounce them off of your heart twice then fold your hands together making a point with your index fingers. It was their way of saying *I love you* when they weren't able to actually talk.

He pointed at her, motioned as if he were waving her through the glass. He was asking. He didn't realize she had no control over the pane of thick glass that separated them. Apparently this was not a normal situation, because everyone that arrived at the glass seemed to be confused by it. That was probably not a good thing.

The browser window was still up, and she could see Jakub watching what appeared to be a sideways pantomime. Since she had Pablo's eye, she pointed at the image of Jakub sitting on the couch, pointed at her heart, pointed at herself, reversed the sequence. Pablo broke into a grin and gave her a smug smile with his raised eyebrow. Almost like a 'good job' look.

"My brother's here," She said to Jakub. "We can't hear each other, and that's why we're doing this weird pantomime thing. It's horrible charades. But he seems to approve of you, so that's good."

"I certainly *do* want your family's approval. That's a good thing to have, I think."

"I'd be very inclined to agree," Veronica said as Pablo waved again and slipped out of view. He was pointing at someone just out of sight, and Veronica was trying to figure out who it was when the figure came back into her vision.

The girl was back. She smiled and waved, walked right up to the glass as if she could just walk through it. Put her hand out, and was deflected immediately. She looked studiously at the glass, re-examining it again, tapping it a few times. She spoke. Veronica couldn't hear her. She spoke again, pointed at Veronica and then pointed at her ear again.

Veronica shook her head *no*, she couldn't hear her.

The girl was looking at the edges of the glass while drumming her fingers on it. Then she held a finger up and shook it.

Wait.

Veronica watched her place her hands together in what appeared to be a prayer position. Then she began to feel a tingling like soda bubbles fizzing in the center of her brain.

Then the voice.

Veronica heard it as clear as if the girl was standing next to her. It was soft, melodic.

Baby Girl, you need a medium. Find a medium.

She released her position and looked back up at Veronica with an expression that seemed like hope. She nodded, and gave the girl a thumbs up. *Yes, I heard that.*

The girl broke into a big smile, and almost skipping, backed away from the glass and out of sight. Veronica knew as soon as she said it who needed to be contacted. One person she knew that had knowledge about mediums and the paranormal.

"You need to do something for me," Veronica said to Jakub. "I want you to listen closely, because you're gonna hafta say exactly what I tell you in order to get her attention. You're gonna need to call the S&L Express. You have to get to Lindsey. I don't care how you do it, but you have to tell her that I have told you to come to her for help, and that you know about Roger and the green teddy bear. Got it? *Roger and the green teddy bear.*"

"What's that?"

"Don't worry about it. But it's the right code that will get her to take you seriously. That's a deep secret only a few people know about. I very highly doubt Sarah knows about it. She knows what to do about all of this. I can't really explain it, and I don't know if she will, but things like this run in her family. At least how to deal with them."

"Okay."

"Do it. Let me know what happens. Go."

worlds out there

"We need to talk. Now," Jakub said into the phone. He hadn't meant to come off harsh, but it was that important. The voice of Sarah was on the other end of the line.

"What happened? Are you okay?" She asked, the concern unmistakable.

"I need to actually meet you. I need Lindsey there too. Y'all are gonna hafta help me sort something out *big*."

"Um, yeah. Come on over.," she said, almost confused, "How far away are you?"

"I'm downstairs."

"Damn. Come on up."

He heard the buzz and the click as the magnetic lock on the door disengaged and pulled it open. He had been to their apartment twice in the entire time he'd known them. Once for the housewarming, and then one other time when Sarah had to pick something up she'd forgotten. Lindsey had been off at work, which was why he'd even been allowed that level of access.

Sarah opened the door as he got closer to their apartment and waved him in. Lindsey was sitting at their kitchen table, which consisted of a glass circle atop a stand, surrounded by barstools, some you might find in a bar or restaurant more than an apartment. She gave him a nominal acknowledgment.

"Can I get you something to drink?" Sarah asked.

"Diet Dr. Pepper."

"You're in California. Try again."

"Diet Coke, then."

"Anything in it?"

"Nope, straight."

She jerked her head to the side and eyed him suspiciously. He realized it might be one of the few times he had *not* been drinking alcohol around them.

He stretched back in his chair and tried to take a moment to figure out how to formulate this so they didn't kick him out of the house in the first 60 seconds.

"Okay. Clear your minds and lemme finish before you say anything, 'cuz this is gonna be a bit wild. I met this girl named Veronica. She's from Texas, too. San Antonio."

"I know at least three Veronicas," Sarah said.

"I only know one," Lindsey said flatly.

"She says she lived next door here," Jakub said, "She also calls you two the S&L Express, she says she used to go to the beach with you, and that originally she was roommates with Lindsey."

Lindsey's eyes shifted down to the table. "You've seen her before," she said, almost without emotion.

"What?" Sarah said, her eyes widening. Then as recognition set in, she exclaimed, "Oh, *that* Veronica! Yes, she was at our housewarming party."

"Yeah, when she was with Lunk." Turning to Jakub she finished, "Back when you were all about that brunette chick..."

"Janet," he finished. Now Jakub remembered. He had blown over her because she was with some beefy guy that he instantly labeled as an idiot. But he'd been with Janet, so he didn't pursue it.

"That was before you hooked up with Ju-Ju Pebbles."

"Mitzi."

"Whatever."

"So you didn't really like my girlfriend, then. Ex-girlfriend."

"Honey, I haven't liked *any* of your girlfriends. And I *have* reasons. Plus, you sell yourself short, and you couldn't clean yourself up. Girl even came up and talked to you because you had that damned hockey jersey on. I wanted to set you two up, but you had your head so deep up that shark's ass. I'm not going to hurt my own friends." She didn't lift gaze from the table. But she wasn't sugarcoating anything, either. He was concerned she wasn't taking him seriously, and he'd hit a sore spot by coming there. Lindsey seemed full of piss and vinegar at the moment, and it seemed somehow to be justified.

She was right. He had seen Veronica before. But he also saw the bodybuilder dude and figured a hot girl with a guy like that, he didn't have a chance in Hell.

Lindsey was still looking down at the glass on the table, probably a reflection. She was processing like she was studying for an exam. She would look over repeatedly at Sarah, figuring out what the best reaction should be for the moment.

"So let me make sure I've got this right," Sarah began, "You are telling me that you're in love with Veronica Salazar, and she's in your VR goggles right now."

Jakub exhaled. He took a moment. "That's *precisely* what I'm telling you."

"Six degrees," Lindsey said with almost a hint of sarcasm, "Kevin Bacon would be proud."

"Ronni also says that I'm supposed to get Lindsey, because she has a secret, and I'm supposed to mention some guy named Roger and a green teddy bear, whatever that has to do with."

That got Lindsey's attention. She stiffened and sucked in slightly, and oddly, she was trying to keep that reaction hidden from Sarah, who was too busy rolling her eyes at Jakub as if he were delirious.

"I'm still trying to figure out if you're pulling my chain or not. So what are ya gonna do, get married and become a video game? Have little Super Mario Brothers kids?" Sarah turned to Lindsey, "What's today's date? Is it April Fools?" Lindsey was staring him down now like a hawk. She waited before she spoke.

"It's not April anymore. He knows someone we didn't officially introduce him to because he was too busy being a knucklehead at the time. Guy's not drinking. I haven't seen him this sober in some time. You do the math. Looks to me like he's not bullshitting here."

She kept gaze on Jakub, her light emerald eyes piercing him. There was something behind them, but he couldn't tell exactly what it was.

"So what's the problem you're trying to work out?" Lindsey asked.

"I know how crazy this sounds. The best we can figure is that it could probably be scientifically explained. We have theories. What I need is someone who can talk to dead people and open this door Ronni keeps talking about. She says that there is a door where she is. It looks like a thick plate of glass. She says she can move all the way around it, and it glowed one time when her grandmother spoke to her. She's seen her dad and a couple other people in it too, but it doesn't actually open. Who can open it?"

"You're asking me a question I can't even begin to fucking answer, Tex," Sarah said with a hint of skeptical shock. She was having a difficult time with this conversation.

"I know someone that can help you," Lindsey said. "She's not gonna be freakish, this'll all make sense to her. She might even be able to see Veronica herself. She's a medium."

"What do they do?" Jakub asked.

"You *must* watch TV," Lindsey prodded, "They talk to dead people, of course! Well, a bunch of them are bullshit, but she's legit. And she'll help you at no charge."

"How do you know that," Sarah asked.

"Because she's my aunt Jeanette." She slung her booted heel up on the table and landed it roughly, like a mic drop. Looking over at Sarah she continued, "There's damned near nothing you don't already know about me, but that was the secret. It runs in our family. Mom's side. We all have *abilities*. I'm not supposed to talk about it, but there it is. That is what my rock collection, as you call it, is about."

She turned back to Jakub and asked, "You said that you were running a feed from the headset to your TV."

"That's right."

"And you are using a webcam with a web app to broadcast the room inside the headset."

"Yes."

"That's a two-way communication. Which means we can see her, and she can see us, too."

He hadn't stopped to think of it that way. For some reason he had thought of it in terms of something he could use, and forgot that anyone else in the room would see it, too. "Yes, I would imagine so, unless I'm an absolute nut job and imagining things."

Lindsey looked over at Sarah, "You still have that PI app on your iPhone that captures datestamps for videos?"

"I haven't changed anything on my phone in aeons."

"Good. We're gonna make us a movie."

"I *like* movies," Sarah purred.

Lindsey gave a glance and flatly answered, "Not those kinds of movies."

Jakub realized that this was the most in two years that Lindsey had actually spoken to him directly, and certainly one of the only times she had maintained eye contact with him. Wonders never cease. He questioned whether it was loyalty to Ronni, or the subject matter at hand that turned her into a more social creature with him.

Taking a breath, he tried to relax as Lindsey stepped out to make a call. Coming closer to his senses again, he took note of the chair he was sitting in, a soft buttery cream leather with what appeared to be cherry wood arms. It was boxy, but extremely comfortable. Like one of those pieces you'd buy at a modern furniture shop.

"Where'd this chair come from?" He asked Sarah.

"You like it? It's part of the Corisande Collection. Cost a pretty penny, but I think it was worth it. Lin was obsessed with it but neither of us knew exactly why. She said it was calling out to her or something."

"It's comfortable."

"It's *her* chair. You're lucky she's letting you sit in it without pitching a blue hissy."

Lindsey came back into the room happier for some reason Jakub couldn't identify. "So, I talked to Jeanette, and she's open tomorrow at about 1PM, right after lunch. So we'll meet at your apartment and do this thing." She paused to examine Jakub briefly, sitting in her prized chair. But she made no mention of it. "Things might be a little different and a little painful by tomorrow night, so expect it. But what we're doing is only going to be good for Veronica. Being stuck is *no bueno.* She's going to be free after that, and although I don't really know what all happens out there," Lindsey gestured with a wave of her hand, "I do know that she'll be free and not in an electronic box for who knows how long. That could have really went horribly, y'know? Think about it. What if something happened to you, and nobody knew she was in there? Then she'd really never be able to get back out. So this is a good thing. Maybe the best thing. And having the six degrees here just made everything easier for everyone involved."

gone dark

"You know, sometimes I feel like I'm just dying all over again. Not that I necessarily knew what that felt like the first time I did it. But you get the point." She heard herself say it. And she felt sadness held deep in the statement. Finally she had what she had always wanted, and had who she was looking and hoping for, and it was too little, too late. She couldn't stay here forever, that much had been made obvious.

It was coming on go time, and she didn't have the slightest clue where it was she was going to. But what she'd figured out was that Papa, Pablo, and Avo would be there. Not to mention that other girl that kept popping up at random like she was trying to irritate the piss out of her. She had to go, because if anything happened to Jakub, it would be doubtful he would be there where she was, and that made it more of a holding cell. Better to get out into the flow of things. That way she had a chance to reconnect, learn how, something.

The fact that there was life after death in the first place had changed everything. She felt his understanding. It was calm, peaceful, but sad. He was the love of her life, but she would never be able to touch him. Only by some slick thinking had she been able to actually *see* him. And she knew *exactly* how he saw her. More than she should ever tell him she knew.

"It's like everything was just delayed, and somehow I got lucky. I got really lucky. I found you on the way out. Or you found *me*. I don't know. I don't care anymore, I'm just glad it happened. I'd give anything to touch you one time. Maybe it's just so I'd know this hasn't been a dream."

"Certainly hasn't been a dream for me," Jakub said, realizing he'd just tripped over his own words. "That wasn't what I meant, I meant..."

"I know what you mean. I can feel you, remember? We share the sentiment, I guess. And maybe there's more after this. I don't really know, but I do know we all gotta die someday, right?" Veronica gave a weak smile. "I'm glad you set the camera up. At least now I can see everything and every one, including Robert over there, so that helps make things a little easier for me, I guess. Nice to be surrounded by the people you're familiar with."

"Have you seen anything else in the glass since I've been gone?"

"The girl showed up again. Pablo waved at me and left. So they know I'm here, and they're waiting to get me wherever they are. I think it's probably outside of here, or it's a really cruel optical illusion of some sort. I think more of the former and a lot less of the latter."

They sat in silence for a few moments. Neither knew what to say or how to break up the quiet. It was like those moments when you know something bad is happening, like when you were sitting at Grandma's deathbed, and you knew there was much to say, but no way to say it.

"Pablo looks good. He's still wearing that damned Tim Duncan jersey," She smiled, "I don't know about that boy. But he was always so sweet, and tried to be macho all the time. I think it's just a Latin thing. He was a great big brother."

Jakub smiled, "Having a good older sibling is half the battle, isn't it? I know Willie would go to the ends of the Earth for me, so I completely understand where you're at. And I have the cavalry coming, but it'll be tomorrow before they show up. You were right about the code phrase. Whatever that was about, it worked. I think it was the first time Lindsey had more than two words to say to me."

"What's she got against you? She never really mentioned anything other than what we already talked about. She didn't seem to really dislike you, per se."

"I don't know. Sarah told me I was sitting in her chair, and she'd have a fit, have my head, something. But she didn't even react that I was in it."

"You mean that white leather one with the wood handles?"

"Yeah."

"Really? She's defensive over that chair like it's her firstborn. No idea what that was about. I wasn't even allowed to sit in that chair, and we were practically sisters."

"Sarah said that they were both drawn to that chair."

Veronica snorted. *Typical Sarah, inserting bullshit to meet her ends.* "Sarah wasn't even heard of yet when Lindsey bought that chair. I was the one that got it with her. I don't remember if it was Grayson or Naurelle, but it wasn't cheap. You gotta watch out for that Sarah. She's a bullshit queen."

They conversed back and forth, chatting about life and what they believed in, topics that were trying somehow to avoid the fact that this could be the last night they would have together. He fought it. Hard. He didn't want to sleep, so Veronica decided to take the reins and began talking more softly and slowly, lulling him into sleep. The more she committed to talking like a hypnotist, the further he drifted off. Tomorrow was going to be a painful for him, anyway. She had no clue what she was looking at, but Veronica knew who was waiting for her when that glass got opened.

For him, it hurt her heart to know that she had to leave him here. She knew that she would miss him every bit as much as he would miss her. The fact remained that there was only one way out of all of this, only one way to find out how they could connect outside of this. Moving through that glass was the only way to go.

It occurred to her that now, with him asleep, she had the free rein on the web browser, and he really wouldn't have a clue what she had in mind, and wouldn't ever think to look.

Veronica began going through her social media accounts. Someone, and she wasn't sure who, had managed to turn them all into memorial accounts. She knew that alarm bells would go off if she logged in and made any moves. If she sent him a message on social media, she knew the chat feature would ping him and wake him up. That could be saved for a little later.

In sudden burst of inspiration, she checked the shopping account that she used heavily when she was alive. It was still open. No one had touched it, amazingly. There was still a gift card balance.

B-I-N-G-O.

She stopped to think of what she wanted to do, but where was she going to send her final shopping spree once she ordered it?

Wait. Jakub had to register this headset to begin operating it. One of the requirements. Being a normal user, he wouldn't think twice of using his *real* address in it. She went to the headset settings panel, and it was there. She knew most of the address, and made a mental note of the numbers she needed to recall.

Now it's time to go shopping.

She still had a gift card balance from the night she died. She examined that first, and with a sigh of relief saw it was enough for what she had in mind.

Glad I packed that shit on the regular.

Two searches later, she had the selection in the cart, and checked it out with a shipping address. She decided to pick the slowest delivery, because he would have no clue when it was arriving, and it would appear on its own out of the blue.

That would be good. It would help after she was gone, one final act to let him know that she loved him and would miss him. Maybe there was something after this that could bring them together, and she was willing to take any steps that she needed to take to get there.

Looking at the time, she saw it was 4:44AM. Wouldn't be too bad of a time to ping him, and if he woke up where he was snoozing on the couch, it would be okay. Entering her social media account, she gave him full permissions to everything and shot a connection request to him with a short message.

A few seconds later, she heard the alert go off on his phone, but he only slightly stirred.

That's about the best I can do from here, she thought.

And then she did the thing she had never been able to do before.

She watched him sleep.

anything else

Jakub was not sure what to expect when Jeanette came to his door. He had in his mind a vision of what a "medium" would look like, flowing wild dresses, bangles, probably the Madame Weirdo Whatsis whole thing. What he was looking at was a later middle-aged blonde woman that seemed like she had picked up groceries after a day of shuffling kids around.

She was so normal you would have never selected her out of a crowd in a million years. He knew where Lindsey got the short hair from, Jeanette had a pixie cut with the matronly makeup and soft canvas shoes, loose blue jeans, California t-shirt and a designer dress shirt layered on the top. She looked like any high school mom in the Deep South.

He had apparently taken too long to sum her up, because she smiled at him gently and broke his thoughts with, "I'm Jeanette Falkner. I know, I get it a lot. It's perfectly okay. No harm done. People always seem to be surprised when they see me for the first time because they're expecting one of those wacko crystal ball readers from the beach."

"God, I'm sorry. I think I've lost my mind. Please come in. Can I get you anything to drink?"

Thankfully, she opted for a diet coke and took a seat on the couch. She didn't wait to talk business.

"I'm not sure how much Lindsey has spoken to you about this situation you have. We don't discuss this sort of thing very much in our family. Even though it *runs* in our family. Had some bad experiences in the past, and the poor girl has blocked a lot of it out. I, on the other hand, work with the paranormal quite a bit. As you can imagine, we have our share of detractors and skeptics. This girl, Lindsey said you had a two way connection going with her..."

He motioned to the television, curious how she hadn't noticed it before. He saw that it had timed out and shut off by itself.

I'm gonna hafta fix that, he thought.

As the screen came back up, Veronica was seated cross-legged on the floor. Or what was serving as a floor.

"Ronni?" Jakub prodded.

"Yeah?" She answered, looking up.

"I have someone here to see you. Someone that can help. This is Lindsey's Aunt Jeanette."

The excitement washed over her face as she bolted upright.

"Hi, sweetie," Jeanette said, "It's been a while since I've seen you. How are you holding up in there?"

"Well, I'm relieved to know there's life after death. I can say that."

"I can imagine. This would probably be a bad time to say that I told you so, but I'm glad I *can* say it. I always liked you. So tell me about the door. I understand there is a glass door, plate glass?"

"Yes."

"Describe it to me."

"It's like a solid sheet of glass, like that bulletproof glass you see in the corner stores on the bad parts of town. Just a sheet of glass. You can walk around it."

"Does it ever glow? Any light inside it?"

"Sometimes. That's when people show up."

"Who are the people? Do you recognize them?"

"Yeah, Papa has showed up, my brother Pablo, and some girl I don't recognize. She's been here two or three times. It glows, they show up, and I can't get to them, they can't get to me. We can't hear each other, either."

"Okay, that's your portal. So I'm gonna explain something to you real quick. You've passed on, but you haven't crossed over. That's what's going on."

"What's the difference? Passing on is being dead, but crossing over is getting to somewhere else beyond this?"

"Exactly. When we pass, we really don't have the energy to create our own portal. That's when people like me become important. Lindsey and Sarah should be here soon, and then we can all get together and try to supercharge that glass for you. Don't worry, sweetie. It all gets better from here."

Jeanette seemed amazingly calm, like this was something that she did every day. To her this conversation appeared to be as natural as talking to the next door neighbor over the fence.

Another knock at the door produced Lindsey and Sarah. Lindsey entered the room brandishing a camera tripod as Sarah followed along less enthusiastically. "Sorry we're late," she said, scanning the room until she saw the television and burst into a wide smile Jakub had never seen before.

"Hey, you!" She exclaimed at Veronica.

Veronica threw her arms out like she could actually hug her and brandishing that beautiful grin Jakub was now so familiar with answered, "Sissy! It's you! I knew you'd come!"

He could see Sarah out of the corner of his eye, looking as if she were trying to swallow a golf ball. She seemed to be wildly jealous of a person who was already dead.

Why? That doesn't make sense.

Lindsey affixed her phone into a clamp and screwed it down on top of the tripod, aiming the camera at the television. She aimed the phone until she got a clear view of the television spreading across her screen and said to Veronica, "Okay, Sweetie. This is so we have a record of you. We can see you, and you can see us. I killed a lot of games on this thing so I'd have the space."

Veronica smiled and said, "I can appreciate that. I know how much you love your games."

"Do you know what today's date is, and can you say it out loud?" Lindsey asked her, looking onto the phone screen.

"May 5th, 2019. It's a Sunday." She pointed up, "It's on the main menu widget right there. I know. *I* coded it back in the day."

Veronica interrupted his thoughts.

"Jakub? When I said to get rid of your momma and take mine, I meant it. *Do it*. Worked for Jesus."

"Speaking of," Lindsey interrupted, "Do you have anything you want to say to your mom? Not that she'll ever see this, but you never know."

"Well, Mama, if you see this, I love you, and I really miss you. I also love Jakub very much, too. If I'd had the chance, I'd have married him. So if you get to meet him, I hope you'll give him all the love you gave me and Pablo, because his momma really sucks. He needs a new one. Someone like you. I told him to take care of you, so doncha go fighting him about it. It's what I told him to do. I know how defiant you can get." She laughed.

"And just so you know, I've seen Papa and Pablo... they both look like they're doing fine. And there's some girl keeps showing up. I don't know her. She calls me 'Baby Girl for some reason'. She looks like those pictures of you when you and Papa first met. So everyone's okay, and now you have proof it's not a bunch of fairy tales. I love you!" Veronica stopped to think for a moment and continued, "Where's Luna? I hope nothing bad

happened to her. I trust you, whatever happened."
She then returned a smile to her face.

"I need everyone to grab a hand. We need to all be together in this so that there's enough energy flowing around to help Veronica." Jeanette said, as she reached out with her right hand to grab Jakub's. Lindsey was to her left, and as she grabbed her hand, the bottom of the world seemed to fall out.

Not now! I'm doing something here!

Everything disappeared. She was standing in what appeared to be a cemetery. It wasn't a typical church-type boneyard, this one was more like a garden. The blooming flowers trellised in a way that compartmentalized everything without truly blocking them off. A single headstone stood before her, the smell of night jasmine floating.

It was dusk.

Someone had planned this site carefully. She tried to read the headstone, but as Jeanette tried to bring it into focus, she saw Lindsey step into view. Her hair was longer, that was the first thing that she noticed, the shoulder-length blonde hair with a violet and blue streak dyed into it. Some notions never change.

She had a strange Jackie Onassis number going on with her dress. It seemed like the end of summer or beginning of fall. She wore an ornate butterfly brooch on her label, meticulously crafted with some sort of blue and indigo looking stones. Lindsey was stroking the headstone with her fingers softly, tracing the letters with her fingertips like she was touching a face.

Jeanette saw her reach into a pocket and then remove the thin gloves she had been wearing to complete her look, and she closed her eyes in what looked like prayer as she clasped the object in both hands. She was older. Jeanette could tell that she had aged a bit, although she still looked every bit in her 30s, the vibe felt like she was older than that.

The object turned out to be a rose quartz carved skull. Lindsey was charging a crystal, *that's* what she was doing!

Lindsey placed it on top of the stone in a recess that was created for it, she gently gave the stone a prolonged kiss and plopped down on the ground next to the headstone, sobbing until she was shaking.

Something was to Jeanette's left. It seemed like it was made of rubber, but she found that she couldn't turn her head to see what it was exactly.

A voice she didn't recognize spoke from behind her right shoulder. It was a female.

"Think of what you've done," the voice said, "I know it hurts like hell right now, but what you've done is *beautiful*. You know he always loved you. And more than that, he loved you *first*. No one is going to take that away from you. No one, and I mean *no one* would even want to."

Jeanette turned to see the speaker, but all she saw was a thin feminine hand, tattooed to the knuckles. A blooming lotus flower was creeping onto the top of her hand from the wrist.

Lindsey sniffled and nodded. She was trying to speak and couldn't find her voice. Lindsey nodded again. Finally she got it together and said weakly, "I guess everything is about to get interesting now."

"The world is about to get stood on its fucking head. Don't kid yourself. What you've done is *epic*."

The premonition disappeared. As she felt the softness of Lindsey in her left hand, the name of the headstone clicked in Jeanette's head.

JAKUB XANDER RISER

All the air in Jeanette's lungs seemed to vanish. *What in the hell am I starting here?*

"I'm going to give you guys a crash course here. So what we are doing is called *crossing someone over*. It's gonna seem like a bunch of imaginary stuff, and to a degree that's true, but the results of what we are doing in this case will show up on the TV there.

So, I want everyone to take a deep breath, let it out and relax. Visualize a ball of bright white light right here in the middle of us. Feed that light, make it brighter, make it stronger. Does everyone see this light now? Do you have it in your mind?"

The others murmured affirmatively and she said, "Okay, start shifting your focus, move that ball over to the VR headset Jakub has, try to sink that white ball of light down into it. That light is what will open the door for Veronica."

She felt the warmth flowing around the circle, like a wavelength that spun from left to right, moving naturally and growing by the second. The pressure of the energy built and built, and then released.

It was done. Then she heard voices she'd never heard before.

As Veronica moved, it was off the screen to the left. She had turned, looked towards the group in the room, and gave a kiss towards Jakub. He was the only one with his eyes still open. He gave her a kiss back, and it hit him what this meant. The finality of it struck him as the feeling began creeping up his body into his throat. He wanted to scream, to sob, to do anything but watch quietly as the love of his life vanished yet again.

She paused, reached forward, then with an angelic, sweet smile that he tried to burn into his mind like a branding iron, she nodded.

It worked.

A voice that had not been heard on Earth in over fifteen years came gently, softly through the speakers of the television. It was male, it was the sound that only a father could make.

Ven con nosotros, Mija.

As a smile lit Veronica's face, she slipped from view, and through the glass.

Jeanette moved closer to Jakub, and wrapping an arm around his shoulder pulled him close.

He let her. Somebody needed to.

"She's gone now, honey," Jeanette said, the look on her face telling him that she knew exactly what this pain was he felt, losing all over again.

That was the moment the floor seemed to disappear, because Jakub melted into it.

Veronica Salazar had left the building.

soft memory in blue

He put all the travel miles he had accrued into a flight to San Antonio. The vacation time at work was begging to be used, and Jakub figured this was a respectable way to dispense of it. For some reason, he had a more driven attitude as of late, and couldn't find it in him to go to any of those horrific events he had been subjecting himself to.

The night before he headed east, he visited her favorite place. He must have driven by it hundreds of times, but never went in. It was near the freeway, tucked away with a white painted face and bright blue trim. Very Argentine.

It was as good as advertised. Maybe the Texan in him was led to it, but he was still dealing with things. Jakub was in a perpetual state where half of him wanted to laugh and the other half cry. It was ironic how the whole thing played out.

As he landed and was in the process of picking up his car, he had an email alert on his phone. They had found his resume in order up in Austin. They would be speaking with him soon. It was just as well. He couldn't feel California anymore. She wasn't here or there, but this was where they had laid her to rest, and for some reason the closer he was, the better he would feel about life in general. California had been all about getting away from his mother and trying to live the life he'd always seen on TV and in the movies.

You can certainly get something like that, but in the end there is always a question of what you'll truly get out of it. In his case, all of the juice was gone.

The feel of San Antonio had always helped soothe his soul. Part of him wondered if it was because Veronica had been raised here, as if they had been crying out for each other all this time and the connection just hadn't been made until everything hit the critical mass.

He drove the rental out to his hotel on the north side of the city, that was the closest to where he eventually needed to go, and spent the night relaxing in front of the TV. The Spurs were playing. He didn't care much for them before, but he had an idea that that was going to change. It was something else to hold on to. Right now it wasn't serving a purpose of joy other than the monotony and white noise it seemed to create.

The next morning he went to the missions and walked them, took in the feel of the air, the electricity of the history, the sadness and tragedy of the Alamo, the vibration of Tejano and everything that was Texas. Those things spoke to him as if they were a forgotten language. In a manner of speaking, they were.

He was home.

Home involved a lot of Lone Stars everywhere. They were plastered on everything from overpasses to signs, to houses and on the outside any major box store he could think of in Texas that he had ever been in.

Jakub stopped to have a meal and a virgin Mojito by the Riverwalk. He had always wondered how Hemingway had felt in his escapades and adventures, sitting in exotic places and sipping on a Mojito with a cigar. Perhaps this was about how it felt, it was the vibe he was going for in the moment. He knew deep down that he was afraid, and what it was he held the greatest fear *of*.

He had picked the anniversary of her death to come here. If what he knew he was going to see tomorrow *was* there, it would prove he wasn't crazy, and that he had experienced a substantial, unexplainable thing.

It was safer for it all to have been a delusion, frankly. Having all these thoughts, addresses and facts would mean that he had imagined it all, and he could just consider himself not in his right mind. Sure, it would take these moments he had away but would also erase some of this sudden impulsive dedication he had to a girl he'd never met in real life. It was like having a crush on a movie star or something instead.

The ache was genuine. The grieving also. He was in the process of dealing with it, and Jeanette had suggested that he seriously look into grief counseling. As far as she understood, he'd lost a wife given the intensity of their interactions, even in that short of a time.

There was a story that Jakub read once online where a couple had a whirlwind love and desired to become married, only to have the wife die the day of the wedding. They were wed twelve hours. They never made it to their honeymoon.

Her mother had no idea he existed. She couldn't know, either. The family would not understand this, wouldn't believe it, and it would hurt them more than help them to ever be aware of his presence.

Sleeping that night wasn't easy until after midnight. He had gotten used to the "prime time". Jakub had left the goggles in Los Angeles. There was no reason to put them on, since he knew she wouldn't be there. He did know that eventually he would, right now everything was too fresh and he couldn't focus on anything but that, so it would be more pain than pleasure.

He considered the bottom line: she was free, at rest, and something in that fact felt right. He didn't feel lonely, or lost, just hurting. She had loved him, he had loved her, and now everything was a weird matter of timeless time. The thought of it didn't even make sense.

That was the twisted spiral his brain was traveling down when sleep finally overtook him, and he relaxed for the night.

Breakfast the next morning was somber. The constant racket of the grackles was one he had erased from his memory years ago, but they were back. They were as painful for him to listen to as the music at Jermaine's parties. He felt fortunate, no, *blessed* that Willie had driven in overnight with Carl and the kids. He hadn't asked for it, but it was that sibling connection that led her to understand how important this was for him.

Someone had tipped her off. He had no idea who. He didn't really care at this point, either. She'd probably rat on them later, knowing her.

He had collected as many pictures of Ronni as he could find. Because her social media was converted into honorarium accounts, it made access simpler for that. He had one that was his favorite, a shot taken while she was laughing, a smile that exploded over her face and could have instantly lit a room. That was the Veronica he knew.

That was the picture he handed on his phone to Willie.

He was not prepared for her reaction. He expected some soft, soothing comment, because she was good for those, and they were usually perfectly timed. He did not prepare for her to completely lose her shit at the table and break down into a sobbing mess. After all, she had never interacted with Veronica or knew her at all. But the reaction was genuine. She was hurting for *him*.

Willie became uncharacteristically quiet. Carl knew this was something beyond his comprehension, and it showed on his face. He'd learned that you roll with whatever program Willie is in, and you don't argue because she normally knows what's going on. He had a 'I just work here' mentality, and most of the time it worked out well.

Jakub picked up a dozen red roses from an elderly Mexican fellow he observed on the corner of Nacogdoches Road the evening before. It made sense to take them to Holy Cross. Carl had the foresight to keep the kids at the hotel room, even though they had been little angels that morning. The children were likely threatened with some ungodly torture Willie had devised for them if they acted on the urge to behave wildly.

Holy Cross was quiet and had an air of solace. Willow went with him to make sure he would be all right. It was the sisterly instinct kicking in. He saw the paved pathways that led between the rows of plots, the rows of stubby yet full trees that were evenly spaced to provide an extra feeling of calmness and eternity.

Veronica laid at rest in a Catholic cemetery, which made sense.

Her space was nondescript, as was her father's, a space in between them. Willie kept an eye on him, and would frequently place her hand on him in reassurance. The urge hit him, and it was uncontrollable. He split the roses ten and two, and stepped over to her father's plot about ten feet away and placed the two roses in the pair of granite boots that served as a base at the head. They were fitting, from what he knew about him. Alejandro Salazar, *devoted husband and father*.

"Dad?" Willie inquired quietly.

"Yeah. I figure if I was ever gonna ask him, now's as good of a time. He already knows who I am, anyway. Even if I haven't met *him* yet." He stopped for a moment to try and take this all in, to rationalize what he was doing at that moment, but he couldn't. That was the pure and simple truth. Simultaneously, it felt like something was simply flowing into him, a feeling of sad peace.

Calm.

Jakub held the other ten in his hand, and standing at the foot of her plot he uncontrollably looked left. He didn't understand the force that propelled him at this point, but he wasn't going to argue with it anymore, not after what he had seen firsthand.

Pablo Salazar. He laid to the other side, sister and mother's plots sandwiched in between the two males. It was predictable. It was the masculine need to protect, both males were there to keep the family rounded up for the Resurrection, Pearly Gates, whatever. He wasn't certain what they had believed in.

"I'm sorry," he whispered, as he pulled yet another rose from the bundle. She would have wanted it this way. Somehow he still felt like he was taking something away from her. He stepped over and placed the single rose in Pablo's cups. They had sank into the ground, but hadn't been properly cleaned out.

It's hard to keep every plot here clean, as large as it is, he thought.

Jakub took a hand and scraped some of the grass clippings that had settled and pulled them out of the cup, replacing the single rose.

Ronni was there. At least her physical body was. This wasn't a joke, or imagination, or something that he could have ever known about any other way, and the thing that stuck in his heart the most was that he would not have ever cared. The love of his life, and he would not have cared either way whether she was alive or dead because he'd not met her before, and wouldn't have *known* to care.

Perhaps it was guilt, or anger at lost time.

Veronica Luz Salazar
August 31 2017

He took the bronzed plaque in, let the pain flow. If you could go to a national championship and lose, and then multiply that feeling by ten, perhaps one hundred, you'd be close.

Willow watched quietly, a few steps back. It seemed almost like she was feeling this, too. She was more than likely feeling the broken heart of her brother, but it wasn't the first time they'd felt this way together, either.

They were both so much younger and smaller then, so many years ago, the big sister scared to death about her little brother. Somehow, it had always been this way.

No denying that everything was perfectly real at this point. He wasn't completely certain how he felt about it either. There was a nagging part of him that wasn't feeling anything at all, and that was mostly because he was intentionally denying it access, which was still his usual patterns at work.

Jakub knew that it wasn't the way things would stay. He was gonna break, and it was a matter of time.

"I'm coming back," he said matter of factly.

"To Texas?" Willow asked.

"Yup. Got a position in Austin. Friend of a friend, walk in the door kinda thing. I'm supposed to start on the 14th."

"I thought you loved it in California," she probed, raising her eyebrows a bit.

"I did. Then there was this, and I'm just not feeling it anymore. It was starting to get on my nerves anyway."

"We are *not* telling Mom." She said it solidly, like she was laying down the law.

"Not really planning on it, Willow. At least for a while. I'm also going to be harder for her to get on the phone. I think maybe once every two months might be better for me. I'll probably see a lot more of you guys."

"Good boy. You're learnin'. We'd like that. Change your phone number. Just make sure you give it to me."

"I'd just feel better for right now being a little closer to Ronni. I haven't ruled out the future, and I doubt she would've let me, but I need some time to enjoy things, explore a little, calm myself down."

"She didn't drink, did she?"

"Not really. Light drinker, onesie-twosies with food. Why?"

"Because you haven't been."

"How ya know that?"

"I know my own brother. You normally smell like a distillery. There's not a single whiff of it on ya. One of the first things I noticed. Girl's done a number on you, and in a good way."

"I think I am probably gonna be here at least once a year, every year," he deflected, "It feels almost like a divine assignment, if that makes any sense. I'm not sure how much sense it makes to me right now, but we're going with it." He felt her rub her hand at the base of his neck. It was the same motion she'd used to try and console him over Dad. It felt soothing, comfortable.

"Oh, hon. But you now have a purpose... The rest of your life begins now. It's what you're gonna do with it that's important."

"The rest of *something* begins now. That's pretty much clear to me. I'm just not entirely sure what that's gonna be yet. I just know it's not in California, and I've seen too much at this point. I got a lotta things to figure out now. I'm pretty sure I'm gonna need some help. Can't hide forever, I guess. You realize no one's gonna believe this story."

"If I didn't know you, I'm not sure I woulda believed it either."

"I was advised to go to grief counseling. I mean, I *want* to. I watched something that I've always wanted in my life shoved impossibly out of reach, and it was too little, too late. I don't know what to do with it, and if I go try and explain it, they're probably not gonna get it and tell me to just quit playing video games. I have this feeling that I know I can't ever say a word to her family, or what's left of them, because they would never understand, and I would just be an insult to them anyway."

Willow stiffened. "I get it, but don't you *ever* let me hear that come out of your mouth again. For what you had time to do, you did well. Look at how you've held together since then! You're clean. You haven't been clean in about nine years. AA might not hurt ya, though."

He thought about it for a moment. "I know I have the street cred for that one. I could always start there."

enjoy the ride

The cardboard box with the trademark smiley face caught his eye as he began the ascent to his front door. He wasn't expecting anything and tried to calculate if it was near his birthday, or if there was something he had forgotten about. Maybe it was delivered to the wrong place.

What in the hell did Mom send me this time? This had better not be a dildo.

He bent over without touching it at first, as if it were a package that might need the bomb patrol. His mother didn't send the package, and yes, it was in fact his.

Jakub realized that the label should have sent a shock, a chill, something down his spine. Instead he felt warm, like he was standing in the direct beam of the sun, on a beach somewhere, where the winds held heat and sea-foam aloft in a gentle mist.

The sender was Veronica.

He scooped the parcel up as if it were the most natural thing in the world and carried it inside to his kitchen bar. His eyes caught the bottle of bourbon, untouched since Jeanette was there. He still didn't have a taste for it anymore. Who knew how long that would last, but he wasn't feeling it. The glass was now insulting him and taking up his personal space.

Grabbing the bottle, Jakub twisted the cap off and looked at the remaining liquid like he was performing an experiment in a laboratory. He inhaled the fragrance of it, that familiar smell with the sweet, woody notes, and then inverted the contents into the sink and down the drain.

"I think you've rendered your services," he said as the remainder of the amber fluid disappeared down the drain. He stopped to reflect as he replaced the cap.

"You're going with me so I don't forget. And I doubt I will," he announced to the bottle and the empty room as it was returned to its prominent spot on the countertop.

"On second thought," he said aloud to the room, "I think I have a better place for you. At least until I'm ready," and promptly moved the bottle into the trash bin with a clunk.

Some things in life needed to be set right. There was no moving forward without tying up a few loose strings from the past. Enough of those were around, for sure. The two that were the most important were already underway. Keep your friends close, and your enemies closer. Just don't let them know you updated your address.

He focused on this physical box, tried to consider the implications of exactly what he was looking at. No one would believe this. It might not be worth telling anyone. It could be a most cruel joke, but he hadn't shared any of the past few weeks with other than a handful of people. None of them knew half of what he knew about Veronica, and they wouldn't dare do anything like that to him. Neither Sarah nor Lindsey would do anything to mess with his head. They had been part of the process.

Both of them had known her well, but they didn't know *her*. He'd gotten the ultimate crash course in all things Veronica Luz Salazar.

Still, not the faintest clue what might be in the box. She had said to expect a surprise, but no hint at what that surprise might be, and he couldn't recall anything in their previous conversations that was much of a hint either.

Her face came back into his mind's eye, and it stuck Jakub like a needle. He was mourning a girl that had already been mourned by everyone else. But he had also loved her when no one else could, in a way that seemed utterly impossible and that was something that could never be explained or even worse, taken away from him. Unlike everyone else who might have already forgotten her in everyday life, his grief was still fresh.

She was still very real, and it hurt deeper because she was now more than a VR sideshow or an acquaintance. Ronni was someone who managed to see into the depths of his soul in ways he had been able to defend from everyone else that had ever existed in his life.

And then, there was this.

He lined the box perfectly along the corner of the counter, because to him this was an event, rather than some package. Instead of the way you'd open a Christmas present, tearing and hacking away like roots in a jungle. This was a one time event, that had never happened before, and would never happen again.

Jakub sliced the packing tape like a surgeon cutting into a heart patient for the first time. Every motion delicate and precise.

He unfolded the box lids as if he was exposing organs never meant to see open air, or a time capsule ready to fill its spectator with awe and wonder.

Exactly what happened.

The contents of the box filled him up to the brim and over the edge again. As he slid the brown paper away and looked down, he saw the black fur, soft like down on a baby duckling. The beige tag attached was from Kosen. It was a stuffed black Dwarf Lop rabbit. The floppy ears tucked gently down around the jaw.

Jakub laughed, gasped, and choked all at the same time.

"Hi, Luna." He grinned broadly, sensing the pain as the muscles in his cheeks found a new position. The tears that came next burned, wet and hot as they gushed with emotions he hadn't quite released yet. Then he felt himself disconnecting completely.

He hadn't remembered moving to the couch. Jakub woke up with darkness outside, the only light a reflection from the streetlamp outside through his picture window and a solace of Luna cuddled near his chest. She was soft. He could see Veronica again in his memories, the way her curls nestled gently next to her face, that smile when she didn't think he had been paying attention. But he had always been a captive audience.

There had been a note. The recall flashed in his head. He had assumed it was a packing slip, but before he had done whatever the hell that just was, his brain had registered that it was formatted differently.

He slipped off the couch and cradled the stuffed rabbit in his hand as he fumbled his way in the pale darkness over to the counter. Popped on the stove vent light, felt the burn in his eyes like a cutting torch as they adjusted. It was both. The packing list had her now vacated address, but at the bottom was a printed note:

J-
Electricity is wonderful.
So are gift cards.
So are you.
I love you. I'll miss you. I'll see you
"soon".
Be good.
Until then, here's Luna.

V

He decided to not even try to figure it out, to justify it. This changed everything yet again. He drew in a breath, and felt grateful. It was difficult to explain the feeling, that specific emotion. It was close to the times he had been near a waterfall and felt the mist gently needle onto his skin. That feeling that you are truly alive, and in a moment. He could almost hear the soothing roar in his ears.

Everything she had changed in his life, everything he had seen and felt, desired and loved, was created without her breathing a single breath of air. It wasn't closure... It was *opening*.

There was no way to replace what they had experienced, and only one way to get back to it. Only one way to justify it. Jakub felt the whirl begin inside like a torrential storm brewing off an island coast. There were no longer any endings, only beginnings. She had proven that there was more to the life equation that he had ever imagined, and his decision was locked in tight. He knew what he had to do, what she was asking him to do.

Live life. Big and beautiful, sucking every moment for what it was worth, and riding every minute like a stolen horse. Which ironically still held a death sentence in Texas.

Jakub heard the ping from his phone and looked to see the header and first few paragraphs of the email. It was the confirmation for the moving truck and the car trailer the following week. He had gotten a nice price on that, thanks to Jefco, who was apparently useful for more than electronics and appeared both heartbroken and secretly jealous that he was going back to Texas.

But what's done, is done.

"Well, Luna," Jakub stated to the stuffed rabbit, "Looks like you're rollin' with me now. You better buckle in for this one."

about the author

Sion Jones is a Welsh American writer of magical realism and satire.

Born to an engineer and housewife in the Deep South, he was raised in the 1970s to read excessively.

The fact that his mother founded the local library helped.

His first published works were of poetry in 1992, and over the next decade, extended to three full-length poetry books and a novella. He began the Jakub Riser series in 2018.

Sion is also a member of the Society of Professional Journalists and studied Journalism at Michigan State University.